THE NEW ORLEANS ZOMBIE RIOT OF 1866

AND OTHER JACOB SMITH STORIES

CRAIG GABRYSCH

**The New Orleans Zombie Riot of 1866
And Other Jacob Smith Stories**

Published by
Twit Publishing
Dallas, Texas

Edited by Chris Gabrysch
Cover design by Chris Gabrysch

ISBN-978-1-938035-21-0

First Edition paperback 2014

The smell of rotting flesh hit him as soon
as he slipped between the buildings.
He pulled his kerchief from his pocket and covered his mouth. A colored woman's corpse lay to the side, still cradling her dead baby. They'd been left next to a pile of decaying vegetables. The heat and humidity had bloated the bodies. Likely, they'd been dead since the day before. Jacob stopped next to them and knelt down.

The woman had been bludgeoned to death, her head caved in, her teeth knocked out. The baby's mouth hung open, like it'd died mid-cry. Jacob said a silent prayer, stood and walked past her, deeper into the alley. He heard movement ahead.

He stopped at the intersection and looked both ways. Three afflicted crowded to his left over the body of a dead dog. One of them was small and waifish with ragged, straight brown hair. It had been a small boy, a child. The second one was an old colored woman missing her left arm. The third was a younger, busty white woman wearing a torn dress. They ripped out the dog's white entrails and tore into its gut. Canine blood and filth covered all three. Jacob felt a momentary pang of sorrow for the mutt. Jacob cocked his pistol.

For Jill.
You didn't want him dead, so he ain't.

Contents

HILLBILLY HELL

Jacob Smith and Henry Bennett stood on the top deck of the steamboat *Lackadaisical Belle* passing a bottle of rotgut whiskey between them. They were Knights Templar. They had work to do.

Chattanooga slowly came into view as they rounded the bend of the Tennessee River. The skyline looked sparse.

"Mind telling me why we're headed for Chattanooga, Mr. Bennett?"

"Not at all, Jacob. We're here to recover a stolen book," Henry said, taking a drink of the whiskey. He handed the bottle to Jacob.

"Must be one precious book to send us all the way down here."

"It is."

"Oh." Jacob took a big swallow of whiskey and wiped the back of his hand across his mouth. He offered the bottle back to Henry. "How did the forces of Hell manage to lay hands on this book, anyways?"

"A Confederate spy just weeks before the war's end. He absconded with it from Miskatonic University in Arkham, Massachusetts. I positively shudder when I consider what the Confederates would have been capable of if they'd only had the opportunity to unleash its power. Fortunately for the Union, it was stolen en route to General Lee by a rogue Confederate general named William Bedford Forrest. Unfortunately, it has yet to be recovered. Nevertheless, the Order is certain the book resides in this region of the country, though it is uncertain as to the exact location. It will be soon, though." Henry looked down at the bottle and the last finger of liquor for a long moment. Before Jacob could protest, Henry hurled it into the Tennessee River. The older man turned and looked at Jacob, a crooked smile on his lips.

"We're working. I'll buy you a bottle of the finest whiskey in Chattanooga when this is finished. And, believe me, you'll need it. Now, grab your gear. We'll be docking soon, and we still need to find a place to lay our weary heads."

3

*   *   *

They managed to find a room in one of Chattanooga's only buildings of whole construction. Years before, the Confederates had lain siege to Union-occupied Chattanooga for the winter. The battle had resulted in an important victory for the Union, but not before the besieged armies tore down the riverside city for firewood and fortifications. Luckily, their hotel had been constructed primarily of brick.

A few days before he'd left Chicago, the Order's armory had issued Jacob his full armor and a new shooting iron. The armor looked to be straight out of the Hundred Years' War, with a shirt of chainmail and a solid breastplate, but was as new and polished as if it had been made yesterday. Which it had.

The shooting iron was a custom made revolver. It held bullets with no need for percussion caps or paper cartridges, and the cylinder swung out on a sturdy hinge. During the war, Jacob had seen guns like this, but had never been able to afford one. He'd spent the trip down the river getting a handle on maintenance and reloading. It wasn't much different from his previous revolver, but the mechanics of physically loading only one item into the cylinder was paradoxically confounding Jacob as he has sat on the edge of his bed fiddling with it.

Henry entered as Jacob swung the revolver's chamber back into place for the hundredth time.

"Hello, hello, young Mr. Smith," he said, shutting the door. "Col. Winifred's telegram was waiting for us at the agent. He's given us our objective."

Jacob grunted as he reopened the cylinder and emptied the bullets into his hand.

"I know I didn't ask many questions on the trip down," Jacob said, slowly feeding bullets back into the chambers. "But, what book is it exactly that we're looking for?"

"It's the *Necronomicon*."

"*Necro*-what?"

"*Nomicon*. The Book of the Names of the Dead. Supposedly it was written in human blood by some mad Arab named Abdul Alhazred and bound in human skin. Supposedly. Whomever the author, it is, in fact, a tome of unspeakable power and evil. And we're going to take it back from the forces of Hell.

4

As an aside, Jacob, let me tell you of the importance of loading only five shells in that revolver. The hammer is a bit fidgety and lends to misfires if the pistol is not kept on an empty chamber."

"I'll keep that in mind." Jacob removed one of the shells from the cylinder. He closed it.

"Are you confident on reloading with the newer cartridges?"

"Yes sir. I figure they're a lot faster than the old ball and cap, even if I fumble around with them like I've got rheumy fingers."

"Good show, then. Our destination is a day's ride away, so this is your last opportunity to practice with the new weaponry. Have you sharpened your sword already?"

"Yes sir."

"Excellent. We should arrive at the DuBose plantation shortly before nightfall if we leave within the hour."

"DuBose? William DuBose?" Jacob asked.

"Yes. Why?"

"Recognize the name, is all. I heard stories of him during the war. He was a tough man, hard on his soldiers. Worse than Quantrill. Executed Union prisoners. Left their heads on stakes. Hung an entire Negro battalion he'd captured, and so on. Had some interesting beliefs, too, if the stories are true."

"Yes. From your description, he's certainly the man we seek. How quickly can you don your armor?"

"Ten minutes if you squire. We're riding in our full getup?"

"The arrival of two Knights Templar in shining armor loses a certain something if they both stop outside your front gate to put everything on."

Jacob holstered his pistol in the gun-belt that hung at the head of his rented bed.

The ride was long and chafing. True, the war had accustomed Jacob to long rides in poor conditions, but not to ones in poor conditions while wearing a suit of chain mail and a steel breastplate. The two Templars sounded like an entire company of soldiers to Jacob's ears, even while riding without speaking.

Henry broke the silence. "I believe we've been dancing around the subject, Jacob, but we've never truly touched on the heart of the matter," Henry said. "Why did you join up with the Templars?"

"The war."

"Did the gentleman grace the winning or losing side?"

"Winning, I guess." After a moment he went on. "I was a Jayhawker. Left the farm to join up and fight Bushwhackers in Missouri."

"Volunteer or draft?"

"Volunteer."

"How old?"

"Seventeen."

"What about your parents?" Henry asked. "Did they care?"

"Both dead. Pa died in Bleeding Kansas, back in '56."

"Your mother?"

"Kicked in the head by our horse. Died just before I left."

"For how long did you serve?"

"Just over three years."

"A lot of blood on your hands, then."

"Yes sir," Jacob said, taking his eyes off the bend ahead for a brief moment. "And what's your story? What brought you to the order, if you don't mind my asking?"

"Not at all. The usual story for Templars. I'm English, as you may have surmised. I was a gentleman of sorts back in the homeland, so I went off to the Far East and to the Opium War. I fought in China for two long years. But, all that ravaging and shedding of the sick man's blood finally wore its way on me. Realized I didn't have much stomach for killing peasants for the Queen and Tea Company. So I ran. Rather, in interest of exactness, I sailed away on the first ship out of Hong Kong that would take me aboard. Couldn't give two shakes where I was headed, so long as it wasn't for England. Not that I don't love my Queen Victoria. I am, after all, a fine Englishman of excellent breeding and disposition. Except for the deserting part, of course.

"I ended up in California. Stayed there for awhile, until I realized that all the good land was owned by a handful of cattle baron families. So I shipped off for lands further afield. Texas, this time. Still Mexican controlled, but with some white settlers that actually spoke English.

"Then independence broke out there, and war found me again. I was offered land by Mr. Stephen Austin and Mr. Samuel Houston if I'd fight and help gain sovereignty for the good white folk. And before you ask, no, I was not at the Alamo. Most everyone there died. I did know a number of men involved in the fight, though. God rest their souls, even if each death was a sad waste.

"I stayed and helped them fight for slavery, though I didn't realize it at the time. And, to put your conscience at ease, I never owned slaves. One night, just after the Battle of San Jacinto, the battle at which Sam Houston managed a coup by capturing Santa Anna, I watched an officer whipping his supposed property and realized of what I had been part. The next morning I deserted the Texas Army and left for the border."

"Wait. You mean to tell me that you ran to Mexico of all places? Why not the States?"

"Not entirely certain, facts be told. It just seemed like a smashing idea at the time," Henry said, shrugging. "But, good idea or bad, I fell into a monastery. Had the same vision all Templars seem to have, with someone we murdered in war telling us how we could atone. It was a Chinese boy from years back. And now, some couple decades later, here I am riding down a backwoods trail to a plantation with you."

"That's definitely one hell of a story. Mine's more or less the same, but with less years in it and no desertion."

"I mean no offense by asking, but who did you see?"

"I saw a girl I shot in Missouri. She was young. I snatched the life out of her without even thinking before I pulled the trigger. Just saw a movement, aimed, fired. She forgave me in the vision. Gave me my mission. Said I'd gain absolution that way, so that God would forgive me, too."

He turned in the saddle towards Jacob. "It never gets easier, by the way. Never think it will. But the self-loathing becomes more bearable with time. Just remember that you're finally in the good fight. And never forget that neither she nor God would have given you a chance at absolution if you were beyond forgiveness. People like that are the people we hunt. Things like that are what we hunt. They have no remorse. Our guilt separates us from them. Keep it in mind as we ride into Hell itself."

7

"Thought we were riding to a plantation, sir?" Jacob asked, a slight smile curling on his lips.

"A figure of speech. Just a figure of speech."

Evening fell as the two Templars turned down the path towards the DuBose plantation. Oak trees towered over the path, filtering the weak light coming from the west.

"They haven't grated this road in years," Jacob said as his horse avoided a particularly troublesome looking spot.

"Probably had too many people fighting and dying over it to worry about land-grating," Henry replied. Jacob just wiped sweat from his brow."Besides," Henry continued, "the man of the house was away at war."

"Tell that excuse to my horse when I put him down for a broken ankle."

Ahead, a wrought-iron gate guarded the plantation. It had been left open. "Kadath Estates" was sculpted into a metal arch over the pathway.

"Better than 'Abandon Hope,'" Henry muttered as the pair rode onto the grounds, pushing through the overgrown oak limbs that hung over the path.

On the other side of the gate, the plantation grounds spread out before them. The once fine lawn looked like a field left fallow, the grass having grown several feet tall.

"Man of the house, away or not," Jacob said as they rode onto the decrepit plantation, "this ain't no way to keep your homestead."

"I agree. Something about this place is most unsettling. Keep your shooting hand free and your wits about you."

Ancient, dying oaks lined the central road leading toward the mansion. Withered and tired leaves hung from the sickened trees. The mansion across the lawn was a sprawling six-pillared Georgian-style building that, in better times, would have been a whitewashed wonder. Now it was as sad as the trees, its paint yellow and peeling. A carriage road ran past the front door in a circle around a central fountain and continued back towards the gate. Mud and leaves choked the fountain; the brackish water in it now only good for spawning mosquitoes.

The pair rode down the path, Henry ahead and to the left. Someone, or something, moved in the trees on either side of the Templars. Neither man glanced away from the road. They circled the fountain and drew their horses to a halt in front of the mansion. They both shifted in their saddles. Jacob looked at Henry expectantly.

Henry cleared his throat and cupped his hands around his mouth and shouted, "My name is Henry Bennett of the Knights Templar. I've come for the book which you stole, DuBose." Henry put his hands down and looked at Jacob. Neither men detected movement within the house. Jacob shrugged. Henry drew his pistol and aimed it into the air. "DuBose, you can't ignore us." He pulled the trigger. The pistol shot's report echoed back in the stillness. "We are honor bound to hunt you till the end of your days."

Still nothing.

Jacob removed his wide-brimmed hat and wiped sweat from his brow. He slicked his hair back and replaced the hat back. "Think we should go and check the place out?"

Henry sighed. "I suppose so. We have scant available courses of action at this point, wouldn't you say?"

"I'd say so."

"Well, I suspect that we should get to it then," Henry said as he dismounted. He left his shield strapped to the horse, taking only his sword and pistol. Jacob followed suit. They climbed the front stairs cautiously, taking each one with care. The steps creaked in protest as their boot heels knocked heavily against the wood. They approached the door. The lock clicked.

The door creaked open. A tall, emaciated man with greying skin, a dark mustache, and white hair stood in the doorway. He wore the well-pressed, thoroughly cleaned suit of a gentleman landowner, but reeked of grave soil and death, as if the omnipresent odor over the estate came from him. Henry and Jacob stepped back and leveled their pistols.

The man raised his hands, palm facing the Templars.

"Are you Mr. William DuBose?" Henry asked.

"Yes, I certainly am. I presume that you, sir, are Mr. Henry Bennett?"

"Your presumption would be correct."

"And who is this?" DuBose asked, gesturing towards Jacob with a flip of his wrist.

"Jacob Smith," Jacob said.

"We've come for the book."

"Pray tell, Mr. Bennett, which book would that be?"

"The *Necronomicon*."

"Oh," DuBose replied, a tight-lipped smile on his face. "That book. So, you intend to steal it?"

"No. Our intention is to return it to its rightful owners."

"My family is, far as I am concerned, the rightful owners. It was removed from our possession some fifty years ago and placed in a Yankee university. Have you come to return it to them?"

"No, not precisely."

"Then you do intend to steal it from me? And for someone other than those Yankee dogs?"

Henry cocked his revolver. DuBose raised his hands a little higher.

"And shoot an unarmed gentleman in the process?"

"If slaying an enemy of the Lord could possibly be considered shooting an unarmed gentleman, then yes."

"Still," DuBose said, his lips widening to a yellow-tooth-filled grin, "that does seem a mite un-Christian. I propose a more honorable solution to you two good sirs of the knightly order. I challenge you to a duel."

"When'll this duel be happening?" Jacob asked.

"Just after sunset, of course. I would not dare consider forcing you off my land, only to have you return in the morning. It would not be gentlemanly. And, with the current circumstances as they stand, I hope you understand if I do not offer my hospitality this evening. That would just be dimwitted. So we duel after nightfall."

"What do you think, Jacob?" Henry asked, revolver still cocked.

"I think we either trust the word of this man or gun him down. Neither sounds like a good idea, but at least we don't shoot an unarmed man if we do the first."

"Sadly, I think you're correct. We accept, Mr. DuBose," Henry said, uncocking his revolver and holstering it.

"Excellent. I'll prepare my champion."

10

"Hold on just one second. Champion?" Jacob asked as he holstered his own pistol.

"Correct. I may choose a champion to stand in. It is my right."

"He's correct," Henry said.

"Now, gentlemen, as night is falling across the valley, I propose we make our preparations. If you will give me only a few moments, I will meet you at the rear of the house and we can begin."

Henry narrowed his eyes at DuBose. The Templars returned to their horses and remounted.

"I don't like this one bit, sir."

"Neither do I. But you were both right. We couldn't just kill an unarmed man and steal the book, corrupted by evil or not. We play this game his way, no matter what the outcome, simply because we gave our word."

"I agree completely."

The pair circled around the south side of the mansion. The sun gave its final bit of light to the plantation as they rode. An overgrown, mismanaged garden sprawled out behind the mansion. A sparse forest of oak saplings and wild cotton plants surrounded the estate on all sides. Ahead of them, vague shapes moved in the dark yard. They met DuBose and his servant on the rear steps of the house. DuBose's servant held a lantern aloft and its light made DuBose's face look more sickly. The servant was aged somewhere between thirty and sixty years, white, and hunched over with a series of near-crippling deformities. His nose was flat, his eyes set wide apart, and his forehead entirely too large. He was unsettlingly disproportionate. The younger Templar fought the urge to stare.

"My champion will be meeting us at the family plot, gentlemen," DuBose said.

"Family plot?" Jacob asked.

"We'll be playing out our duel in the cemetery. I prefer ambiance when I watch a fight to the death. Now, if you'll be polite enough to dismount, my servant will take your horses."

"What?" Henry asked again. "No slave?"

"Slavery is illegal, Mr. Bennett, in case you had not heard. Martin here is an indentured servant. His great-great-great-great-grandfather gave the souls of his lineage to my family going on two centuries ago."

Jacob sucked in air through clenched teeth. Henry caught Jacob's gaze and shook his head.

"If you'd be kind enough to follow me, gentlemen."

The Templars dismounted, Henry taking his shield. DuBose took the lantern from Martin and the "servant" took the reins of the horses. DuBose led the way through the garden paths.

"If you look to the left, gentlemen," DuBose said, pointing as he walked, "you'll see the pristine farmland that has made the DuBose family such an economic force these past forty years, with the gracious help of Martin's relatives of course."

Jacob followed his gesture but saw nothing except unploughed fields slowly being taken over by the Tennessee forest. He did notice a poorly constructed house on the edges of the garden, though, lit by a series of torches coming from the front door. The greying wood and darkness of evening had camouflaged the squat structure when he looked the first time. Now the new torchlight illuminated it perfectly. He looked to his right and slightly behind him and noticed more buildings like the first. Torches streamed from their doors, filling the garden with a soft, yellow-orange light.

"Mr. Bennett, are you seeing this?"

"Yes, I am. It's a tad bit disconcerting, wouldn't you say?"

"Yes sir, I would say as much."

As they neared the stand of trees at the edge of the garden, Jacob turned his head and looked at the crowd following them. They all shared the same flat nose, incomprehensibly large forehead, and close-set empty eyes of Martin the servant. DuBose led the Templars through the stand of oaks and into the cemetery's center. Granite headstones dotted the landscape.

"You stated earlier that your champion would be waiting, DuBose."

"He should be somewhere around here, Mr. Bennett. I shall return once I've collected him."

Jacob and Henry stood in the center of the cemetery as the silent torch-bearing men and women shuffled in. They formed a loose semicircle behind the Templars, blocking them from the plantation mansion. The two men drew their pistols and checked them over.

"I don't like this."

"You'll grow accustomed to the feeling over the years. When you stop being afraid, you generally embark upon being dead." Henry smiled ruefully.

A low rumble began amongst the crowd, almost a bass hum that collectively emitted from the chests of the men and women gathered.

DuBose's angular form approached through the headstones, one hand holding a chain draped over his right shoulder. A hulking form lumbered behind him. They stopped fifty feet away from the Templar Knights.

"I apologize for the wait, gentlemen. Wyatt, here, was bit by the wanderlust bug and got off his tether. I had to retrieve him." DuBose led Wyatt into the light. Wyatt was ugly; downright hideous. He, or it, stood at least nine feet tall and wore the tattered clothing of a servant. The skull of its bald and bulbous head seemed distended and far out of proportion from the rest of its features. The thing's giant, black eyes bulged from its face. They possessed no properties of the eyes of man or beast. Twitching and thrashing tentacles sprouted from where there should have been a mouth. Its arms were of normal proportion to the rest of its body, except for the razor-sharp talons at the end. Powerful muscles rippled beneath its thick, grey hide.

Yeah, it was ugly by Jacob Smith's reckoning, even for a demon. Of course, it was the first demon he'd ever seen, so he really didn't have much point of reference.

"That a demon?"

"Not like any I've ever seen. But it's certainly not from our world."

"That's for sure. Think we can take it down?"

As they spoke, DuBose reached up, brushed aside the tentacles, and undid the neck shackle to which the chain connected.

Jacob watched Henry size the creature up. "My experience has been that most things, extra-planar or not, capitulate when one properly applies enough of the correct kind of physical force. So, yes, I do think we can take it down."

"Gentlemen, are you ready?" DuBose called across the graveyard.

"We are," Henry called back.

"Then let the duel begin. Wyatt, go on and kill now."

The Templars both drew weapons, a sword for the elder and a revolver for the younger.

Henry Bennett drew a line in the Tennessean dirt with the point of his broadsword. Jacob Smith cocked his revolver. Jacob made the sign of the cross. The demon recoiled.

The thing recovered and began to close the twenty paces of cemetery headstones to the two armored men.

"Is this what I signed on for?" Jacob asked Henry as the demon came at them with deliberation, shoving over headstones in its path.

"You signed up for the Templars, didn't you?"

"Suppose you're right on that count."

"Cover me. Don't close in on it unless you absolutely must."

"Yes sir."

Henry raised his shield enough to cover his mailed torso. He kept his sword's blade out and to the side, giving him free range of motion in case the demon tackled him. Demons liked to grapple, that much Jacob had been taught in training. He'd never been taught just how damn ugly they were, though. That was a revision to the manuals Jacob would mention when next he spoke to the abbot.

"Hell-spawn," Henry barked, advancing towards the demon. "Come at me, you beastly thing."

Wyatt's tentacles flared from its face, the tips flailing and grasping at air. The creature uprooted a tombstone from the moist soil and hurled the hunk of etched granite at Henry. Henry stepped aside from the granite missile's trajectory with grace belying his age.

"Put in a bit of effort on the next toss, Wyatt." Henry shook sweat soaked hair from his eyes. "Let's make this interesting."

The tentacled thing stooped to the ground and ripped another headstone from the ground, a five-foot-tall obelisk topped with an ornate cross. It hefted the weight in its right hand, gave the makeshift club a test swing, and continued advancing towards Henry.

"I believe that's a slight improvement. Jacob?"

"Yup?"

"Is there a reason you're not shooting?"

"I was just . . . I apologize, sir." Jacob leveled his revolver at the thing's torso and pulled the trigger. The revolver roared

14

and leapt in Jacob's hand. The demon took the bullet squarely in the chest and recoiled a step. Black spread on the yellowing buttoned-up shirt. Jacob fired three more bullets. It took more steps back. Wyatt turned and focused on Jacob, hefting its obelisk turned club. It advanced, closing the distance with long-legged strides. "Sir, I don't reckon bullets are working as well as we'd hoped."

"Not a concern. Perchance, could you endeavor to shoot it in the head next time?"

"Yes sir." He adjusted his aim slightly upward and fired again. A fine mist of black ichor sprayed into the air as the demon's head snapped back violently. It stumbled backwards two steps, its club swinging out and away from its torso as it lost balance. A collective wail like the howling of ravenous wolves welled up from the crowd.

Henry took the opening and charged the demon with a roar that would've put Johnny Reb to shame. He slashed across the demon's belly with the outer edge of the blade, ending the cut with his broadsword raised and ready. More of the brackish ichor welled out of the thing's gut. Henry struck again, this time at its exposed left limb. The demon backpedaled, but Henry matched each of its lumbering steps with two of his own. He hacked at the right leg. The demon swung the obelisk, but the Templar met the stone club's base with his shield and absorbed the impact.

Henry kept up the assault, chopping at the demon's right wrist. The demon's hand severed with a sickening plop and an otherworldly scream that sent its tentacles flaring. Ichor sprayed from the stump, leaving Henry's breast plate with a shimmering patina of black slime. Henry danced out of the falling obelisk's path and skirted around the creature to its rear.He sliced across the demon's left Achilles tendon, hamstringing the demon with a practiced barbarism that produced another wail. It collapsed to its left knee, its head falling forward.

Henry huffed and completed his circle, moving to the demon's right side. Jacob glanced furtively around at the now quiet crowd. "Jacob,would you care to do the honors, or shall I?"

"I wouldn't presume to steal your glory on the battlefield, Mr. Bennett. You go right on with that beheading."

"You certainly have my gratitude," Henry said as he raised his blade. With a roar, the Templar swung the blade down at the demon's neck. A gunshot rang out just before Henry's swing connected. Henry stumbled backward, stunned. The broadsword tumbled from his shattered right hand. The Templar went to his knees, the color drained from his face.

"Drop your firearm, Templar," a raspy voice said from the other end of the cemetery. "Or I end Mr. Bennett's life at this very moment."

Jacob swung his revolver towards the shadowy source some thirty paces away.

"Consider the course of events you are about to set in motion, Mr. Smith. I know you have already fired six shots at Wyatt. Which leaves your pistol empty, if I am not mistaken, and you surrounded with only a sword for defense. Bennett, handless as he is, will be of no help in this fight," William DuBose said as he stepped from the shadows, a tightly held revolver pointed at Jacob. Jacob pointed his own revolver back at DuBose's angular, pallid form.

"Wrong, DuBose, I only fired five shots," Jacob said and pulled the trigger. The hammer clicked on an empty cylinder. "Shit," Jacob cursed, closing his eyes. He never should have taken Henry's advice. He dropped the pistol at his feet. "Thought this was supposed to be a fair duel for the book, DuBose. Us verses your thing there," Jacob said, gesturing at the grey demon on its knees.

"I lied, Mr. Smith." Grey lips twisted and curled on DuBose's drawn face. "Take him," he snarled at the crowd. "We'll use them for the ritual tonight."

Martin's kinfolk obeyed with gusto. The circle closed in on Jacob.

Consciousness came back to Jacob Smith. He lay on a dirt floor. His head felt like he'd tried to catch a six-pounder's cannonball in the teeth. His left leg felt like it'd taken a kick from a horse's hindquarters. It reeked awfully strong wherever he'd awakened. Jacob smelled something sickly sweet. Cooking pork, maybe? Below that was body odor and sweat.

Not the most appetizing of fragrant combinations. Jacob kept his eyes closed, just hoping this would all go away. He groaned.

"Quiet, Jacob," Henry whispered.

"Mr. Bennett? You're still kicking?"

"Yes, barely," Henry replied, his voice jagged and full of rasp. "I'm still alive. My thoughts are that being well is another matter entirely. Now stay quiet. Our jailers don't know you're awake yet. I'd prefer it remained that way."

Jacob opened his eyes and turned his head to look in Henry's direction. The movement ratcheted up the pain. He winced. They were in a filthy cell. Henry sat propped against the metal bars in the corner opposite Jacob. Dirt, blood, and Wyatt's foreign ichor covered his armor and clothing. Henry wheezed with each breath, his face was pale white. Blood-shot eyes, sunken, with deep, black circles beneath, gave the impression of a raccoon rather than an English gentlemen. He cradled his shattered right hand, swaddled in yellowish gauze, to his chest. The space below the elder Templar's left knee was empty. They hadn't even bothered to dress the wound, they'd simply seared it at the stump. Jacob shuddered.

"What did they do to you?"

"It's not nearly as bad as it looks. Keep that upper lip stiff. How are you faring?"

"Fine. Headache from hell, and my left leg is injured, but manageable. But, you . . ."

"Quiet, Jacob. Understand that I don't have much longer. Do you smell that cooking? I can't be certain," Henry said, coughing weakly, "but that may very well be my leg. You have been out for over an hour and—"

"We gotta get you to a surgeon or doc—"

"No," Henry said. The hissing severity shut Jacob right up. "DuBose came into gloat earlier. They're starting a ritual tonight, a ritual you must stop. They're tearing a hole into some place other than Hell. I won't live much longer, whether or not you can drag me back to Chattanooga. You've seen wounds like this as often as I, and you know that oftentimes they prove fatal. So be a good chap and shut the fuck up. I have a plan to help you escape, boy. After that, it's up to you to stop DuBose. That ritual must not be completed."

Jacob sighed. "Yes sir. Wait. Did you just cuss?"
Henry just smiled and laid back his head against the cell bars.

After ten minutes, or maybe five, or even twenty, one of Martin's cousins, brothers, or uncles came to the cell door. Jacob couldn't see them, he kept his eyes closed, but he could tell it was one of the inbreds from their shuffling, shambling steps they all seemed to have in common. Keys jingled, someone fumbled with the lock, and there followed a neat click as the key turned the tumblers.

"Hello, mate. Come to take my hand? Quite the feast your kinfolk seem to be having this evening."

"Leg," the Martin replied.

"Sure you wouldn't want my arm instead?"

"Leg."

"Fine, fine. But you'll have to fight me for it."

There was a soft thump and the sound of something heavy landing on the dirt floor, followed immediately by a horrendous howl. Jacob's eyes snapped open. The servant was hunched over, clutching his privates. A heavy, rusted meat cleaver lay on the floor in front of Henry. Jacob clambered to his feet, his bad leg almost giving way. He braced himself and stomped on the right side of the Martin's knee.

A satisfying crunch sounded and the inbred crumpled, his yowls reaching a crescendo.

"Jacob." Henry handed the meat cleaver to Jacob.

Jacob took it quickly. He grabbed a handful of the Martin's greasy hair and pulled the distorted head back, exposing the throat just like he'd done to cattle on his grandfather's farm. The man's eyes went wide with terror. Jacob chopped the cleaver, sinking it as far into the exposed throat as possible. Blood welled up from the Martin's mouth and around the blade. The blood ran down the servant's worn shirt, pasting it to the skin.

"Hurry, there may be more coming."

Jacob began desperately wrenching the cleaver's blade from the inbred's neck. Jacob hoped there weren't any more of Martin's kinfolk as he worked the blade back and forth. He finally yanked the cleaver free.

18

Jacob hefted the cleaver in his right hand and exited the cell. He walked the short distance to the corner. He couldn't hear anything, but he couldn't be for sure. Jacob drew himself up against the wall and took a half-step back from the corner and steadied his breathing.

Nothing. Just a room with a firepit in the middle and Henry's leg roasting slowly on a spit. Jacob shuddered, then turned and went back to the cell.

"Mr. Bennett? Still with me?"

No response. Henry stayed against the bars, unmoving. The older Templar's head leaned forward, his chin resting on his breast. Jacob's stomach sank. He walked forward and put a hand below his nose. No feel of breath on his fingertips. Jacob sighed. He hunkered down next to the older Templar.

"Mr. Bennett," he began in a low voice, "I've really appreciated our time together. It's awful we couldn't get to know each other better. I'll tell the abbot of your valiance and sacrifice when I get back to Chicago."

Standing, Jacob turned and walked over to where his hat lay on the ground. He picked it up and went back to Henry's body. He laid it over the Englishman's face. He made the sign of the cross, whispered a short prayer for Henry's soul, and left the cell.

Upon seeing Henry's leg again, Jacob felt a queasiness in his stomach. The sulfurous, sickly-sweet smell of the cooking flesh suddenly hit him, driving its way into his nostrils like a wagon train heading West. It coated the inside of his nose and mouth.

Before he could choke down the vomit, he'd doubled over and begun heaving. It had been a dry heave. Jacob suddenly realized he hadn't eaten anything since a few bits of jerky on the ride to the plantation. The thought of food made his stomach churn again. He stood and, wiping saliva from his mouth, began searching the small hut.

"What do we have here?"

Across the firepit, next to the front door, hung Henry and Jacob's gun-belts. On a nail next to the pistols someone had stored a hunting knife in its sheath. Their swords, still sheathed, were propped in the right hand corner. Opposite from the swords, a double-barreled shotgun leaned against the wall.

19

Jacob walked over and strapped the belts in a crisscross. He drew and reloaded his revolver, holstered it once more, before making sure that Henry's was still fully loaded. Grabbing his sheathed blade, he slung it over his torso and tightened the belt. He checked to make sure he could draw the sword over his left shoulder. Satisfied, he took the hunting knife from the wall and stuffed it in the shaft of his right boot. He removed Henry's leg from the fire and propped it against the wall. The queasiness set in again, but this time the heaves didn't come. He picked up the shotgun and went back into the cell. Rifling through the pockets of the inbred's corpse laying on the cell floor, he found four shotgun shells.

Better than nothing.

He stuffed them into his breast pocket and went back to the front door.

Jacob opened the door a crack and surveyed the area outside. The servant cabin they were in was set quite a ways back from the garden they'd walked through earlier on their way to the duel. Judging from where the house was in relation to him, he was on the south side of the plantation. And, considering the chanting and activity on the east side of the plantation, the ritual was somewhere in the general direction of the cemetery. He eased open the door, flattened himself against the wall of the house and crouched low till he was sure he was out of line of sight from the garden. He moved into the forest, careful to not make any more noise than he had to.

Between his wounded leg and the spiderwebs, thorns, bramble, low hanging trees, and deadfall trees, the trip through the woods was a slog. It seemed like everything tried to slow him down. Maybe it did.

The chant increased in tempo the closer Jacob got. Finally, he reached the edge of the clearing where the ritual had begun. The Templar gripped the shotgun tightly and surveyed the grounds.

The clearing was easily eighty feet across. The grass and brush had been cleared here and what remained had been stomped down by a multitude of feet. In the center was a bonfire that crackled and roared, with a tongue of flame reaching some fifteen feet into the night sky. Surrounding it were a group of figures clothed in grey and black robes. On the east side of the clearing to Jacob's right was a stone altar that looked as black as DuBose's soul. Flanking the altar were two demons similar to the one he and Henry fought in the cemetery.

Two. Jacob gripped his shotgun tighter. On the north edge, he could just make out a pair of wagons outfitted with prison bars. People were inside.

As he watched, one of the figures strode imperiously to the altar with a massive tome in its hands. It rested the book on the altar and took up position behind it, facing the bonfire. It drew back its hood. The figure was DuBose.

"CTHULHU SHADDUYA! ISHNIGARRAB IA! PH'NGLUI MGLW'NAFH CTHULHU R'LYEH WGAH'NAGL FHTAGN," DuBose shouted at the crowd. The crowd responded in kind.

Jacob backed into the trees. He stayed low and circled around to the backside of the altar. "I should have just stayed at the monastery," he whispered.

"PH'NGLUI MGLW'NAFH CTHULHU R'LYEH WGAH'NAGL FHTAGN."

Jacob crouched and moved to the edge of the clearing. His leg throbbed in pain. He raised the shotgun and braced the stock against his right shoulder. He stood, took a deep breath, and limped into the clearing behind DuBose and his two things.

Whatever they chanted, it sure had their attention. Stopping fifteen feet from the trio, he turned to the thing on the right, aimed the shotgun at its head, and pulled the trigger. A load of buckshot erupted out of one barrel and tore a hole in the side of the creature's head, black ichor spraying. It stumbled forward and to the right, black blood streaming down its backside, tentacles waving in the air.

Jacob didn't wait to see the creature fall. He turned immediately to the left and hopped back a stride, favoring his good leg.

The other creature began turning to engage him.

The chant continued.

Jacob fired again, but only winged it. Pellets tore into the creature's shoulder and shredded its face tentacles, but it only broke stride for a moment. He cracked open the shotgun and pulled the spent shell casings out, singeing his fingers. He reloaded and snapped it shut. The Templar took aim and fired again.

The creature's face caved inward and the back of its head exploded. It toppled backwards, its body beginning to melt into greyish unidentifiable matter on the way down.

The chant grew louder, with all voices joining in.

Jacob took a hit to his right shoulder. The force of the blow sent him spinning into the air, flinging his shotgun away. Pain flared out from his shoulder as he landed facedown in the dirt. The Templar scrambled to his feet and turned to see a massive grey fist bearing down on him. Jacob flung himself to the right, regretting the decision immediately as he landed heavily on his hurt shoulder.

The first creature, its face distorted from the buckshot, connected with the empty ground. Jacob came out of the roll, almost losing his footing as his left leg nearly collapsed, and drew his sword.

With a curse, he hamstrung the thing like Henry had earlier in the evening, cutting swiftly across the exposed Achilles tendon of its left foot. He spun to the right, pivoting on his good leg, and hacked his broadsword into the right tendon. The creature crumbled.

Jacob clambered onto the creature's back, sword held in both hands, and plunged the blade through the thing's neck. He twisted the blade and rode the swiftly decomposing corpse to the ground. Ripping his sword free, he spun awkwardly to meet any oncoming foes.

They all kept on chanting. Jacob drew his pistol in his left hand and limped towards DuBose. He shouted over the crackling of flames and chanting, "DuBose. Stop the ritual or I'll shoot."

DuBose looked back over his shoulder at Jacob. "You're too late, Templar. The ritual is almost complete. There ain't nothing you can do now." William DuBose pointed above the bonfire. "Look."

Jacob looked up. A green and purple shimmer had started to form over the bonfire. As Jacob watched, a single tentacle slithered out from the gate. Another one appeared soon after, wrapping itself around the edge. They began pulling at the tear, widening it farther.

"Really? Well, shit." Jacob raised his pistol and shot DuBose in the back of the head. The Tennessee gentlemen collapsed forward onto the altar.

The creature on the other side roared its disgruntlement as the rift closed with a moist pop. The chanting stopped abruptly. The bonfire continued to crackle.

"You know," Jacob said to DuBose's corpse, "that was a lot less morally troublesome than I thought it'd be." He dragged the body off the altar and unceremoniously dropped it on the grass.

"Alright, ya'll, fun's over," Jacob shouted to the crowd. "Get on out of here."

A dozen sets of confused eyes turned towards him. "I said get!" Jacob raised his pistol and fired into the air. The group dispersed, running for the closest edge of the clearing. Just for good measure, Jacob fired over their heads.

When the area had cleared, Jacob looked down at the book on the altar. DuBose had opened the *Necronomicon* to a page covered in foreign, crimson sigils. He reached out a hand to the vellum page, feeling the strange warmth and humming of the words. Something inside Jacob told him that this was even less like other books than he'd thought. He drew back.

He knelt down next to DuBose's corpse and cut a large swatch from the black robe with the hunting knife he'd taken from the servant shack. The piece of fabric measured three feet on each side. He laid it down on the altar next to the *Necronomicon*, then used the knife's edge to flip the book onto the cloth. Jacob wrapped it up, tucked it under his arm, and headed to the captives.

They were a pathetic lot that numbered a dozen or more. Jacob shot the locks off the prison wagons and released the captives. "Get on home now," he told them. "And watch out for them folks in dark robes."

The people stared at him from within their cages. Jacob just stared back. He shrugged and limped back to the mansion, wincing with each step. The group followed, not knowing where else to go.

Jacob had never been so happy to see such a ragged town. Chattanooga may as well have been New York City in the dawn's early light. He stopped his horse and funeral sledge in front of the undertakers and removed what remained of Henry's body. He explained to the man that they'd both been attacked by a bear, and that the undertaker should prepare the body and send it to Chicago immediately.

He left the address of the Templar abbey and went to purchase a ticket on the first steamboat leaving town for Chicago. Hopefully, the boat would leave before the undertaker could get around to telling any interesting stories.

Jacob went back to the room they'd rented on arrival. The ship home didn't leave till that afternoon and Jacob figured he could at least get a few hours shuteye. He ordered the finest bottle of whiskey from the bar downstairs. He didn't know if it was the finest in Chatanooga, but it sure was quality.

He tipped back a glass for Henry and one for himself before laying down on the bed. He closed his eyes, exhausted.

In his dreams, tentacles slithered out from a purple void into his vision. Jacob opened his eyes and sat upright, gasping. He looked over at the chest where he'd stored the *Necronomicon*. Nothing had changed since he'd put it there hours before.

He got up and walked over to where his sword hung. He took it down and retrieved his whetstone from his traveling bag. He went back over and sat down on the edge of the bed. He drew his sword and spat on the stone. With one eye on the chest, he began sharpening his blade.

He'd sleep on the way home. Failing that, there was always the monastery outside Chicago.

THE RENAISSANCE
OF JACOB SMITH

The purplish-grey tentacles grabbed hold of Jacob Smith's leg and began pulling him closer to the mass of swirling, gnashing teeth at the portal opening. Acrid fluid burned through the leg of his trouser and shaft of his boot . The chant of CHOGTHATHA CHOGTHA CHOGTHA reverberated in his ears and vibrated his sinuses, as a steady back beat began: *pound pound pound.*

Jacob, eyes wide, sat upright in bed. The sheets and his long johns were both drenched through with cool sweat. His eyes tracked around the unadorned stone walls across from him, looking for whatever had invaded his dreams.

He breathed deep. He was back in the monastery, miles and miles away from the graveyard of Kadath Plantation. The pounding at the door started again, *bang bang bang,* barely keeping pace with his heart.

"Jacob, open up," someone said through the door.

"Hold your damn horses," Jacob yelled back. "Let me get some clothes on."

He tossed the thin covers and sheets off and got out of bed. He shivered as his bare feet touched the flagstone floor. Damn, it was cold for spring. He grabbed his trousers and shirt from the back of the room's only chair and dressed. Clothed, he padded across the room and opened the door.

Christopher Freeman stood, leaning against the door's frame, arms crossed.

Jacob let the door swing open and walked back to the chair to pull on his boots.

"We kept some vittles on the table."

Jacob wondered if he'd been screaming in the waking world. He'd had complaints from some of the other passengers on the steamer trip from Tennessee.

"Thanks." Jacob began tugging on the first of his old boots.

"How was it coming back?"

"Lonesome," Jacob said, pulling on the next boot. He sighed and stayed seated in his chair.

"Yep," Christopher said, entering the room. He leaned back against the wall and recrossed his arms. "Know that feeling. It's painful to lose a comrade." He leveled his gaze at Jacob.

"Yup." Jacob returned Christopher's look. After a moment, Jacob stood and walked over to the empty water basin. He poured some fresh water in and splashed his face. He toweled off and looked back over his shoulder at the other man. "What'd they fix for breakfast?"

"Sausage and grits."

Jacob went over to where his holster and sword-belt hung from a wall peg . He pulled both down and began to strap them on.

"Coffee?"

"Hatsuto made sure they left a cup."

"Good man," Jacob said, cinching his belts tight. Christopher walked out into the hallway and Jacob followed. "When did Mr. Bennett arrive?" he asked Christopher as he shut the door to his cell.

"Few days ago," Christopher replied. They walked down the hallway to a set of spiral stairs at the end.

"Had a service yet?"

"Not yet. Didn't seem right without you here."

"Why? Ain't like I knew him all that well."

"Guess you didn't," Christopher said, scratching at his beard. "But you were with him when he fell. Figured you got some words to say." Christopher led the way down the stairs.

"I reckon so." Jacob followed after Christopher. "How many of the others are here?" They entered the corridor which led to the dining hall.

"We got Hatsuto and the colonel."

"And the book's safe?"

"Put in the vault as soon as you delivered it."

"Good."

Ahead, the dining hall's double doors stood open. Monks sat quietly breaking their fast. Jacob and Christopher walked in and headed for the back corner reserved for the Templars. The colonel and Hatsuto were both already there, their plates cleaned of any food morsel. They sipped tea and spoke to each other in low voices. As Jacob and Christopher approached, the other two men stopped talking and stood.

"Jacob, sir, it's good to have you back," Col. Winnie said, offering his bear paw of a hand.

"It's good to be here, sir," Jacob replied, taking his hand. He turned to the Japanese man, Hatsuto, and bowed. Hatsuto bowed in turn and offered his hand. They shook. All four sat at the table. The three others focused their attention on Jacob.

"Did Henry go down fighting?" the colonel asked.

Jacob hesitated a moment. "Yes sir."

"Good. The thought of him falling from his horse and breaking his neck, or some other variety of needless death, wouldn't have sat well with him. Henry was a proud man."

"He got me out alive."

"And that damnable *Necronomicon* is safely in the vault as well."

"What are we going to do with it? Return it to Miskatonic University?"

"No," Col. Winnie said, patting the table for emphasis, "a replica will be made and sent in its place. Mark my words, men, I'll not again risk having that tome fall into the wrong hands."

There was a round of nods around the table.

"You men eat your breakfast," Col. Winnie said, standing. "Jacob, when you're finished eating, go see the abbot, then come down to my office. I'd like to discuss our next move."

"Our next move, sir?" Jacob asked, looking up at the colonel.

"Certainly, son," Col. Winnie said, putting a reassuring hand on Jacob's shoulder. "We must rally the troops."

The older man excused himself and left the room, heading back through the double doors to the corridor. None of the monks watched him go, their gazes remained fixed on their plates.

"Rally the troops?" Christopher asked. "For what?"

"What is 'rally the troops'?" Hatsuto asked, a bushy eyebrow raised.

"Means to bring all your soldiers together," Jacob said as a monk brought over a plate each for Christopher and him.

"Ah," Hatsuto said, taking a sip from his mug of tea. He made a face. He still hadn't gotten used to black tea, but they could rarely find green anywhere in Chicago.

"Why do you think he said that?" Christopher asked before he started digging into his food.

"Reckon DuBose, the man we took the *Necronomicon* back from, wasn't acting alone? Maybe there's other rebels like him that are stockpiling artifacts?" Jacob asked, digging into his own plate. He was starving.

"Maybe," Christopher said around a mouthful of food. "Wouldn't put it past 'em, what with the way they tried to hold on."

"If a man picks up arms and fights another man," Hatsuto said, setting his mug down, "do not expect him to stop fighting when beaten one time."

"But we whooped 'em good," Jacob said. "Sherman marched right through there."

"The Union whooped 'em," Christopher said. "We ain't got nothing to do with it. May have been a boy in blue before, but you ain't now."

"Fine," Jacob said. "The Union did it. Figured they wouldn't have much fight left in 'em, that's all."

"I think Hatsuto's right. South thinks the North is telling 'em how to live still. That's what the rebellion was always about, the South thinking they was fine to buy and sell my people and them not wanting no lip from the other side. Sherman marching to the sea ain't likely to have made 'em anymore willing to take to it. I think we're gonna see more like that DuBose."

"Reckon so?"

"Yep. Bet my poke on it."

"Likely right." Jacob forked a link of sausage and bit into it. "What do you think Col. Winnie wants to talk to me for?"

Both of the Templars looked at each other and shrugged.

"Beats me."

"I do not know his intentions, either," Hatsuto said.

Jacob went back to eating.

Jacob breathed deep and knocked cautiously on the door to the abbot's small office. It was nestled in one of the top corners of the monastery. Abbot Jean Marie Ouellet was the head of the Jesuit order in these parts. The Templars, for their part, weren't necessarily part of the Catholic Church, but they did receive most of their funding from them. They operated out of this monastery, and the abbot

30

was considered their caretaker of sorts. Like Congress does with the military, the Church controlled their purse strings. And, just like in the normal military, the chain of command could get foggy.

"*Entrez.*"

Jacob pushed the door open. The room was spacious in comparison to the monastic cells Jacob was accustomed to. The walls on all sides were hidden behind wooden bookshelves stacked with leather-bound tomes. Fur rugs covered the flagstone floor, making it feel more like a hunting cabin than an office.

Abbot Jean Marie Ouellet sat behind his desk. He was a birdlike man, all frailty and sharp edges. Even his little bald head looked like an egg to Jacob, with its skin stretching tight over his fragile skull.

"Jacob," the abbot said, looking up at him through bifocal lenses, "thank you for coming. Allow me to complete this letter, and I will be right with you. Please sit."

In front of the desk were two wooden chairs. Jacob took the one on the left and crossed his legs, idly looking about to the rhythmic accompaniment of the abbot's scratching quill.

"I am concluding my letter to M. Bennett's sister. It is customary to write such letters in the military, is it not?"

Jacob had written plenty of letters like Ouellet's during the war, though not as a commanding officer. Always as war buddies to a girl the man knew or loved, or thought he knew and loved. Sometimes to sisters, too. They gave a brief respite to some, but Jacob had never been glad to perform the duty. But that was duty's definition, wasn't it? Something you did despite its joylessness.

"Thought that was the colonel's responsibility?"

"Oh, it is. My letter will accompany his. I feel it is my duty."

Jacob nodded absently and looked at the titles on the shelves. History texts mostly, but with treatises on mathematics, philosophy, and naturalism scattered throughout the collection.

"It is a sad day when one must send such letters, do you not agree? I wrote of your involvement, and your returning of M. Bennett's body to our care. It is good that he will be buried on sacred soil."

"Yes sir, it is."

"I would, if you feel comfortable, Jacob, like to ask about what happened in Tennessee."

"Yes sir," Jacob said.

The abbot put aside his quill and closed his inkwell's lid. He folded his hands on his desk and looked at Jacob. Jacob looked back.

"The colonel wrote his report based on what you told him of the events. What did you see at Kadath Estates?" the abbot asked, his lips pressed together in a distinct line.

"A bunch of folks trying to cause the Apocalypse."

"Yet you halted it, did you not, by taking this DuBose's life?"

"Yes sir. I did."

"Are you fine with your decision? The colonel said you shot him without second thought."

"Yes sir, I did. I shot him in the back, too, if that makes a difference."

"*Un peu,*" the abbot said, making the gesture for a little bit with his right hand. "Do you feel guilt?"

"I took a man's life, Abbot. I'd never lie and say it was noble, shooting him the way I did, but I stopped him from doing the same all over the north."

"Perhaps all over the world. Any, how do you Americans say, second guessing?"

Jacob thought about it. He hadn't really considered it yet, so he figured he might as well just for the hell of it. He looked off to the side at all those books of history and their chronicles of a world which might have ceased existence if DuBose had finished his ritual.

"Were I forced to relive it," Jacob said, looking the Abbot in the eye, "I'd do it again. DuBose belonged in a sanitarium or in the ground, and I didn't see no sanitarium around."

Jacob walked down the final flight of stairs to the floor of the monastery's cellar that served as headquarters for the Knights Templar in America. The Order covered as much of North America as they could from this small space, with Col. Winfred Hitchcock sending the knights to the four corners of the continent whenever there was something in need of being taken care of. The colonel, Col. Winnie to his men, served as their spiritual guide, as well as their commander, bringing the total of the Knights Templar membership to nine. Well, eight, since Henry Bennett had died in Tennessee.

Jacob had only met a few of the other Templars: The colonel, Christopher Freeman, Hatsuto Watanabe, Henry Bennett, and Five Feathers. The other four were on distant missions, and generally stayed gone. Blake Hardy, a crazy mountain man from the sound of him, stayed in the Pacific Northwest hunting werewolves, werecats, windigos, sasquatch, and the like. Pedro Hernandez stayed in the Southwest, killing chupacabras, vampires, and such. Finally, there was an Irishman in New York named Conner and another Templar, Jean, in Quebec.

Jacob walked down the dank, close-walled corridor to the colonel's office. Water dripped somewhere in the labyrinth of dank halls. Damp and mildew filled Jacob's nose and coated his skin. Gaslights burned on the walls, a recent addition, but they didn't do much to ward off the sense of being entombed. Jacob stopped at the door to the office and knocked.

"Enter," Col. Winnie bellowed from the other side.

Jacob puffed out his chest a little and opened the door. Maps made of vellum and books older than Jacob's dead grandfather fought for the tiny space offered by the shelves and table tops. Towering over it all like a spectacle-wearing grizzly was Col. Winnie. He was stuffed into the scant space he'd set aside for his desk. He glanced up from the stack of letters spread in front of him.

"Jacob," he said, waving at a chair which a stack of books had won from the maps, "take a seat. I was just going over a letter from Mr. Hernandez." Jacob looked warily at the plain chair, weighing whether it was worth trying to find places for all the amassed words just so he could sit. He looked back at Col. Winnie, who seemed engrossed.

"My Spanish is far from impeccable, so this could take a moment," Col. Winnie said without looking up from the letter. Jacob began moving the books from chair to shelves. He sat down when he was finished. "How went the interview with the abbot?"

"Fine. Asked me about DuBose."

"What about that man?"

"Whether I regretted shooting him or not."

"Do you?" the colonel asked, looking up from his letter for the briefest of moments.

"No sir."

Col. Winnie pursed his lips and considered Jacob for a moment more before going back to his reading. More time passed.

"Care for a drink?" Col. Winnie asked after a while, pulling open a side drawer and reaching in for a bottle of bourbon whiskey. He set the spirits on the desktop in front of Jacob.

"Just crept past noon, sir."

"Asked if you cared for a drink, son, not the time of day."

"Reckon I'll have one, then."

Winnie stuck his hand back in the drawer and grabbed two glasses. He set them next to the bottle. Jacob poured them each three fingers and took a sip of his. It was good. Smoky. The younger man took another sip. Winnie kept reading.

Ten minutes passed. Col. Winnie sighed and took off his spectacles. His chair creaked as he leaned back. The colonel began to chew on the ear piece of his spectacles. He looked from his untouched glass of bourbon to Jacob. The young Templar was already beginning to show signs of the whiskey's affection. Jacob poured himself another glass.

Col. Winnie sighed and looked at a bookshelf in the corner. It reached to the low ceiling and was so crammed full of books and tomes that any false pull may set off an avalanche.

"See those books on that shelf, son?"

Jacob turned and looked back at the shelf. "Yup."

"There is one on the second from the top shelf. Its spine is unmarked. Bring it here, please."

"Yes sir," Jacob said, downing the last of his whiskey before standing. He walked shakily over to the bookshelf, knocking over a stack in the process, and pulled the book Col. Winnie had indicated. Luckily, no bookslide started.

Jacob looked down at the plain, leather-bound book in his hands. He turned it over so he could see the back. There was no marking on the other side either. It was thin and old, but well cared for.

"What's this?"

"The *Annals of the Knights Templar*."

"All the way back?"

"Just from our reinstatement by Pope Pius in 1780. When our founder left from Europe to come to this monastery, he brought a copy. Our histories diverged from that point, you understand."

"Mind if I look at it? Still don't know much about the order. Just, you know, the vision I had and what y'all have told me."

"It is your right."

Jacob opened the book at the beginning. It was filled with plain, cream-colored, unlined paper. There was no dedication on the first page, just a simple date at the top left, "4 March, 1780," like a journal, followed by a long stream of florid script which swam and danced in Jacob's vision. Jacob tried to read the first few words, but they wouldn't connect.

"God," he said under his breath, "I'm drunk already." He shut the book carefully and took it to Col. Winnie.

"Feeling alright? You look a bit flustered, son," the colonel said around the earpiece of his spectacles as he took the book from Jacob. Col. Winnie thumbed through it till he stopped on the first blank page he reached.

"Yup. Well, no, not feeling so right. Whiskey of yours kicks like a mule." He looked down at the colonel's untouched glass, and back to his. He picked up his empty glass and smelled the remnants.

There was bourbon and notes of something else, something slightly acrid. His eyes widened. Jacob sat down, barely catching the edge of the chair, his gaze still fixed on the bottom of the empty glass. He looked at Winnie again.

"Feeling alright?" the colonel asked again, leaning forward with his fingers expectantly steepled at his chin.

"You . . ." Jacob said, his tongue feeling like a bud of cotton. "Didn't . . ." The words wouldn't come. He closed his eyes and tried to force them out. If he could just get the damned thought out, he'd be fine. Jacob opened his eyes and attempted to speak again, but there was still nothing. Winnie blinked slowly.

The room abruptly slanted to the left. Jacob grabbed hold of his own thighs in an attempt to stay seated. The young Templar struggled to stay upright, fighting the floor's incessant tugging. He raised an accusatory finger at Winnie as his vision again lurched to the left.

"You've plenty of fight, son," Col. Winnie said, putting his spectacles back on. He took his pen from the desktop and began filling it from an inkwell. He began to write in the book.

Jacob stood, but his legs couldn't resist the spin of the room. He tried to maintain his footing in broken stamps and stomps, but the pull from his left was too much. Jacob tried to draw his pistol, but his arms were lead and unresponsive. He staggered backwards into the chair, knocking it over. He fell to the floor in a sitting position.

"Stay down," Col. Winnie said from behind his desk. Jacob heard the distant groan of the chair as the giant man stood and came around to hover above him. The younger man looked up at the older. Winnie still had that grim, tight-lipped look. "Only gonna make this harder on yourself if you try to get back up."

Jacob looked at the desk. He reached for the corner and tried to stand at the same time. He made it to his feet, but unable to get any purchase on the desk, toppled forward. He collided with the oak desk and slid to the ground. Jacob's vision faded.

"Told you to stay down, son."

"He's coming to," Christopher said. At least Jacob thought it was Christopher. His vision was still blurred. Jacob shook his head from side to side, trying to shake himself out of the fog. He was naked, almost completely submerged in some sort of liquid.

"Let him have a bit more then," said the colonel. "Only need him out for a bit longer."

"You sure, sir?"

"Course I'm sure."

A figure moved in the darkness. It pushed a balled up rag over Jacob's mouth. He held his breath. He tried to struggle, to thrash at his captors, but his arms felt weak as a foal. They grew weaker as he finally broke and inhaled from the rag.

"*Shhhh,*" whispered Christopher as Jacob drifted back into the darkness. Jacob heard stone grind on stone. A dull thud followed.

Jacob awoke again. Well, at least he reckoned he did. He floated in a vacuous world of nothing. He groped outward with his hands, trying to get a grip on the dimensions of his confinement. He touched something solid. Trying a different tack, Jacob felt at his own body, but he struck something soft, but firm and unyielding when he moved his arms more than a half-inch or so.

"Hey," he hollered, trying to kick and thrash, his voice echoing in the bleakness.

Questions rolled through his mind. Why had his comrades done this? Why had the colonel poisoned him? Where was he? Was this because he'd let Henry Bennett die? Was it because he'd killed DuBose? Was this some sort of punishment?

He tried to keep his breathing steady. Jacob didn't know how much air there was.

How long he stayed that way, just thinking and breathing, Jacob couldn't say. With no sun or pocket watch, there was no point of reference to measure time. The same thoughts of reasons for his imprisonment rolled and rolled through his mind, till his thoughts seemed trivial. Eventually, because eventual was all he could think to call it, his trivial thoughts became nothingness. They simply ceased. His mind quieted. And then he was . . .

. . . standing naked in a roughly hewn stone corridor. Air so hot it might as well have been from a steam engine rushed past Jacob, almost knocking him to the ground. He covered his nakedness with his hands as he looked around. Amber light emanated from strange lichen covering every surface and hanging from the ceiling in great clumps. Light came from ahead. Jacob looked behind him, but the tunnel wound around a corner and went out of sight. Confused, Jacob stumbled ahead, following after the beacon . . .

"Hello?" Jacob called as he walked forward, gravel and sharp bits of stone digging into the soles of his bare feet. He followed the curve of the cave.

"Christopher? Hatsuto?" No response but his echo. Jacob kept walking.

The tunnel straightened out after thirty or forty paces. Jacob saw a great, white light emanating at the end. He looked behind him. He shielded his eyes and looked back into the light.

"Anyone?" Jacob walked on, stepping into the light. It was as bright and warm as a summer day.

* * *

"We made you," said the voice. Jacob opened his eyes and looked around. He was strapped to a table of some sort in an impossibly white room.

"Hello?" Jacob asked.

"We made you."

The walls shimmered the same way windows do in a rainstorm. Out of the base of the walls around him came a legion of small beings, only a foot or so high. Hundreds of them, pooled together in a great crowd of dark eyes and featureless faces. They pressed near where Jacob lay on the table. They stopped and looked up at him. Jacob craned his head to each side and looked back down at them.

"You will defend?" asked all the creatures together.

"Defend? Defend what?"

"Everything."

"Against what?"

"That which would undo all we have wrought."

Jacob, his neck strained, relaxed and let his head thump against the table.

"Yes," he said to the ceiling, "I'll defend."

"This is the Truth, Jacob Smith. We are the *sophia* of which your ancestors spoke." Jacob looked back down at the featureless creatures. Each now held aloft a ball of distorted *otherness* which bent the light around it. "This is the *logos* of which your ancestors spoke. It is the Truth. Accept it."

Jacob blinked. When he opened his eyes he was fully clothed and girded in his helm and chain tunic. He stood in the center aisle of an empty chapel, the comfortable weight of his revolver and sword hanging from either hip. In front of him stood a giant of a knight clad from head to foot in green-tinted plate mail.

The armor of the giant was inscribed with scrollwork and pictures of events and great battles depicted in a medieval style. His helmet was one of the old flat-topped pot helms which fully enclosed the wearer's head and only had a thin opening to see through. The knight's hands rested on the pommel of an enormous great sword, larger than any blade Jacob could ever lift.

Jacob looked away from the knight and around at the empty chapel. Light shone in through a myriad of stained glass windows, each of them a single instance in the long history of the Knights Templar. He recognized the images from some of the books he'd looked through in Col. Winnie's study.

"Where am I?" Jacob asked quietly. His words did not echo in the silent chamber.

"The Chapel of St. George, the heart of my order," said the knight, his voice louder than a battery of cannons. "Who are you?"

"I am Jacob Smith."

"Why have you come here? To join the *Pauperes commilitones Christi Templique Solomonici*?" Jacob hoped he didn't have to fight this knight. One swing from the sword he carried would cut through an anvil, let alone Jacob.

"You mean the Knights Templar?"

"Aye."

"Then, I reckon so," Jacob replied as he repositioned his feet to a fighting stance.

"Prepare yourself, mortal." Jacob drew his sword as the giant raised his own blade and began advancing with a lumbering gait. He covered the space in a few long strides, swinging his great sword in a horizontal arch at Jacob's neck.

Jacob ducked the clumsy swing, but the knight caught him in the face with a backhanded slap from his right gauntlet. Jacob flew through the air, over and into the wooden pews. He tried to tuck and roll with the impact, but his landing space was too confined. He landed hard on his left shoulder, his collarbone snapping with a profound crack.

Fire shot up his arm as he slid three feet down the smooth seat, his legs splayed behind him. He gripped his sword tight and scrambled out of the pew.

"Goddamn," Jacob said, trying to move his left arm. All he got for his trouble was agony. The knight reached down and effortlessly cleared the pew with a brush of his right hand, throwing the wooden pew off and to the left.

Jacob scooted backward towards the side aisle, his left arm hanging useless by his side. Gritting his teeth against the pain, he sheathed his sword and drew his revolver.

"Face me," the knight bellowed from the center aisle. Jacob stopped on the other side of the pews beneath a stained glass window emblazoned with a medieval depiction of two knights riding the same horse.

"Think I'm stupid?" He drew his pistol, cocked it single-handed, and aimed at the knight's head.

The knight stopped.

"What are you doing?" The knight looked both ways. "That is dishonorable."

"Dishonorable?" Jacob asked and fired a shot. The knight's head snapped back, the metal of the visor dented. Jacob switched positions, moving to his left to flank the giant. "You must be three times my size." He fired another shot, this time aimed at the side of the giant's head. The giant stumbled sideways, losing his footing.

"One punch and you broke my damn collarbone." Jacob moved as quickly as he could through a pew towards the center aisle. He fired another round. The bullet hit the giant in the shoulder. The giant knight lost his footing and stepped forward to regain his balance. Jacob thumbed back the hammer. The gun boomed as he fired into the giant's backside.

The armored man fell forward, sounding like a pots and pans covered bull plowing through a barn wall. His great sword fell to the stone tile of the aisle. Jacob holstered his pistol and drew his sword. He rushed the giant with a roar.

The giant rolled with surprising quickness, trying to bring an arm up in time to meet Jacob's charge, but it wasn't any use. Jacob already stood over him, broadsword clenched in his right hand and ready to drive it downward and through the giant's neck.

"Yield?"

"No," the giant said, a touch of surprise in his voice, "this is not the way it should happen."

"Wait. What do you mean?"

"No one ever has won."

"I ain't supposed to win? Really?" Jacob grunted his own surprise. "How does anyone ever join the Templars?"

"It's a sacrifice on your part, this duel. The initiate is to lay down his life for honor, and to leave behind their old life. Only after that can they be reborn into their new," the knight said.

Jacob grunted. "Well shit."

"May I remove my helmet? The dents make for an uncomfortable fit."

"Fine." The knight reached up cautiously and undid the strap beneath his helmet. He removed the helmet, revealing a gentle, topaz-hued face surrounded in long, blonde locks of hair. His eyes were golden, but human in shape and appearance.

"Thank you. I seldom have to wear the armor. One forgets how hot it can be. May I stand?"

"Your word you ain't gonna make a move?"

"Yes, my word as an angel." Jacob raised an eyebrow and stepped back. The angel rose to his feet.

"Woah there. Angel? Got any proof?"

The angel sighed. He puffed out his chest, his breastplate groaning with the strain, and stretched his arms to his side. As he leaned forward, a great wrenching of metal sounded. Feathered, white wings sprouted from the rends in the armor, stretching two dozen feet in each direction. Jacob stepped back as the angel twice beat his wings in the air.

"Does my proof back my assertion?"

"Yup," Jacob said, sheathing his sword. Wincing, he cradled his useless arm to his chest.

The angel sighed again and bent down to retrieve the helmet at his feet. He picked it up and inspected the depressions left by the bullet and looked at Jacob. "None of the others used pistols, you know."

"Why not?"

The angel shrugged.

"So, I was supposed to lose?"

"Yes."

"I wish someone would've mentioned that beforehand. Reckon this is all new." He looked around the structure. "Nice chapel, by the way."

"Thank you, but it's not mine. I'm merely it's guardian appearing in a way you wish to see. This place belongs to the Knights Templar." This close, Jacob realized just how tall the angel really was. Jacob only rose to his chest.

"They own this place?"

"In a manner of speaking. It's difficult to explain, but this is the ideal Chapel of St. George. The perfect one,

41

upon which all others depend. As long as the other chapels exist, this one will as well. All the others previously built across Europe and the Holy Land by the Knights Templar were just shadows. You should have seen this place three centuries ago. The daemons almost reclaimed into the ether."

"Demons?"

"Allow me to clarify. *Daemons*. They are neutral, and have no bearing on the fight for creation. They come through like stable hands and wipe out old, unused ideas and constructs."

"Right." Jacob pursed his lips. "How do you reckon we get this thing moving forward then?"

"I could kill you."

"What'd that take?"

The angel made a chopping motion with his hand.

Jacob shook his head. "Not a chance."

"I am no Jack Ketch, sir. A well-placed, clean strike should do the trick neatly."

Jacob looked askance at the great sword laying a few feet away in the aisle. He looked back up at the giant through squinted eyes. "Your word as an angel?"

"My word," the angel said, holding up his right hand and beating his wings once for emphasis.

"Alright, then. Guess we should keep tradition." Jacob sighed. "How do you want to do this?"

"You can just kneel right where you are."

"Alright," Jacob said, getting down on one knee. He settled in with the other while the angel retrieved his sword. "One quick question."

"Yes?" The angel asked as he spun the sword with ease.

"What's your name?"

"Michael."

"You're Michael the Archangel?"

"I am."

Jacob grunted and closed his eyes.

"A request of my own, Jacob?"

"What?" Jacob replied, eyes still closed.

"Could you not tell the other Templars you won?"

"Reckon I could keep it to myself." Jacob sighed.

"Thank you," Michael the Archangel said just before beheading Jacob Smith, the newest Knight Templar.

Images and experiences pressed together in Jacob's mind, squeezing themselves into his awareness.

"Papa, I wanna ride," Jacob saying, holding his hands up to his father.

"You sure, son?" his father asking as he reaches down to pick up Jacob before the boy can reconsider. Jacob sitting in front of his father on the horse, the saddle's hard leather being uncomfortable, the smell of fresh grass and barnyard filling his nose. His father's warm presence behind him as they both rode out from the Kansas homestead and into the prairie.

Jacob's first taste of coffee, his mother scowling when he spit it out, his brother laughing at him, his little sister screwing up her face in distaste and saying, "I'll never try that."

Jacob decking his brother with a hard right hook, riding off the farm for the last time, going past the lonesome tree where they'd laid his mother, father, and sister to rest.

Then the war, three hundred days of rain and cold nights, three hundred more of heat, all of them full of thirst and hunger, the soft crying of the new recruits, his own depression and lonesomeness in those early days, the ache in his gut because his parents would not ever come back no matter how many Rebels he killed.

Jacob shooting the young girl in the face, the way the ball from his revolver entered below her left cheekbone and exited through the back of her skull in a bloody crater, his mustering out from the raiders afterward when the war ended.

That same girl forgiving him a lifetime later while he sat breaking fast with the other monks. The abrasion of his vocal cords as he screamed, waking up from his first vision.

Henry Bennett teaching him how to swing a sword properly. Jacob talking to Hatsuto about meditation, Bushido, and the Buddha. Talking to Christopher Freeman about the South. Hatsuto whooping him at practice, the feel of the Japanese man's wooden kendo sword across his wrist. Jacob outshooting the Japanese man at the target range, and Jacob's gloating afterward. Chanting in some foreign, cthonic tongue, tentacles,

43

Jacob shooting DuBose in the back, the relief of safety, the pain of his leg.

Then somewhere. Somewhere he had certainly never been, and had never dreamed before. He was floating above it all. A spangled mash of pinwheeled stars spun far below him in the echoless, silent vacuum. It spun so quickly, Jacob imagined he could scoop it into his hands. So he did. He reached down with his right hand and plucked it from the soft, velvet-like backing and held it up to his eye.

The Templar blinked and saw he was now floating above the rambling sprawl of wooden structures that was Chicago. Jacob looked over the whole of the city. Judging by his position near the lake, the monastery would be due east. As Jacob realized this, he was already there, above the stone compound.

He looked down upon it and felt a tug, a sort of wail which filled his senses. Jacob followed the pull through the ceiling of the monastery, down past the dining hall, beyond even the basement levels, far into the earth till he reached the catacombs below the structure.

Jacob was in a giant room, far larger than the dining hall and bigger than any room Jacob had ever entered, filled with pillars and tombs. Scores of lamps and torches fought vainly against the shadows. Dozens of sarcophagi lined each side of the chamber, each carved with an individual likeness of a man laying in repose, eyes closed, hands at the hilt of a sword resting on his chest. Blurry figures swirled through the room so fast they seemed elongated and solid.

The figures centered on a single sarcophagus in the corner. Jacob watched as one blur would come in and stop, become a human being, then would leave after another blur came and joined it. At times it was Hatsuto or Christopher, and at others it would be Col. Winnie. After some watching, all three blurs came to a halt together. They arrayed themselves around the sarcophagus. Jacob was dragged in closer.

The three men reached down and, with effort, slid off the stone lid of the sarcophagus. Jacob, or his body at least, lay inside, naked and submerged in some sort of liquid with closed eyes and an empty expression. Only his face protruded into the air.

"Think he survived?" Christopher asked.

44

"He is strong," Hatsuto replied.

"Hatsuto's right," the colonel said. "Besides, if he doesn't make it, he was never meant to join us."

Jacob floated in closer, looking down at his face. He looked so different from outside himself. Like a stranger he'd known his whole life. Jacob reached down to touch his own shoulder. The middle of his forehead opened and a great, sideways eye protruded, blinking rapidly and sucking in the light.

The floating Jacob drew back, gasping. Then he was there, laying in the water and staring up at the faces of the three men who had imprisoned him.

Jacob, eyes wide, sat upright in the sarcophagus. Salt water ran in rivulets from his naked chest and hair, cold air striking his skin with suddenness. He was alive, good God, he was alive!

"Woah there, son," Col. Winnie said, putting a towel over Jacob's shoulders. Jacob, unblinking, looked at each of the three men. "Do you know who we are?"

"Y-y-y-yes." The three Templars looked at each other in expectation. Jacob screwed his face up, tried to remember the order of the words he needed to say. "You're Christopher, the colonel, and . . . Hatsuto."

Col. Winnie clapped him on the back and the two other men exhaled in relief. "Damn good for a first try, son. Damn good. Do you know who you are?"

"Jacob Smith."

"Even better. Let's get him out of this thing."

The four men sat together in the burial chamber. The three senior Templars had brought down chairs when they came to retrieve him from his initiation. Jacob was naked beneath a blanket as he sipped from a cup of broth the colonel had given him.

"Did you understand any of it?" Col. Winnie asked.

"Not really."

"I didn't neither," Christopher said. "Still wonder about most of the bits."

"Feel same?" Hatsuto asked.

"No."

"That is good," the Nipponese man replied.

"Sorry we had to do you like that," Christopher said. "It's the way it's written is all. Supposed to show us our true selves and sever us from the past. Whatever that means."

The four men sat in the quiet.

"I did have one question, though. Why wasn't it more . . ."

" . . . religious?" Col. Winnie finished.

"Yup."

"Because we only appear to be a religious order? Because God isn't real? Because religion is about life, and life is about religion, and the two often look the same?"

Jacob and the other two subordinate Templars just looked at Col. Winnie.

"I don't know, son."

Jacob looked from Col. Winnie down to his broth, then back to the colonel again. "God ain't real?"

"I have no idea," Col. Winnie replied, shrugging. "We're only backed by the Church. Hatsuto's a Buddhist. Five Feathers still follows his tribe's ways. Freeman here's a Southern Methodist."

"But just the things I saw at Kadath, those creatures. They weren't from here. And the tear DuBose made . . ."

"The things I've seen, you wouldn't believe neither," Christopher said. "That don't make the Catholic Church and the Papacy the final word on nothing. Just makes 'em one interpretation."

"I wrastled with an angel, though. And demons, too? Sounds pretty much like the Church to me."

"I fought a *kami* in my vision," Hatsuto said. "Guardian warrior spirit."

"I went against a *loa* named Ogun," Christopher said. "They're like angels and demons in voodoo. My aunt practiced."

All four men looked at each other.

Col. Winnie sighed. "We don't know what they are. We just know there are places . . . beyond. Some of these creatures, like the one you saw at Kadath, come from a different land. Others, like the ones you studied before, come from a place the Church already knew of. 'There are more things in heaven and earth, Horatio, than are dreamt of in your philosophy.' There are ancient things, son, things we haven't seen in our life. Hopefully, we won't have to, either."

"And we gotta stop 'em? How? There's only a handful of us."

"Just gotta believe," Christopher said.

"Believe? In what? Y'all just told me God ain't real."

Christopher leaned forward, forearms on thighs, saying, "The colonel misspoke–"

"He ain't 'misspoke,' he just said there ain't no God."

Christopher held up a hand. "He gave you his version." He spread both hands as if his thoughts were an offering to Jacob. "Truth is, we just don't know. We just gotta trust that whatever sent us to the order sent us for a reason, that's all. Whether it's God or an angel or just something else, that's all open for debate. Hatsuto here thinks we are cursed for our sins."

"'May you live in interesting times,'" Hatsuto said. "Old Chinese curse."

Jacob grunted. He took another sip of his broth.

"So what is this place?"

"You won't believe us," said the colonel.

"Try me, sir."

"The monks found a door from the cellar. This was here before any of the Templars came. It was here when the monastery was built by the French." He paused for a moment. "The French didn't build it, though."

"I'll be damned if you weren't right."

"But it's real," Christopher said, "as real as anything else we've told you."

"The dimensions match up perfectly with sites in Acre, in the Holy Land, and others across Europe," said Col. Winnie. "And the architecture is similar to the chapel you probably saw in your vision."

"St. George's?"

"Of course. That is the thread for us. And those little creatures, of course."

Jacob looked around the circle at the other men. "Who built this place then?"

Christopher and Hatsuto just shrugged.

"No one," the colonel said, leaning back in his chair, "has taken possession of that dubious honor."

"Alright, I've done heard enough," Jacob said, rising to stand on quivering legs. "I'm gonna get some sleep. Some normal sleep." Hatsuto stood and took Jacob's cup of broth and Christopher offered him a shoulder. Jacob wrapped the blanket around himself, shivering against the damp. "Colonel, you can fill me in on all this stuff in the morning. For now, I'm dead tired and worthless as a Confederate dollar."

"Agreed," Col. Winnie said, staying seated. "Get some rest, son."

With that, Christopher and Hatsuto led Jacob from the room.

GRACE

Jacob Smith and Christopher Freeman rode through the starless night, their hats pulled down against the sheets of rain pouring down on them and rolling off their oiled greatcoats. The mud-covered morass of a road seemed to stretch on forever through the thicket of oak and hickory trees.

The two Templars had set out from Chicago for St. Louis by a combination of riverboat and train. In St. Louis, they purchased horses and set out straight for Ft. Smith, Arkansas. Why Col. Winfred and the abbot sent two Templars, rather than just Jacob, was a mystery. Christopher was a colored man, formerly a slave, and right now the South wasn't exactly amenable to his presence. Hell, Hatsuto, the Nipponese Templar, would have been a safer choice than Freeman.

But, Jacob was sure they had their reasons. Their superiors always had their reasons.

Jacob convinced Christopher to push on to Grace, the next town. He'd figured they could make the trip before the storm hit. He'd been wrong, of course, and the going was rough. That's what Jacob got for making a rush of things.

"Christopher," Jacob said, raising his voice over the torrent.

"Yeah?"

"We gotta find somewhere to bed down for the night. Horses are dead tired, and we might as well be riding through a pig sty."

Lightning ripped overhead like it was Lucifer's own ax splitting the sky. Thunder cracked like that same bastard's whip. Jacob and Christopher both held tight to their horses and tried to calm them.

"One of us is like to get thrown, too."

"Well," Christopher said, patting his horse's neck, "it was your damned idea to keep going. You see any place to bivouac for the night?"

Jacob sat a little straighter in the saddle and peered through the torrent. "Not as such."

"What about that over yonder?" Christopher pointed westward, through the trees.

"What do you see?"

"Looks like light. Maybe a cabin. Must be a cutoff up ahead."

They rode on till Jacob spotted a trail that led through the trees. The two men urged their mounts down the winding, wagon-rutted path. The light ahead was clearer from the trail. It looked to be coming from a fire outside the house, not from a light within. Christopher stopped and Jacob rode up next to him.

"What do you reckon it is?"

"Maybe the house is afire. Lightning is hell tonight."

Jacob shook his head. "Looks like it's in front of the house. Take a closer look?"

"If it gets us a dry bed."

They both kicked their horses gently and continued down the trail. As they neared the house, the trail went around a bend, blocking their view of the yard. There was a loud crack nearby. Jacob and Christopher looked at each other. Lightning split the sky again.

"Thunder?"

"Came before the lightning." Christopher put heels to his horse. Jacob followed.

"Y'all niggers stole this land from our people," a man's voice called out from somewhere beyond the trees. "We've come to take it back."

The Templars turned the bend and came out into the yard of the house, reining in their horses not more than fifteen paces behind a mounted group of men wearing peculiar white robes. They'd covered their heads with hoods cut from the same cloth. Some of the men had bull horns or deer antlers protruding from their temples. There were seven of them, with three bearing torches against the darkness. Three rested revolvers across their saddle horns. Six rode coal black horses that drank in the flickering light. The one up front, the one doing the shouting, rode a plain bay and appeared unarmed.

Beyond the crowd, Jacob and Christopher could see a typical one-roomed, frontier cabin with a covered porch spanning the front. A young, black man stood on the porch guarding the front door, wearing an undershirt and suspendered trousers with a Navy Colt stuffed into the waistband. He aimed a shotgun at the lead figure.

"Over my dead body, mister," said the black man. He cocked back one of the hammers on the shotgun.

"Well there's seven of us and one of you, Washington, and you already fired a shot in the air."

Thunder rumbled again.

"Not quite," Christopher said.

The crowd's heads moved as one, their horses wheeling around to face the Templars. Christopher flipped open his greatcoat to expose the two revolvers that hung below his arms. Jacob drew his 10-gauge double-barreled shotgun from its saddle scabbard and laid it across his lap.

"There's two of us," Christopher said, "and only seven of you boys."

"Ain't none of your concern, nigger," one of the robed men said to Christopher in a voice hollow as the grave.

"Unfortunately," Christopher said above the roar of the rain, "it is my concern." He sat up in the saddle. "Now, y'all boys can ride on out of here safe as you please, or Jacob and I can find a nice elm to put you 'neath. Your choice."

The white-robed man who was the first to raise his pistol was also the first to be shot from his horse. Jacob didn't even see Christopher draw, he was so fast. Jacob took the cue just fine.

He raised the shotgun to his shoulder and shot down the nearest man. The gun kicked against Jacob's shoulder like a mighty pissed bronco. At this range, the load of buckshot ripped through the robed man's left shoulder, severing the arm and sending a cloud of dust and cloth into the air. Jacob's victim lurched to his right, losing his footing in the left stirrup, and tumbled to the trampled yard.

Jacob trained his gun on the next nearest man and fired, hitting him square in the chest. The man rocketed free of his stirrups and flew backwards into the rider behind him. Jacob sheathed his shotgun as Christopher spurred his horse forward, firing into the crowd of men with discrimination, shooting down first the ones with pistols drawn.

White-robed men fell from stamping, snorting coal-black horses, their bodies riddled with bullets. Christopher holstered his empty revolver and drew the other, switching hands on the reins. Jacob drew his own pistol as the black man on the porch, Washington, fired his shotgun into the crowd of night-riders.

Jacob cut his horse to the left and tried to flank the crowd so he could push them back towards Christopher. He looked down at the man he'd shot first, the one whose shoulder had come clean off. Mud encrusted the back of his white robe. The man had picked up his left arm and began awkwardly climbing back onto his horse.

Jacob shot him again, this time in the head. The man stumbled forward into his horse's flank, but still groped for the saddle with his right hand. Jacob roared and drew his sword, riding further into the crowd.

On Jacob's left, one of the men drew a revolver. Jacob cut off his white-gloved hand. The man looked down, almost curiously, at his hand still clutching the revolver on the ground. He looked back at Jacob. The Templar struck him again with his sword, slicing through his upper body.

There was no blood.

Jacob wheeled his horse around and went after another rider, a torch-bearer with an eight point set of buck antlers sticking out from his hood. He struck the man's head, antlers and all, from his shoulders. Jacob watched the man's headless body kick legs into his horse's side and tighten his grip on the reins.

The decapitated rider galloped out of the yard and into the night. Jacob turned his horse to find another assailant, but they'd all begun following after their beheaded comrade. Jacob wheeled his horse around as he sheathed his sword. He put heels to his horse as he began to reload his pistol.

"Hold up, Jacob," Christopher called out. "Woah, there."

Jacob reined in his horse and circled back around to where Christopher, still mounted, was reloading his pistols.

"Dammit," Jacob said, holstering his pistol. "They're getting away, and we ain't gonna be able to track 'em in this weather."

"Yep. You're right. But we got a spooked family to deal with," Christopher said, holstering his guns. They rode back the short distance to the house where the owner and his wife stood on the porch.

"G'night sir," Christopher said to the family.

"G'night, mister," said Washington. "God bless y'all for the help, even if it ain't gonna do much good."

"They'll be back," said his wife with a shake of her head.

"Maybe that's the case, ma'am, but they ain't here now," Christopher said. "My friend and I originally came by to see if we could get out of this downpour for the night. We've had a long ride and we're soaked through."

Washington looked at his wife. She sighed.

"I'll warm some blankets," she said, turning to go inside, "and see to the children."

"There's a barn round back for your horses. Fresh hay, too," said Washington.

"We're obliged, sir," Christopher said. The Templars turned their horses and went around to the back. They dismounted in the muck and led the horses into the small barn. Christoper began forking fresh hay into a manger as Jacob began wiping down his horse with a handful of hay.

"Did you notice anything funny about those men?" Christopher asked.

"Aside from the robes and horns?"

"Yep."

"Now that you mention it, fellas didn't seem to wanna die."

"Well that ain't funny or surprising." Christopher stopped his forking and wiped an arm across his brow. "Ain't many out there that wanna die."

"You know what I meant. I shot one in the head and he just climbed right back up his horse and rode off. Cut another one's head off, and he did the same."

"Without his head?"

"Yep."

"Did you notice them not bleeding?"

"It was like shooting one of them sand dummies in the practice yard."

"I wonder," Christopher said, setting the pitchfork against the barn wall, "if it's still out there."

"His head you mean?" Jacob asked as he moved onto the next horse and began wiping it down.

"Yep. Might help us figure out what's going on here."

"Thought we were headed for Arkansas. Col. Winnie ain't gonna appreciate us tarrying."

"We'll send a telegram ahead and one back to Chicago. The relic in Fort Smith can wait a few more days."

"Who do you reckon those men were?" Jacob asked, throwing down the soaked hay.

"Not who. What. Come on, let's talk to Mr. Washington."

"First time they was here, but this sure as hell weren't the first place to get a nighttime visit," Simon Washington said. He'd leaned back in his chair. He kept one eye on the cabin door.

The four of them sat at the small table near the fire. Ruth had taken the Templar's soaked greatcoats and hung them by the fire to dry. She offered Jacob a bowl of stew. He took it with a nod of thanks.

"Not the first place?" Christopher asked. "Where were the others?"

"Other freedmen in the area. When Mr. Lincoln emancipated us, we just left the fields. Ruth and I grabbed the children and headed north."

"One in the lead said you were squatting," Christopher said, taking his own bowl of stew from Ruth.

"If you mean the one that was doing most of the talking," Ruth said, "you mean Cyclops Justicar. He's their leader. Well, whatever that nasty man thinks, this place was just sitting with the fields fallow and coons living in the loft." Ruth turned back around to the fire. "We made this place respectable, Mr. Christopher. Cleaned the place out and planted last month. Y'all want some cornbread?"

"Yes ma'am, thank you. This homestead was just abandoned?" Christopher asked.

"Missouri never seceded," Jacob said. "A lot of guerilla fighting, partisans, Bushwhackers, and Jayhawkers going after each other and their families." Jacob took a piece of cornbread from Ruth.

"Like the men you rode with?" Christopher asked, turning to Jacob.

"Never ran any men off their land, if that's your point, but other groups sure did. Rebs all over the state ran loyalist families off if their men had joined up with the Union, and the same went for the other side. Plenty of the groups were never official, or they were disowned for outlaws by their own sides, like Quantrill. Good stew, ma'am. What's in it?"

"Squirrel." Ruth wiped her hands clean on her apron. She pulled out the chair next to her husband and sat.

"Ain't had squirrel since the war, ma'am. Much obliged."

"Been telling my Simon here that we should go to Kansas. Plenty others are leaving for there."

"Kansas is a right fine place," Jacob said, "but Missouri is good, too."

"What happens when the owners come back? Maybe with the law?" Christopher asked.

"Been a year since Appomatox," Jacob said, sopping up the last of the broth with his cornbread. "If they ain't back yet, they might never be."

"Perhaps that's the case, but that still don't explain these men," Christopher replied. He turned back to the Washingtons. "They sounded white, like maybe ex-Confederates. What have you heard from the other freedmen?"

"Depends on who you ask," Simon said, leaning forward and resting his elbows on the roughly hewed table. "Some folks are saying they're just men, ex-Rebels like you just said. Others are saying they're ghosts. About a fortnight back, a group of those riders rode up to another house. They called up to the house and asked for water. Sarah, Frederick's wife, went out and gave them water. She said the thirsty one, the one calling for it, drank a whole bucket, just upended it and pretty as you please asked for more."

"Did he now?" Christopher asked. "Sure Sarah wasn't letting herself get away?"

"Frederick swore by her word, said he was there," said Ruth, clearing Christopher's bowl from the table. "Frederick ain't book read, but he's as bright and honest a man as I've ever met."

"Well," Jacob said as he pushed his empty stew bowl forward, "I think I've heard enough. You, Christopher?"

"I have. Let's go look over the yard. Y'all folks stay inside for the rest of the evening. Jacob and I will take turns on watch tonight, too, and sleep on the porch. If they come back, we'll be ready."

Simon and Ruth thanked the Templars as they pulled on their coats from where they hung near the fireplace. Jacob and Christopher went out to the porch. They put on their hats and looked at each other.

"What do you think?" Jacob asked.

"I don't know yet. Let's take a gander at this head."

The white peaked-hood stood out in the middle of the yard like a lonesome cone of surrender. It must have rolled to an upright position after the tumble from the owner's shoulders.

The Templars stepped down off the porch and into the yard. They walked through rain which was still coming down like a waterfall. Mud sucked at their boots with each step as they made their way to the head.

They stopped a few feet away from it and looked at each other. "Hear that?" Jacob asked over the driving rain.

"Like some kinda rattling." Christopher drew his sword and extended the tip to the hooded head, poking at it.

Nothing happened.

"Pick it up," Christopher ordered.

"What? Why do I have to? You pick it up."

"I got seniority," Christopher said, narrowing his eyes. "Pick up that damn head."

Jacob circled around to the front of the hooded head, eying it like it was a moccasin ready to strike. He stopped in front and looked at Christopher. "Go on," said the other Templar. "Pick it up." Jacob looked back down at the hood. Two eye holes had been cut in front, and the whole of it was splattered in mud.

Jacob sighed and crouched down, hand outstretched to the peaked hood. He pulled it off, revealing a desiccated head beneath. The Templar leaned forward, hood still in his hand, and eyed the shriveled husk and its long strands of dry, twine-like hair. He looked back up at Christopher. "Ain't a way this is the head," said Jacob.

"Why not?"

"Look at this thing." Jacob looked back down at the decapitated head. "Looks almost a skeleton already."

Jacob reached forward with both hands and picked it up. He stood and walked over to Christopher.

"See?" Jacob asked, holding it out to the other Templar. "You'd think it had been in the ground for years already."

"That's because I *have* been in the ground for years, race-traitor."

Jacob yelped and dropped the head. He drew his pistol and had it cocked before the dessicated thing landed with a squelch.

"No," Christopher barked, stepping forward, hands raised in front of him, "don't shoot."

Jacob's eyes flicked back and forth between Christopher and the disembodied talking head on the ground.

"Put your gun away, I want to talk to it."

Jacob licked his lips uncertainly and eyed the head again. Its eyes glowed the same red as those coal black horses' had. Hesitantly, he uncocked the revolver and holstered it.

"Did you know it was going to do that?" Jacob asked as Christopher bent down to pick up the head.

"Reckoned it might. Ain't never seen one of them talk, though."

"Run across something like this before?"

"Yeah," asked the head, "run across a Kukluxer before?"

"No, I've run across a zombie before. But, you, you're something completely different. A Kukluxer, you say? Whatever that is, must be bad juju too. Come on, Jacob, let's get this back to the barn."

The head looked even more awful in the lantern's light. Glowing red eyes, set deep in skeletal sockets, glared out at the Templars from the middle of the small work table. Christopher poked the head with the tip of his hunting knife.

"Feel that?" he asked.

"Dammit, yes!"

"How about this?" Christopher cut into the exposed forehead bone.

The head wailed.

"Interesting." Christopher set the knife on the table. "How can you talk?"

"How can you, nigger?"

"Learn some manners," Jacob said. "What's your name?"

"Cpl. Aloysius Tate," the head said, then, almost as an afterthought added, "race-traitor."

"Alright, Corporal. What's a Kukluxer?"

The head somehow cleared its throat. "We, sir," it began in its vacant, echoing voice, "are a chivalrous and knightly order dedicated to the protection of Southern values and virtue."

Jacob snorted. "Can I shoot it yet?"

Christopher held up a hand. "Who made you?"

"The Lord, you cretin, same as he made everything."

"Fine, I'll concede that. But who raised you up from the dead and put you in this present form?"

"The Grand Wizard, of course."

"Grand Wizard, huh? Who's that?"

"None. Of. Your. Business. Nigger."

Christopher didn't flinch. "Who's Cyclops?"

"He's our lieutenant. I got a question now."

"Fine."

"How'd a monkey learn to talk?"

"We could always grind it down and use the bonemeal for Ruth's garden," Jacob said.

Christopher sighed and rubbed the ridge of his nose. He stood, put on his coat, and left the barn. Jacob followed after him.

"What's the matter?" he asked as they stepped out into the rain.

"Plenty," Christopher said, walking back to the house. "We need to get some rest. First light, we're going into town to send a telegram to Col. Winnie."

"Thought that was already the plan," Jacob said, walking with him.

"It was. But now we need to tell him we might've found the Grand Wizard."

"Who is that anyway?"

"Don't know for sure. But we need to let Col. Winnie know we've got our first lead."

Jacob and Christopher, tin cups of coffee in hand, stood together looking at the now inanimate head. The burlap sack they'd kept it in all night lay on the table beside it. Crisp morning light shone in through the open doors of the small barn.

"Little critter couldn't stop talking last night to save his own hide."

"Nope," Christopher said, nodding. "Sure couldn't." He walked out into the small barnyard and watched Ruth feeding the chickens with her children. It was a fine family, if a little tired. He took another sip of coffee. Jacob joined him after putting the burlap sack over the head, walking out and looking up at the perfect blue sky.

"That head seem a little off to you?" Jacob asked, spying a band of ravens in a nearby tree.

"Other than the obvious?"

"Reckon I mean aside from that. Just seemed real particular in its agitation. Had plenty of rebel soldiers we captured during the war. None of 'em seemed so full of venom."

"War changes men." Christopher took out his pocket watch and checked the time. "Speculation aside, we need to get the horses saddled and head into town soon. Simon said we can reach it by noon if we leave within the hour."

"Get a bit of lunch packed?" Jacob asked, stretching backwards, hands at the small of his back.

Christopher nodded. No sense in fighting evil on an empty stomach.

They rode into Grace just before noon. As small as the town was, they could have ridden out the other side just a few minutes after. There was a saloon, blacksmith, and general store clustered together on the main street, in addition to a small sheriff's office. The livery and a handful of clapboard houses were set back a little ways from the rest of the buildings. Few folks were around. The roads had been bad coming in, which meant farmers in the surrounding area would likely stay at their own places for the day. A few old-timers stood on the porch of the general store, which had a big hand-painted sign reading "KETCH GENER-AL" hanging over the eaves. They were smoking hand rolls and jawing at each other.

Jacob and Christopher hitched their horses in front of the sheriff's office. It was a plain, wooden building like the rest and looked to be in need of some new paint. Its front door was open.

"Ask around and see if there's been anything funny going on," Christopher said. "I'm going to send those telegrams." Jacob nodded and Christopher walked away, headed for Ketch General.

Jacob hiked up his gunbelt and stepped out of the muddy street and onto the porch. He stomped his feet, knocking the mud from his boots. There was the blustery sound of a man coming awake and the creek of an old chair readjusting inside the office.

"Hullo?" called a voice from within. "Someone out and about?"

"That'd be me," Jacob called back as he stepped through the door.

He glanced around the office, taking everything in. Holding cell towards the back of the office, a gun cabinet with a half-dozen rifles locked inside, a desk covered in piles of paperwork with an older, medium-built gentleman sitting behind it. From the skin hanging at his jowls, he looked to be a man that had gone to fat at one point and since lost the weight. His hair was wispy and grey, and a tin star was pinned to his chest.

"Name's Jacob Smith," he said, removing his hat. "You the sheriff round here?"

"Sure am. Sheriff Richard Coleson." The sheriff heaved himself up from the chair and, smiling, offered his hand to Jacob. Jacob took it. "What can I do you for, sir?"

"Just passing through, Sheriff. Was bedding down last night and saw a band of men go racing through. Bunch of men in white robes and such, strange hoods with horns on 'em. Just wondering about them is all."

"Not heard much about them in these parts. Further north, near Jefferson City, they're all over." The sheriff turned and looked out the window. "I'd hoped Grace would stay free of 'em, though."

"Who are they?"

"Call themselves Kukluxers, ex-Confederates going after scalawags and carpetbaggers and," he paused for a moment before continuing, "colored folk. Got a lot of 'em round now, you know."

"I heard."

"Why the interest, Mr. Smith?" Sheriff Coleson asked, turning back around. "You don't look like a lawman."

"Curiosity. Why they going after 'em?"

"Aside from their side losing, and them not getting to vote or hold office anymore on account of that new state constitution's Ironclad Oath?" the sheriff asked with a shrug. "Don't expect you to understand, sir, but this state was torn apart by the war.

We never left the Union, but there was plenty who went and fought for the South, just like plenty went and fought for the North." The sheriff went and sat back down in his chair.

"Men left their families behind to go to the war," the sheriff said, leaning back, "and families got run off the land for the man's trouble. Plenty of folks went to St. Louis or down to Texas. Some ain't come back yet, but they will eventually. Where'd you say you were from?"

"Didn't." Jacob replied. "Chicago."

"Yankee, huh? Where ya' headed, if you don't mind my asking?"

"Arkansas, then maybe Texas. Reckon I don't know yet."

"I remember being that way when I was your age," Coleson said, smiling. "Full of the wanderlust. Pretty soon, though, you'll just wanna be done with it and have a family, making a life for 'em. Be in a quiet place."

"Oh, I'm sure I will. But back to them men in the robes," Jacob said, looking around the office. "You aiming to do anything about 'em?"

"Me?" the sheriff asked, chuckling. "Likely not."

"Why?"

"There's dozens of 'em out there, Mr. Smith. 'Sides, most are like to be just all full of piss and vinegar from the war still. Feel like they done wasted those years of their life over nothing. Once those boys settle back in and get back to their farming, it'll all peter out. Mark my words."

"Well, while you're waiting for that to come to pass," Jacob said, putting on his hat, "you still got folks at the mercy of these Kukluxers." Jacob tipped his hat to the sheriff and walked over to the door. Before he walked out, he turned and said, "You know, seems to me that I remember people saying the same thing about Bleeding Kansas."

"Thought you said you were from Chicago," Sheriff Coleson said.

"I most recently am. Kansas by way of Chicago."

"Then you know how bad this state was," said the sheriff, eyes narrowing.

"I also know how people took matters into their own hands. Now, if you'll excuse me, I got some supplies to purchase," Jacob replied, tipping his hat again. He turned and walked out the door.

Jacob walked about twenty feet before Sheriff Coleson came out onto the porch.

"Mr. Smith," the sheriff called from the doorway. Jacob turned and looked at him. "You leave this be. I'd rather not bury another man over this war. One man ain't gonna make a lick of difference against those Kukluxers."

"That's why I got a partner," Jacob hollered back. He turned back before the sheriff could respond. Ahead, Christopher Freeman walked out of the general store. He saw Jacob coming and walked to meet him.

"What were you hollering about?"

"Men from last night been hitting Northerners and freedmen all over," Jacob said as they headed back to the horses. "Sheriff Coleson's concerned we'll end up in the ground if we keep after 'em. He reckons this'll all just blow over before too long. You find out anything?"

"Nothing," Christopher said, spitting to the side. He began unlooping his reins from the hitching rail. "Sent the telegrams ahead and behind and found out where some of the other freedmen families are living. I'll ride out to them and have a talk, see if they know anything. Maybe give us a line on that lead Kukluxer." He swung up into the saddle. "Ask around town, see if you can find anything. Surprised me that the general store owner was polite enough to talk to me, but he clammed up soon as another customer walked. Seems to me some of these folks got a mean streak to 'em, so you be careful. No telling who's for these Kukluxers and who's against."

"Alright, I'll be careful," Jacob said, looking up at Christopher. "Meet you back at Washington's tonight?"

"Be there by nightfall. If not by then, then soon after. Remember, you be careful." Christopher put heels to his horse and trotted off.

"You too." Jacob watched till the other Templar disappeared from view. He walked to the saloon.

It had seen better days. Those better days had likely been sometime before the war. The front entrance, a set of double doors, were open like the sheriff's office.

He climbed the short stairs out of the mud and clomped his boots clean on the porch. He stepped inside.

The outside almost looked better. Round tables with stacks of cards beneath the legs to balance the wobbles were scattered around the place. In one corner was a badly, and likely often, used craps table. A rickety looking set of stairs climbed to the second story walkway which ran along the far edge of the drinking hall like a balcony. The bar itself stretched across the far side from end to end, a scratched and smokey mirror behind the length of it. Dust lay on everything. Few liquor bottles were in evidence behind the bar, though a sallow middle-aged man was wiping down glasses as he eyed Jacob inquisitively. Seemed wiping down glasses was all bartenders ever did west of the Mississippi. Other than the bartender, the place was deserted.

"Howdy," said the barkeep.

"Howdy," Jacob replied, tipping his hat. "Y'all serve whiskey?"

"You in Missouri?"

Jacob walked across the uneven floor. His toe caught a protruding board and he stumbled forward a step.

"Careful there."

"Thanks for the warning," Jacob said as he leaned forward onto the bar with his elbows. "I'll take that whiskey now."

"Sure thing. Want the bottle or a shot?"

"Shot. Bottle would give me too much liberty with the libations."

The bartender set a shot glass and poured it to the brim. Jacob put down a dollar coin.

"Ain't seen too much of that around here," the bartender said, raising an eyebrow. "You from up yonder?"

"North?" Jacob asked.

The man nodded.

"Chicago," Jacob said and took the shot. He hissed through his teeth as the cheap liquor burned down his throat and into his chest. "Passing through on our way to Arkansas."

"You and that nigger of yours? Saw you two in the street talking."

"Understand you're the proprietor," Jacob said, teeth grit together, "but I don't cotton to that language. I'd appreciate you not using it in my presence."

"Look, mister," the bartender said, his eyes wide as he raised his hands palm out, "no offense meant. Just what folks say in these parts. You're right, I am the proprietor, but I don't want no trouble neither if you're a paying customer. Seems to me some folks don't like me calling 'em Negroes, others don't like colored, and then there's the folks such as yourself as can't stand to hear nigger. Hell, can't even call 'em fucking freedmen sometimes. Never know who is which, so I beg your pardon."

"My apologies for barking like that," Jacob said, looking out the saloon's windows, "but I just saw a mob of men try and burn some folks out of house and home last night. We fought a damn war over slavery, and we can't even decide what to call freedmen now that it's done."

"Want another drink?" the bartender asked. Jacob shook his head and kept looking out the window. "Well, seems to me that the best trail to follow has always been the middle road. Came out west so I could find my fortune, you know, and I didn't intend on running for office. I'm one they call non-partisan. Seems to me Jefferson was right about slavery being a wolf, and us not having much choice on the matter. We let its ear go, and now everything's coming back round. Sure you don't want another one?"

"Got any cider or beer?"

"Just cider. Beer's been hard to come by, even in St. Louis. Would you believe it? Even them lop-eared Dutch been using their grain for eating. Sad day in a German house when the man's gotta drink water rather than beer."

"Gimme a cider then."

The bartender pulled a mug of cider for Jacob from the giant cask behind the bar. He set it down beside Jacob, who took a drink. It was good cider.

"Now, other side of the eagle, like my pa said, is that we got that damned oath. Seems to me, the Republicans do away with that, we put this all back together and leave the problems on the battlefield," said the bartender.

"Problems don't get left on the battlefield, mister. People that have never fought like to think they do, but they don't. And, problems or not, some men never come home from the battlefield even if their bodies do."

"You was in the war then?"

"Don't care to discuss it."

"Suppose that's fair."

"Think there's other men about who see it your way?"

"What way is that?"

"Rebuilding and moving on from the war."

"Just letting bygones go bygones? Not likely. The blacksmith, Sam Fulton, came back from war to find a dead wife and children. He's in a bottle most nights now. Eliana Reid that runs the livery stable, her husband died in the war on the losing side. She saw her own fair share of fighting round these parts. Kept partisans off their land throughout, defending the homestead."

"What about the sheriff?"

"Coleson, that old pissant? He's worthless," the bartender said, putting down the glass he'd been polishing. "Eliana Reid did more to keep the border ruffians outta Grace than that yellow bastard, and she's a woman. Why you asking anyway?"

"Heard of the Kukluxers?"

"Rebs settling up old scores? Who ain't, leastwise in these parts?"

"They've come to Grace, I reckon. Probably gonna be bad for business."

"You're probably correct on that. Not much my problem, though. Folks can go at each other all they want for all I care. Like I said, I'm middle of the road."

"What about when you ain't got any choice?"

"Guess I'll ford that river when I come to it, mister. Now, you'll excuse me, I got some counting to do in back."

"Guess we all will." Jacob stood up from the barstool and walked out of the saloon. He tipped his hat to the bartender as he left.

Who was it? They'd heard a voice, a normal, human voice, the night before. Someone was at the head of these Kukluxers, keeping a hand on the reins and boots in the stirrups. Jacob paused on the front porch of the saloon, looked back at it for a moment, then back over the town of Grace. Who? Christopher had mentioned something about the general store owner seeming amenable to talk. Jacob walked down towards Ketch General.

The Templar pushed open the door to the general store. A bell over the entryway rang, jangling like a lost cow stirred to action. Merchandise was spaced out evenly on shelves behind the counter that ran the length of the back and sides. A small, miserly looking man stood behind the counter at the far end. He appeared to be examining the books, a ledger spread in front of him on the pine countertop.

"Hullo," Jacob called as he walked in.

"Afternoon, sir," the man replied. "What can we get for you today?"

"Needing cartridges for my pistol." Jacob was lying. The order gave them plenty of ammunition for their revolvers, full well knowing that some things just didn't want to die when they were told to.

"Ball and cap?"

"No. The new rimfire cartridges."

"Had a man come in earlier who was asking for the same. Forty-fours?"

"You named 'em."

"You riding with that gentleman?"

"I am," Jacob replied after a moment's hesitation.

"You two in town to do some business," the man asked, eyes peering down at Jacob's gun-belt and sword, "or just passing through?"

"Was just passing through," Jacob replied, walking up to the counter. "On our way to Fort Smith. Ran into a bit of trouble last night, though. Gonna stick around and see it through."

"Trouble's been growing like weeds in spring since the rebellion was put down. Name's John Ketch. This is my shop." Ketch offered his hand across the counter. Jacob took it and shook.

"Jacob Smith. Christopher said you seemed willing to talk."

"I am. Almost talked to your partner before, but Abraham Fields came in to pick up his groceries for the week. Fields is a mean, nasty piece of work. What was your partner's name?"

"Christopher Freeman."

"Seemed a good man, by any standards you can judge a man these days. He fight in the war?"

"We both did. What was that about Fields?"

"Said he's a mean one. Trash, you ask me. The whole of that family is wanting for dignity and respectability. Lucky I give 'em the credit, else they'd be eating vermin and stolen mule the year round."

"You give them credit?"

"They're nasty, Mr. Smith, but they're people same as me. Wouldn't be Christian to deny them provisions."

"Think this Fields is nasty enough to ride with the Kuklux?"

"Wouldn't come as a surprise, that's for sure," Ketch replied, twisting the tip of his mustache with an idle finger. "But he's got a streak of yellow wide as the Mississippi, you ask me."

"Color of a man's belly doesn't matter much when it comes to being part of a mob. Doesn't take a lot of sand to run colored folks off their land in the dead of night," Jacob said. "How do you feel about the Washingtons?"

The storekeeper seemed to look out beyond Jacob Smith for a moment, scanning the windows. Jacob could have sworn he stopped and almost sniffed for danger, as if his thoughts on the equality of race would catch flight and the rest of the townsfolk would be able to sense them escaping out into the street.

"Don't think much on it, tell you the truth."

"You extending credit to them?" Jacob asked.

"Yes." He paused. "I need not add that I'd appreciate other folks in the town not getting wind of that."

"Run off your other customers, you think?"

"That, or my customers would run me off."

"Well, I appreciate the tip on Fields, sir," Jacob said with a nod. "Whereabouts is their cabin?"

"You thinking of riding out there?"

"Maybe."

"Well, luck to you on that. Don't expect tea and cookies from that man, though. Like I said, he's trash."

Ketch gave him directions to the cabin. It was a fair ride out of town, but Jacob figured he could make it there and back before sundown. He tipped his hat to Ketch and thanked him for the warning and the information. He walked down to the sheriff's office and mounted his horse.

Jacob rode out of Grace.

Fields's cabin was a rundown derelict. It hunkered in the middle of some cleared land, its roof sagging and the eaves drooping over the windows like a drunk's swollen eyes. Firewood was stacked haphazardly in all manner of places, but mainly surrounding a large firepit set in front of the house. Three unwashed children, two boys for sure and one that might have been a girl if her hair was ever brushed, played at soldiering around the ashes.

Jacob rode up as the two boys were arguing over why one of them had to be dead. The girl stood off to the side, her stick-for-a-gun dangling idly. He rode up, ignored wholly by the trio.

"No, you nigger-loving Yankee, I done shot you," shouted the bigger of the two.

"Nuh-uh," shouted the other. "You missed me, Jimmy. 'Sides, I shot you twice already."

"Nuh-uh." The bigger one pushed the other. The smaller one leaped and grabbed a handful of the bigger boy's hair. They tumbled to the mud together in a heap of elbows and knees, yelling, thrashing, and pulling at each others' mangy hair.

Jacob brought his horse to a stop a dozen or so feet from where they were rolling in the mud. He watched in silence while they tugged and yanked and hollered. He cleared his throat. The girl-thing looked up at him with piercing green eyes. Jacob and the girl locked gazes. She couldn't have been more than six years old, but her eyes looked distant and sad, like she'd been on the battlefield with Jacob, watching this same brother-on-brother fight three years before. She turned and ran silently for the cabin, dropping her stick on the muddy earth. The boys stopped fighting long enough to look up and see Jacob. They scrambled to their feet. The bigger one eyed Jacob's big pistol.

"Hey," shouted the smaller one, "who are you?"

"Jacob Smith."

"Don't know no Jacob Smith," the bigger one said.

"Reckon you wouldn't. Abraham Fields your pa?"

"Yeah. What's it to you, mister?"

"Here to see your pa, kid, not you."

"Pa know you?"

"No. Need to see him all the same, though. Go on up to the house and get him for me."

"Go to hell," said the smaller one. "We don't do nothing for nobody."

Jacob swung down from his horse and snatched the smaller boy's left wrist almost a breath after he'd finished speaking. The Templar swatted the boy hard on the seat of his pants, eliciting a sharp squawk of surprise. The bigger brother abandoned the younger and ran straight through the grey mudhole of a firepit.

On the other side, he headed right for the house. The boy Jacob had hold of struggled vainly and hollered for his pa.

"Boy," Jacob said, swatting the boy's behind again, "don't sass your elders like that. Now get your pa like I told you." Jacob let the flailing boy go. The boy spun away, his feet tangling and tripping him into the mud. He clawed his way back up till he was able to break into a staggering run towards the house. Jacob walked slowly around the mudhole, eyes fixed on the ramshackle cabin. The bigger of the two boys was already at the front door, hollering for Fields.

"What in the fucking hell are you goddamn kids making so much fucking racket for?" Fields yelled from inside the cabin.

"There's some man saying he wants to see you," the kid on the porch yelled back, his voice keening a little, "and he hit Eli and run me off and I reckon he's armed and I bet he's—"

"Shut up, boy," Fields yelled. Jacob walked a few paces closer and stopped. Abraham Fields finally arrived at the door. He was a grizzled man in his early fifties, hard and lean like Jacob remembered his own pa. Fields wore poorly fit long johns and hastily pulled on ragged trousers. Suspenders hung at his sides. Jacob could see the sharp edges of his cheek and collarbones pushing against his skin, the sun reflecting brightly from his cleanly bald pate.

Abraham Fields stepped out onto the porch. He held a rifle.

"Permission to approach the house?" Jacob asked.

"Not till I know what you're here for," Abraham called back. He turned to his son and barked at him to get inside. When the boy didn't move, Abraham cuffed him a good one on the ear. The boy scurried inside.

"Came to ask you some questions."

"Is it about that damned piece of shit woman of mine?" Fields asked. "Told the sheriff she run off to Texas. Think I'd willingly raise these damned kids by my lonesome?"

"It's not about your wife, Abraham."

"What about then? You the law or something?"

"Not as such, but I'm trying to find some people been running some . . . Negroes off their land."

Abraham Fields raised the rifle to his shoulder. It was an old cap and ball squirrel rifle. At this range, Jacob figured, it would still be deadly.

71

"You with them black-hearted Republicans in St. Louis, then?"

"No," Jacob said, right hand hanging by his revolver.

"Who you with, then?"

"The Catholic Church."

"What? You some kind of Papist? We're Methodist round here, you asshole."

"Ain't looking to preach, Abraham, just looking to talk."

"What's your name, asshole?"

"Jacob Smith."

"Why're you damned Papist cannibals looking to help them niggers, Jacob Smith? Ain't you done enough troublemaking with converting them redskins?"

"Just trying to protect some innocent people."

"Squatters and niggers, you mean." Fields spat to the side.

"People all the same. People with children were almost burned out of house and home last night. Children, Abraham. You know anything, you should help me."

"So your God'll smile on me or some such?"

"God's all the same no matter where you go. But that's beside the point. You know any of these Kukluxers been riding around?"

"No," Fields yelled back, "I do not."

"Look, my voice ain't up to the task on this. Reckon I can come up a little closer?"

"You stay right fucking there and we'll all be happy as bedbugs. 'Sides, I think it's about time you got gone, Smith. We eat plenty of varmint round this piece, so I'm a pretty good shot."

"You come clean on this, and about who you're running with, and I can let you alone. No need to get Sheriff Coleson and the law involved. We just put this to bed here and now and keep it between us men."

"I appreciate the offer," Fields yelled, "but I still ain't got no fucking idea what you're talking about. So, like I said before, you better go lest you want a bullet twixt your eyes."

"Fine, Abraham." Jacob began backing up slowly. "But this was the only chance you got. I find out you were involved with those men, I'm putting you in the ground."

"I ain't, but I'd like to see you try all the same." Fields cocked the squirrel rifle's hammer back. A few backward steps later,

Jacob turned around and walked back to his horse. He mounted and turned back to eye the cabin one last time. Fields still stood on the porch, the rifle raised to his shoulder. Dark eyes glared down the barrel at Jacob.

He turned his horse around and rode back to Grace.

Jacob arrived in town a few hours later. He couldn't find Christopher, so he walked into Guffey's and sat down to a late lunch. They had enough to give him a fair chunk of cornbread, some salted meat, and a bowl of greens. He mentally ticked off the likely suspects while he ate. To this point, they had Abraham Fields. But, truth be told, they probably couldn't discount half of Southern Missouri and Arkansas. Too many people round here hated too many others.

Abraham Fields had probably been just some pathetic drunk, made even drunker and sadder by his wife leaving him. Eliana Reid, though, Jacob had no idea. Maybe he'd go by the livery before he left for the Washington's farm. He finished eating his meal and had the owner pack up some more meat and cornbread for later in the day. He walked back out to his horse and put the paper-wrapped bundle of food in his saddle bag.

"Smith," a voice said behind Jacob. Jacob, looking back over his shoulder, saw the owner of the voice approaching. Sheriff Coleson. "Smith, a word with you please?"

"Sheriff? What can I do for you?"

"Word is," Sheriff Coleson said, coming to a stop a few paces from Jacob, "you been asking folks round here questions."

"I have. Ain't no law against it."

"Told you to leave it be."

"You did."

"Why're you still in Grace then?"

"Passing the time, waiting for my partner."

"Heard he's been riding out to some of them Negro farms asking questions his ownself."

"Has he? Christopher got curious too, I guess."

"Listen, Jacob," the sheriff said, walking a little closer, "you seem to me to be a good man, if a bit headstrong. If you leave it be, we'll forget about this. You just get out of town and let me handle the situation."

"Sheriff," Jacob said, taking a step closer to the other man, "the problem is that you ain't taking care of it. Now, pardon me, but I got to go see a stable mistress." Jacob walked past the sheriff, headed for the livery.

"Dammit." Jacob could feel the older man's eyes boring into his back as he walked down the muddy street. He didn't look back.

The livery stable looked to have been painted in the last couple years, and was still well put together. The barn doors that faced the street had been thrown wide, the damp mustiness of the hay and horse shit wafting out. A woman wearing a man's shirt, trousers, and thigh-high boots mucked out the stables inside.

"Afternoon," Jacob called as he approached. "Would you be Eliana Reid?" He stopped at the barn door and leaned against the frame. The woman stopped what she was doing and looked up at Jacob. She was solidly built, with good hips and strong arms. A deep tan covered her exposed skin. She'd pulled her hair back into a tight, silver-streaked bun. Her cheekbones were high and pronounced. She rested the pan of her shovel on the ground and wiped an arm across her sweat-shined forehead. She was a handsome woman by anyone's measure.

"I am. You got a name?"

"Jacob Smith."

"Well, what can I do for you, Mr. Smith? Got a horse to put up? Or you in need of hiring one?"

"Neither. Wanted to ask you about the Kukluxers."

"Don't know nothing about them, except that them damned Partisan Rangers still won't let well enough alone. War's done. Men need to put down their arms and let families get back to peace."

"I agree. Heard you fought off your fair share of border ruffians during the war. Figured you might know some of those guerillas who've gone to ground."

"I fought any side what was wanting to confiscate my property and leave nothing but a receipt. I own horseflesh, which means both sides came to my door."

"Did you sell to the Confederate government?"

"I did. Got what was a fair price at the time, too. Course, damned Confederate money is worthless now. Should have bought gold with it. Listen, who are you?"

Craig Gabrysch

"Told you."

"Well, you look, walk, and talk like a marshal, but I don't see a badge on you. Till I see one, I think we're done talking."

"You're right. No badge. Answer one last question and I'll go."

Eliana Reid looked out the back of the stable at her corral, then back to Jacob. She sighed deep and long.

"I'm gonna say one thing before you ask that question," she said, looking Jacob squarely in the eye. "I've seen your type round here before. You were one of them partisans weren't you? Well, if you're here to settle old scores, I ain't gonna help you. I'm tired of being hungry, I'm tired of watching my children's backs go bare for want of clothes, and I'm tired of men who thought it was my dead husband's responsibility to keep Negroes either free or picking cotton. Whatever it is, Smith, you let it go and you leave me out of it. I'll not bring more violence to my family by choice. They had enough for these past four years from both sides of the Mason-Dixon. Now ask your damned question."

Jacob looked into Eliana Reid's eyes.

"I apologize for the bother, ma'am," Jacob said, pursing his lips. "You're right. You can't help me."

Eliana Reid sighed again. This time it was a sigh of relief.

Jacob turned and walked away. Eliana went back to mucking out the livery.

Jacob figured there was nothing left to do but return to the Washington house and wait to see what Christopher had come up with. Hopefully the other Templar had done better with his afternoon. He walked back to where he'd tied his horse in front of the cafe and discovered Christopher, still mounted, waiting for him.

"Find anything?" Jacob asked as he approached.

"Might have. Waiting for you before I rode out, though."

"That bad?"

"Maybe. Let's get moving."

They rode south out of town towards the Fields's place. A few miles down the road they cut off east and into the woods. They had to get off and lead their horses initially.

"What are we looking for again?"

"Talked to a couple of the freedmen families. No one wanted to talk to me about the Kukluxers. Folks are terrified of 'em. Some of the children, though, they told me about this place.

"About a fortnight ago some boys were out playing, running around in the middle of the night, and they saw a beam of light shoot out of the woods and into the sky."

"Light? What kind of light? Like a lighthouse?"

"Said it was red. Also said it scared the dickens out of 'em. Ran home soon as they saw it."

"Reckon it has something to do with them Kukluxers then?" Jacob asked as they broke through the underbrush onto a broken, unused road that was little more than a deer trail.

"Reckon so," Christopher said as he mounted his horse and headed down the trail. "You have any leads on men from the town?"

"Not as such," Jacob replied, nudging his horse's flanks to follow after Christopher's mount. "Almost got shot by some man named Fields, though."

"You didn't, I see."

"Could have, though," Jacob said. "Which is why I don't think he's our man. He's ornery and old and a drunk, but not the type to go running with them Kukluxers. Saw the livery woman also."

"No luck?"

"No luck. Just like most of the other folks around here. Tired and sick of the war. Besides, she's a woman."

"Women can kill, too."

"But our Kukluxer sounded to be a man."

"True," Christopher said, nodding. "Children said the place is just a mile or so in."

"What is it?"

"Some kind of abandoned settlement. There was a battle out here during the war, they said. Children come out here to dig out musket balls, that kind of thing."

"Sad times."

"Why's that?"

"Children playing where men died."

"Well, least they get to play. I got put to work in a field, remember?"

Jacob didn't know how to respond, so they rode in silence. A while later the trees thinned and they broke into a clearing. A handful of derelict buildings were spread around in the dying sunlight. Some of them were burned, others knocked down to their cellars. Not a single one remained whole. A sapling grew out the window of one, its branches reaching for freedom. A bunch of underbrush grew in another. At the far edge of town stood a giant of an elm.

"Must be from the French days," Jacob said, his voice hushed, "back when they tried to settle these parts."

"Must be." Christopher dismounted. "Keep a sharp eye. This place has got some bad juju. Gives me the willies."

"You know, last person said that to me was Henry Bennett? We both know how that turned out." Jacob got down from his horse and hobbled it. Christopher did the same for his. Jacob grabbed his shotgun from the saddle sheath. He cracked the barrel and made sure it was loaded. He snapped it closed.

"Ready?" Jacob asked.

Christopher led the way into the ruins.

"So what are we looking for?"

"My guess is anything out of place. If this actually is related to them Kukluxers, there's probably going to be some evidence left behind."

The wind blew softly, rustling the trees. Jacob's finger inched towards the trigger. Christopher drew one of his pistols. A building to their left groaned as it shifted and settled. They kept walking, eyes scanning their surroundings.

"I don't like this," Jacob whispered.

"Think I do?"

They walked through the small collection of cabins and out the other side again. Jacob looked back through the small township. Their horses were still there. He breathed a little easier. That was a good sign.

"Would you lookie there?" Christopher asked.

"What?" Jacob asked, turning back around to face Christopher's back.

"That, there." Ahead of them, set a piece away from the town, was the elm they'd seen before.

The dying tree looked to have been lightning struck multiple times. It towered above the small clearing at its roots. A murder of crows perched in its branches, and their caws filled the air. A dozen weathered and worn grave markers covered in indistinct carvings and writing surrounded the tree's base. No two leaned the same way. Mounds of mud and dry, brittle grass covered the ground below the tree's low-hanging branches.

"Well, I'll be."

"Let's take a closer look," Christopher said, holstering his pistol and striding out to the dug-up burial grounds.

"Think this is where they came from?"

"As likely a place as any." They stopped below the tree and looked down into the nearest open grave. They were only a few feet deep. Graves of dead soldiers buried in haste.

"We got some open graves. Don't prove anything, though."

"You're right," Christopher said. He circled around to the back of the tree while Jacob glanced back towards the horses. They still grazed where the Templars had left them. "Jacob, come here."

Jacob circled around to the back of the tree.

"Look here," Christopher said, pointing down at a little hollow where the roots dug into the ground. "What do you reckon that is?"

"I don't know. Looks like something burnt it, though, whatever the hell it is."

"Might be a piece of bone."

"Yup." Jacob squatted down in front of the object, "think you're right. Looks like a finger or something." He reached out a hand.

"Don't touch it. No telling what it is."

"It's probably just a bone. What's the worst that can happen?" Jacob asked, reaching forward and picking it up. It was warm to the touch. Not quite as warm as a human being, but still warm enough to be a little disconcerting.

"Jacob, no!"

Nothing happened. Jacob pushed up the brim of his hat with one finger and looked at Christopher. "See? Nothing," he said. Holding the finger-bone between two fingers, Jacob looked at it. "Feels a lot lighter than it should be. Like it's mostly charcoal now."

"That's strange."

"How so?"

"Bones don't burn easy."

"How do you know?"

"Believe me. I know."

Jacob stood and offered the bone to Christopher, but Christopher declined with a shake of his head.

"Reckon this had something to do with whatever happened here?" Jacob asked.

"Certainly a possibility," Christopher said as he looked around. Day's last light began fading away. "Getting dark. We should get back to Washington's soon."

"Think the Kukluxers'll show up there again?"

"If they're dead Rebels they will. Not going to take to being sent scurrying by a Colored man," Christopher said, walking back around the tree.

"Likely right," Jacob said. He placed the burnt bone in his shirt's breast pocket and followed Christopher. "Or a 'race-traitor.'"

They stopped in their tracks as they came within sight of where they'd left their horses. The riderless coal-black mounts of the Kukluxers stood between the Templars and their grazing horses. The early evening light retreated from their presence, the shadows around them becoming longer and darker. Jacob gripped his shotgun tighter. Christopher grit his teeth and drew his revolver.

"Come on," Christopher said, striding towards the horses and into the settlement. Jacob followed him, finger on the trigger of his shotgun.

They weren't five paces from the tree before they heard the calls coming from the abandoned buildings. Both men had heard them before, years and years ago, out on the battlefields of the war between the states. It was a curious yipping, howling, almost warbling, bark.

It was the Rebel yell.

The yell had chilled Jacob during the war, that wild and inhuman noise, but not now. He'd seen and fought demons, had even looked into the tentacled maw of madness itself, and survived. Some dead soldiers doing some yelling and yipping like bird dogs? This was nothing.

He and Christopher kept walking, their eyes on the surrounding buildings.

They were just about to pass the first building when Jacob heard movement behind him. He spun, saw a swath of white cloth, and fired both barrels from the hip. The Kukluxer couldn't have been more than a few good strides away and caught both loads of shot mid-chest. He flew back in a cloud of smoke and dust, his arms thrown wide and his feet clearing the ground. He landed on his back inside the tumbledown building, swearing loudly.

Jacob cracked the barrel and reloaded his shotgun. He turned back around and followed after Christopher, who had already drawn a bead on one of the white-cloaked men on their right. Christopher fired twice, hitting the Kukluxer in the head and shoulder, driving him back under cover.

"You fine?" Christopher asked as they kept walking.

"Yeah. Only got these two shots, then I'm down to my pistol and sword."

Christopher nodded and fired a shot ahead at one of the men on his right. Jacob shouldered his shotgun and kept pace.

Two of the white-cloaked men appeared from buildings on the left with rifles in their hands. Jacob shot down one. Robes flared out as the creature spun to his right and fell to the ground in a tangle of white. Jacob only grazed the other, though.

The Kukluxer fired, hitting Christopher in the left shoulder with the dull thud of metal hitting meat. Blood misted into the air, spraying Jacob's right side. Christopher stumbled back a step, grunting, right hand covering his shoulder.

"Dammit," Jacob swore, throwing his shotgun aside and drawing his pistol. "You alright?"

"Graze. Hurts like a sumbitch, though." Christopher raised his gun again and fired, missing his target. He fired again and, this time, hit.

A pistol fired from somewhere behind Jacob, and he felt the bullet tear into his left calf. He took a knee, a curse on his lips. Christopher spun and fired at the attacker, the Kukluxer Jacob had first shot. Christopher holstered his pistol and drew the second one from below his left arm.

"Can you stand?"

"Yeah," Jacob said, "reckon I can." His boot had already begun filling with blood. "Gotta bandage this. Bleeding bad."

Still on one knee, he drew the straight knife from his belt and cut his left sleeve at the upper seam. He ripped the cloth off his arm and wrapped it around the boot as tight as he could. He stood and put some weight on it. The leg wouldn't take all the weight, but it would take some. He hobbled along beside Christopher.

"Can you make it to the horses?" Christopher fired ahead of them into the growing night.

"Hope so." Jacob grit his teeth against the pain as he limped forward. He again shot down the Kukluxer that had winged Christopher. "This is useless," Jacob said, fanning his revolver and gunning down another. "They just keep getting back up."

"Yep." Christopher shot another. He reloaded his revolver. They'd gotten nearer to the horses than they had been before, though. That was something.

"Were they just sleeping here all day?"

"Might have been. Maybe they're not active in the daytime? Maybe the magic doesn't work?"

Christopher fired two more shots. The Kukluxer stumbled backwards, but righted itself in record time.

"They gotta be getting their energy from somewhere, though. If that finger-bone was the source, it ain't anymore. Thing was almost burned up."

Christopher fired two more shots.

The coal black horses ahead looked balefully at the Templars as they drew closer. They didn't move, they simply followed the two men with their eyes as Jacob and Christopher limped and walked past. Jacob hadn't ever considered horses to be capable of hate, but, then again, these weren't your normal horses.

Their own horses were, though. Thankfully, Christopher and Jacob had hobbled them before they'd gone into the settlement. If they hadn't, the gunshots would have driven them to flight by now.

"Get the horses ready," Christopher said, wincing as he reloaded, "I'll cover you." He opened fire on the Kukluxers and their horses as Jacob limped around releasing his and Christopher's horses. "Don't think I can hurt their horses, Jacob, which means you gotta hurry up if we wanna get ahead of 'em."

"Hurrying." Damn his leg. With every step or jostle, it felt like someone dug a hot poker into his calf. He finished releasing the horses and climbed on his. His shot up leg throbbed painfully as he swung it over. The makeshift bandage he'd made had soaked through already. "Come on," he shouted, pulling his horse around.

"Goddamn," Christopher swore as he swung up and into the saddle. The Templars spurred their horses, bullets streaking through the air and whizzing past as they rode through the trees to the main road.

Darkness covered all of Grace, except the saloon. The Templars drew their horses up in front of the sheriff's office. Jacob felt lightheaded, and was having trouble staying upright in the saddle. He could still wiggle the toes of his left foot. That was good. But blood also soaked into his sock and the bandage. That wasn't so much so. His boot was heavy with blood.

Christopher shouted for the sheriff to come out. When there was no answer, he dismounted and walked to the front door of the office. He peered through the window with both hands cupped to keep off the glare from the lanterns across the street. Seeing nothing, he tried the door. It was locked. He came back and looked up at Jacob.

"You going to be alright if you get down?" Christopher asked. Jacob nodded. "Good. We gotta get you into that saloon and see if we can find someone to clean that leg while I head to Washington's."

"No. You ain't going anywhere without me. We get this boot cut off and a new bandage on this leg, then we'll ride out there together."

"Got the first part right," Christopher said, leading Jacob's horse around to the saloon. He hitched Jacob's horse and helped Jacob down from the saddle. Jacob, leaning on Christopher's good shoulder, hobbled up and into the light.

The saloon was almost empty. The bartender stood behind the counter. John Ketch, the general store owner, sat at the counter drinking a cider. A saloon girl, dressed in all her finery, lounged around at one of the tables. It was a slow night in Grace.

"Need some help here," Christopher called out.

"Well goddamn!" the bartender shouted. "What in the hell happened?"

Ketch got down off his stool and came towards them.

"Kukluxers ambushed us at the old settlement outside of town," Christopher said, helping Jacob to a long, rectangular table not far from the door. He helped Jacob get on the edge. "Jacob got shot in the leg. Need someone that can take care of the wound."

"Mattie," the bartender hollered at the saloon girl, "go see if Ms. Reid is at the livery."

"But why do I gotta go, Josiah?"

"Cause I'm here minding the place, Ketch is gonna go get some of that magical patent medicine of his, and I got a goddamn man bleeding on my table. Ain't telling you twice, woman."

Mattie left in a stomping, huffing flutter of silk and lace.

"Did it get the bone?" Ketch asked, coming over.

"No, don't think so. I can put some weight on it."

"Good. If anyone can help you, it'll be Reid. I'm gonna get some of those medicinals Mr. Dench was just speaking of." He left the saloon at a jog.

"You seen the sheriff?" Christopher asked.

"No. Ain't seen him since before sundown."

Christopher nodded, lips pressed together.

"He's probably just down at the house, though. Coleson closes up at sundown, lest he's got a prisoner in there with him."

"I'm gonna go get the sheriff," Christopher said to Jacob. "You let these people help you best they can. I'll be back. Dench, you get him some whiskey and some clean water to wash that wound. Get some bandages too."

Christopher left the saloon. Dench went and got the materials as Christopher had ordered. He set the water and bandages to the side and popped the cork on the whiskey bottle. He offered the bottle to Jacob. Jacob took it and had a long pull.

A few minutes later, John Ketch arrived with his pills.

"Don't take more than one," he said, giving them to Jacob. "It'll get you higher than Monk's Mound, you take more than that with whiskey."

Jacob put the pill in his mouth and washed it down with another swallow of the liquor.

Mattie and Eliana Reid walked in the saloon.

"Told you settling up old scores was a bad idea," said Eliana, walking over to Jacob's makeshift operating table and drawing her big hunting knife. "First thing, we gotta get this boot off and get that wound cleaned out."

"We don't think the bone was hit," Ketch said.

"That's good, Mr. Smith. Might still be able to walk the land when everything's said and done. Now roll over on your belly."

Jacob rolled over.

Eliana began by removing with a quick snick of her blade the makeshift bandage Jacob had made from his shirt sleeve. Next, she started cutting up the outside lining of Jacob's trousers with her knife. The razor sharp blade parted the heavy cloth like butter. When she finished, Jacob's trouser leg hung open from the mid-thigh down.

The men looked at Mattie, the saloon girl, who stared with open curiosity.

"What?" she asked. "I seen it before, boys. I just ain't ever seen it all shot up, that's all."

Eliana started cutting through the upper tube of the boot. It had been tooled from tough leather, so Eliana had to put in some effort. Jacob winced at the jostling. Pretty soon she had the upper-half peeled back from the blood-soaked wound and surrounding skin. She whistled low.

"Pass that bowl of water here," she said.

Ketch passed her the water and she soaked some of the clean towels in it. Jacob hissed as she gingerly cleaned the wound with gentle but firm dabs from the edge of the cloth.

"Well, Mattie, today ain't your day. He ain't shot up too bad. I can see it, Mr. Smith. Ball must have bounced off the ground and flattened fore it hit you." She dabbed a little more. "We'll have to get it out. Your boot slowed it. That's good, but like I said, the ball can't stay in." Eliana picked up her knife again, saying, "This is gonna sting a bit." She began digging into the wound, trying to get the ball out.

Eliana was wrong; it hurt like hell. Jacob sucked in a breath, held it, and grit his teeth.

Christopher came back just as Eliana dropped the flattened lead ball on the table.

"That wasn't so bad, now was it?" she asked as she started to bandage the leg again.

"Any sign of the sheriff?" John Ketch asked Christopher.

"No," Christopher replied, shaking his head. "If he's home, he ain't coming to the door. Ms. Reid, I hate to impose further on you, but reckon I can rent a horse? Mine's exhausted and I need to get to the Washington place before them Kukluxers."

"Make it two horses, Ms. Reid."

"You're not going, Jacob," Christopher said.

"I am. It's what I joined the order for. Pack the wound and cut me loose, ma'am."

"You two are imposing a mite on me, ain'tcha?"

"We wouldn't normally," Jacob said, looking back over his shoulder, "but we gotta be quick or the Kukluxers'll get there first."

"Fine," Eliana said after a long pause. "I'll get you the horses. I got two real runners who'll beat anything in the county. Don't want some receipt. Just give me your word and we'll be done with it."

Eliana went and got the horses as Jacob cut the rest of his trouser leg off. He felt a fool for having his leg exposed, but there wasn't much to be done for it.

Dench and Mattie found him an old push broom for a crutch. He hobbled outside while John Ketch and Christopher changed saddles and gear between the horses. When the two men finished, the Templars mounted their fresh horses and rode from Grace.

Jacob and Christopher reined up their horses in front of the Washington's barn and dismounted. They went inside and pulled the sack from the Kukluxer's head.

"Hello, boys," the head said, the dry skin of its hollow cheeks stretching queerly from its rictus grin. Its eyes were bright red coals. "Back so soon?"

"What is this?" Jacob asked, pulling the burnt finger-bone from his shirt pocket and holding it out in front of the head.

"Got the Finger-Bone of Lazarus, do you? So what? Damage has been done, boys, and cats are out of their bags. We're out of the grave, and we ain't going back in one."

"Oh, you're going back," Jacob said, "even if we have to bury you under six more feet of dirt."

The head cackled, its grave voice sounding like the grinding of stone.

85

"Don't matter if you get me, race-traitor. You still got five of my friends to worry about."

"Just five, huh?" Jacob asked. "Not six?"

The head stayed silent.

"Cause the way I figure, one of you out there last night wasn't raised by the relic. See, I think you're drawing your life force from someone else, and I think Cyclops Justicar is that person. Am I right?"

The head stayed silent, its eyes gleaming dully and defiantly. Jacob and Christopher exited the barn.

"Who do you think they're stealing it from?" Christopher asked when they were outside.

"Dunno for sure, but I've got a hunch."

"Let's go inside before they get here."

The Templars walked around to the front of the house and knocked on the door. Simon came to the door, Navy Colt held in a shaking hand.

"Howdy, Simon," Christopher said, hands raised a little, grimace on his face. "Just us."

"Jesus," Simon Washington said, "scared me to death. What's wrong? Y'all come in, now. Ruth, get a hunk of bread and some buttermilk for the men."

"Ain't got time," Christopher said, stepping inside. "Men from last night are coming this way right now." He pointed at Simon. "You need to get Ruth and the children into the woods in case Jacob and I can't stop them."

Ruth came walking up, eyes wide with fright. Jacob could see the children peeking over the edge of the loft, a line of bright, curious eyes.

"Coming here?" Ruth asked.

"Right now," Christopher replied.

Simon's eyes flickered back and forth, his breathing deep and labored. "Alright. Ruth, take the children into the woods."

"Maybe you didn't hear us," Jacob said, "but you all need to go."

"Honey," Ruth said, turning to Simon, "I know you want to stay and fight, but if they're worried, then I'm worried. You ain't no soldiering man. You a farmer and a father."

"We know you built a life here that's free," Christopher said, putting a hand on Simon's shoulder. "But now, we got a job to do. It's your choice to stay or go, but just remember we can't protect you in a shootout. Who's gonna protect the children after you're gone?"

"Get them children wrapped up, woman." Simon sighed. "We're leaving, and we're leaving quick. They forget something, they might as well lost it forever." Ruth, the grip of fear still on her, turned and called for the children to get ready cause they were camping out for the night. Simon turned back to the Templars. "You two real worried, ain't you?"

"Not any more than normal," Christopher said.

"Reckon we've seen worse."

Simon nodded and went to grab more ammo for his shotgun.

After a short while the family was packed and ready. They stood out on the porch, all five of them, arrayed in loose formation. The eyes of the parents were determined, the eyes of the children alight with the prospect of adventure.

"Remember," Christopher told them, arms folded across his chest, "no campfires, no lights, no loud noises. These men are killers. They finish with us, they'll come for you. You understand?"

Simon and Ruth nodded.

"We do," Simon said.

"Alright," Jacob said. "No matter what you hear, don't come back till first light."

The quintet tramped off into the night, circling around the back of the cabin and going into the woods. Jacob and Christopher checked their guns one last time and sat on the porch to wait. It was nearing midnight already.

"You worried?" Jacob asked after ten minutes or so had passed.

"Any man with a bit of brains should understand he needs to worry before a fight."

"For what it's worth," Jacob said, shifting his left leg to get it more comfortable, "I am too."

A quarter hour or so later, Christopher saw the first glimmer of fire out on the cutoff. The torches rode solemnly through the night like a funeral procession. The Templars went inside the cabin and dimmed the lights. They'd wait there.

Hooves clip-clopped outside in the yard. Jacob took his hat off and peeked out the window. The gang was all here, including the one with a missing head. Six white-robed men holding torches, with the headless Kukluxer slumped across the back of another rider's horse.

"Jacob Smith and Christopher Freeman, we know you're in there," Cyclops Justicar shouted. His voice sounded dry and hoarse, as if he'd been shouting a week straight. "Come on out and we'll let the family be."

"No," Christopher hollered back. "Gonna have to come in and get us."

"We'll just light the house afire, then."

"Then we'll just be roasted, Sheriff," Jacob yelled back. Silence followed. Jacob popped his head back up and looked at the men. The horses shifted uneasily. "I'm sure you got your reasons, Sheriff Coleson," Jacob continued. "But this is still wrong."

"Know who I am? That's just dandy. See what good it does when my boys put that house to the torch."

The Kukluxers spurred their horses forward, torches raised. As they rode within range, Jacob and Christopher came out from behind cover and shot them off the backs of their mounts. The torches fell and sputtered on the ground beside the white-cloaked men.

The Kukluxers stood right back up, though, and grabbed the extinguished sticks from the yard. Jacob shot one on his left. It didn't slow the white-robed thing down as he walked back to the group and again lit the torch. The creatures all laughted as they, torches held high, began their steady, calm walk back towards the house.

"Aim for their arms," Christopher said, taking a bead on the one to his right. "Maybe we can sever them and keep the bastards from being able to carry those damn torches."

"Caliber's too damn small," Jacob said, shooting into the Kukluxers. Most of his shots missed entirely because of the robes. "Only chance we have to stop these things is go after 'em with swords or shotguns, and all we got are swords. They'll cut us down before we even clear the yard."

Christopher reloaded one of his pistols methodically, reflexively. "I only have a dozen or so rounds left," he said.

"About the same here," Jacob said. A thrown torch shattered

the front window on the side farthest from Jacob. It landed on a rug and immediately began smoldering.

"Well, this ain't exactly the way I pictured my dying. Fitting, I reckon."

"Fitting? Why's that?" Jacob asked, popping up to take a few shots.

"Tell you if we live," Christopher replied. "Listen, Jacob. We get down to our last few shots, I'm charging the bastards."

"Sounds alright to me. I'd rather die in the open than have a house burn down round my ears."

Another torch came crashing in through a window. This one landed near the potbellied stove. What could have only been a third torch thudded on the roof. Jacob leaned out and took a few more shots. The Kukluxers weren't even bothering to shoot back anymore.

Both men took kerchiefs from their pockets and tied them around their faces as masks. They wouldn't filter all the smoke and soot out, but they'd help some.

"Almost ready for that charge?" Jacob asked through his makeshift mask.

"Just about. You're gonna look pretty silly, you know that? Charging with that crutch-broom of yours."

"Yup." Jacob smiled a tight-lipped smile. He changed his pistol from his left hand to his right and offered his free hand to Christopher. "Wanted to say it's been a real pleasure, Christopher. You're just fine in my book."

"You too, Jacob." Christopher accepted the offered hand. They shook.

"Getting hot enough in there for you boys to come out and talk?" Sheriff Coleson called from the yard.

"Why don't you talk to us instead, Sheriff?" yelled a voice. Saddles creaked and tack jangled as the Kukluxers shifted.

"Hold your fire, men," called Coleson, "hold it. I know them. What the hell you folks doing out here?"

Christopher and Jacob looked at each other. Jacob popped his head back up for a second.

"Ms. Reid, John Ketch, and Dench, that barkeep from the saloon," Jacob said.

The sheriff rode his horse back through the group of Kukluxers to where the folks from town had arrayed themselves in a ragged line. Jacob could see them and their shouldered shot-guns and rifles illuminated in the glow of the burning cabin.

"Figure that same question's on our lips, Coleson," Reid said.

"I'm doing this for the good of the community, Eliana. Don't you see that?"

"See what? Your burning folks out? Take off that damn mask. You look like one of my children playing as a spook." There was a pause. Someone spoke, but the crackling of the flames kept Jacob from understanding what had been said.

Jacob coughed raggedly. The smoke had gotten heavier and their kerchiefs weren't enough to cover their noses and mouths anymore.

"We gotta get outta here," Christopher said.

Jacob nodded and the Templars stood and went out on the porch. They both pulled down their kerchiefs and breathed in great lungfuls of air. The men split and went to opposite sides of the porch.

"Jesus," asked John Ketch, "what the hell did you do to your-self, Coleson?"

Jacob could only barely make out the sheriff in the light, but he saw enough to know that the sheriff was in a bad way. Only a few strands of thin hair remained on his head. His ears seemed bulbous in comparison to his skull. The fat and muscle had been eaten away, and his skin hung in loose flaps from his face and neck.

"Justice requires sacrifice. You all know that."

"Justice?" Eliana Reid asked. "Justice? You want justice, you go to the courts. You're just a vigilante, and you ain't better by any reckoning than the men that ran the original folks off this homestead. You're sick, Sheriff, and the war's over."

"I know that. But these niggers were here squatting. I'm just doing what's right and running them off so folks can come back to what they built. And I ain't sick, I've just sacrificed what none of you were prepared to."

"Just cause you couldn't protect the folks lived here before don't mean you can make it right this way," John Ketch said. "Reid's right. You gotta halt this before it gets out of hand."

"No," the sheriff roared, "this'll only be over when everyone comes home."

"Sorry, Sheriff," Dench said, training his shotgun on Sheriff Coleson, "they're both on the mark. You got to play dress-up and scare people for a mite too long. Throw your guns down and come on in. I believe folks deserve their peace."

Only the crackle of flames and the creak of leather could be heard. Christopher and Jacob looked at each other. Both men stepped down from the porch and into the yard. They began hobbling towards the Kukluxers.

"You going yellow on us, Coleson?" one of the Kukluxers asked after a moment.

"Knew the price when the Grand Wizard laid this burden on your shoulders," said another.

"Niggers ain't even people, Sheriff. Deserve what they get for stealing land the way they have."

"You ain't getting rid of us anyhow."

Sheriff Coleson raised his pistol slowly. Eliana Reid fired, the shot from her big Army Colt sounding like a cannon in the night.

The ball from Reid's revolver entered through the bridge of the sheriff's nose, right between his eyes, and exited out the back of his skull. His head snapped violently back, the upper vertebrae of his neck compacting and breaking with the force. A sound of tearing, like the Heavens, Hells, and the Earth itself being torn asunder, ripped through the air. The sheriff slumped in his saddle briefly before his horse reared, its hooves pawing at the air, and threw him to the yard.

The Kukluxers looked at each other. They went to raise their guns but stopped. In unison they threw their heads back to the sky and howled. Hellish light, the color of rage and hate, burst through their white cowls and washed over the whole of the yard, bathing it in the brightest, most unearthly red imaginable.

The horses of the townspeople reared in fright, spinning on their hind legs, neighing in rejection of what was happening, and pawing at the air. Smoke, wisps at first and then a billowing plume after, poured from the sleeves of the Kukluxers' white robes and their eyeholes as they thrashed violently, writhing in agony. White-gloved hands dropped torches, pistols, and rifles and reached for the sky, clenching and releasing and gasping. Their robes burst into flames, the tongues licking through the

91

white cloth and devouring them. And, all the while, that howl coming from their desiccated lips soared through the air like a single note of harmonious anger and loss.

And then it was over.

The Kukluxers had gone, transformed to grey ash that the wind quickly caught and blew away into the Missouri night. Their coal black steeds, silent as ever, looked briefly at each other with eyes colored that same hellish red as before. They turned and trotted out of the yard, around the splayed out body of Sheriff Coleson, and past the stunned townspeople.

The Templars just watched the horses go, too, full well knowing it would be a waste of time to try and stop them.

"Huh," Jacob said, holstering his pistol.

"Reckon the head did the same?"

"Likely," Jacob replied. He began hobbling over to the townsmen. "Y'all alright?" They didn't respond at first. "Hey," Jacob yelled, "asked if you were alright?"

Eliana Reid shook the stupor and shock first, and she did so physically. She came out of it with a tremor that shot through her body like a breath of wintery air had blown up her trouser legs.

"I'm alright," Reid called. "What the hell was that?"

Jacob shrugged and said, "Your guess is as good as mine, Ms. Reid."

"Place is gone now," Christopher said. He was facing the cabin.

"Huh?" Jacob asked.

"The house," Christopher said, pointing back at the cabin. Jacob turned and looked back. "Ain't no saving it."

Jacob spat to the side. "What do you think we should do with the sheriff's body?"

"We'll take care of it," John Ketch said. He dismounted and walked over to the sheriff's corpse. "He was one of ours, even if he acted a fool near the end." He scuffed at the dirt with the toe of his boot, his head down. "Were those demons or devils or some such?"

"No," Jacob said. "Whatever they were, just be happy they didn't have tentacles. Gonna check on the horses and that head, Christopher." Jacob limped off to the barn.

He went inside and grabbed the now-empty sack from the workbench. It was filled with soot and bone dust, but, nonetheless, empty. He tossed the burlap sack back where he found it and went over to the horses.

They were a bit spooked, but still in good shape. Better shape than him, that was sure. "Well," he said to the horses, patting the side of the one he'd ridden in on, "just glad I didn't have to shoot the sheriff. One less man on my conscience."

Jacob heard boots coming up to the barn. He hobbled over to the door and looked out at Christopher coming up from the yard.

"How's that leg?" Christopher asked.

"Hurts like Hell itself's burrowing into my calf. Your arm?"

"Almost as bad, but without the exaggeration."

Jacob grunted and went back inside. He started checking the tack on the horses. "What's next?"

"Figure we'll get the Washingtons a wagon from Eliana. If she'll extend some more credit, that is."

"Then?"

"Fort Smith. Trusting you can ride, of course."

"I can ride," Jacob said, scratching at his horse's muzzle. "Might need me some of them patents from Mr. Ketch, though. Christopher, can I ask you something?"

"I suppose."

"Back there, in the house, you said it'd be a fitting way for you to die."

"I did."

"Also said you'd tell me later."

"Yep, I did."

"Well?"

Christopher sighed a long, exhausted sigh.

"You don't have to if you don't feel the need."

"No, I should." He walked over to the barn door and looked out at the burnt, smoldering pile of ashes that once was a home. "My wife and child died in a house fire. I couldn't save them, though."

"How did it happen?"

Christopher just grunted. "Maybe some other time. We need to get back to Grace."

They led their horses down to the townsfolk. Ketch and Reid were finishing throwing Sheriff Coleson's body over the back of his horse.

"It sure is a shame," Ketch said. "He was a good man."

"Amazing," Eliana said, walking over to her horse.

"What?" Ketch asked.

"How fast we pass into platitudes after a man's death. I thought he was yellow, through and through."

The Templars and the townspeople rode back to Grace soon after. The sun's rays were creeping over the eastern horizon and through the doors of the livery as Jacob and Christopher settled up on the horses with Eliana Reid.

They bought a wagon on credit from her and drove it back to the Washington place. The small family would need one to get to Kansas. This time around, they wrote a receipt for the purchase.

A week later, after Christopher's arm had mended a bit and Jacob could handle the ride, they began readying to leave.

"Mr. Smith?" Ketch called from the porch of his general store. "Mr. Freeman? Telegram for you men."

Jacob tightened down the flap on his saddlebag and turned towards the shopkeeper. He removed his hat and slicked back his hair.

He went and met Ketch in the middle of the roadway. The older man handed Jacob a slip of paper. Jacob read it.

"New Orleans?" Jacob asked no one in particular. Ketch shrugged his shoulders.

"What now?" Christopher asked.

"Says to forget Fort Smith. We gotta get to New Orleans by the end of the month. Meeting some Pinkerton with a relic so we can deliver it to the monastery."

Christopher swung up and into the saddle with a grunt. "Guess we got a boat to catch, then." He guided his horse around till they were both pointed back to St. Louis. Jacob mounted and fell in beside the other Templar.

They rode out of town together.

THE NEW ORLEANS
ZOMBIE RIOT OF 1866

July 26th

Jacob Smith hated New Orleans. He hated the heat, the humidity, the smell, and the trash in the street. Most of all, though, he hated the mosquitoes.

He swore as he squashed one on his neck. He looked at the little starburst of blood on the palm of his hand. Why anyone would build a city on a swamp was beyond him, but built it they had. He took a sip of his coffee and went back to reading a copy of the New Orleans *Daily Crescent*.

"Almost ready?" Christopher Freeman asked as he walked out of the small cafe and sat down with Jacob. He was armed, just like Jacob, and just like most of the men on the street. The police were less than dependable in New Orleans. Jacob couldn't remember the last one he'd seen, in fact.

"Almost," Jacob replied from behind his broadsheet. "Still don't like the coffee in this town."

"Locals say it grows on you."

"Tastes like milk, sugar, and dirt mixed with ground coffee."

"Well, you stay boarded up in your town behind a Union blockade for a couple years and we'll see what you do to make your coffee last."

"You'd just think," Jacob said, taking a sip of coffee and making a face, "they'd go back to the good stuff, the real thing, when the war ended."

"People are strange. People round here in particular."

Jacob went back to reading.

"Anything interesting?"

"Radical Republicans are reconvening the Constitutional Convention. Some folks seem pretty upset about it. Saying it's illegal."

"Well, lots of people don't want me to get my vote."

"Yup. Heard anything more about them Kukluxers?"

"Col. Winnie sent a telegram. Says they ain't been moving," Christopher replied. "So that's one thing we ain't gotta deal with."

"They're either licking their wounds, or collecting themselves for another push," Jacob said, flipping to the next page. "Yellow fever's coming back, by the way."

"Starting to sound like a preacher talking about the end of the world."

"Says here fire and brimstone are expected next week."

"You keep reading that, I'm gonna shoot you."

"Let's get this over with and get back to the monastery," Jacob said, folding the paper and tossing it on the table. He stood and stretched.

"Don't like New Orleans?" Christopher asked, following suit. They walked down Canal Street in the direction of the river, merging with the stream of early morning pedestrians.

The street ran as a divider in time. On their left stood the French Quarter, full of old Spanish buildings from seventy and eighty years before. The first French Quarter had burned when the Spaniards controlled the city. They'd rebuilt in their own style. The more modern buildings, the ones that had been erected when the American settlers came after the Louisiana Purchase, spread out to their right.

"Between the mosquitoes, the mugginess, and everyone seeming on the verge of drawing pistols on you? No, don't cotton to it much. Gimme the prairies or the mountains."

"Country boy."

They turned left on Levee Street and headed to the docks. Traffic was heavier here. Horse-drawn and push carts wheeled their way through the streets. Empty wagons headed downriver, towards the ships waiting to unload. Full carts headed upriver, back to Canal and the shops beyond. People entered and left hardware shops, boutiques, and shipping offices. It bustled with activity, and the din it raised reminded Jacob of the docks in Chicago.

Three blocks later they came out on New Levee St. The docks and its forest of ship masts stretched out in front of them in a southward bending arch. A fine mist was creeping in from the other side of the river.

"Know where we're headed?" Jacob asked, peering at the stretch of ships.

"Telegram said it would be on the *Isabella*."

The Templars kept walking, horses and their carts trundling by, as they checked the names of each ship they passed. They finally came to the *Isabella's* berth.

She was a two-masted side-wheel steamship, one built for travel on the open water. Cargo covered the deck, with men moving it off as quick as it appeared from the hold below. Smokestacks from the steam engine rose on either side of the pilot's bridge near the center of the ship.

Crewmen pulled crates and bushels of goods up from the hold and their fellows moved the dry goods to the dock. One of the sailors was talking to a teamster on the pier. They both took turns signing off on a bill of lading. Their transaction finished, the teamster came up the pier. The sailor turned around and looked out across the river. The Templars walked down to him.

"Beg your pardon, mister?" Jacob asked the sailor's back as they approached. He was short, but solid-built. "We were wondering if you could help us find someone?"

The sailor turned around. His clean-shaven face was sun-beaten and weathered, but his eyes were cool and clear.

"Who might you be looking for?" the man asked in an indistinct, vaguely British accent.

"Name given to us was Mr. Gibson," Christopher replied.

"Gibson, eh? As chance may have it, we've a Gibson aboard."

"Mind if we see him?" Christopher asked. "He has a parcel for us."

"I'll have one of the boys bring him up," he replied, a smirk dancing on his lips. The sailor hollered to the men working the cargo. Another sailor, this one taller, thinner, and younger came running over to the pier. "Tell the passenger they've a guest," the first sailor ordered.

"Aye, Captain," the second sailor replied.

"Begging your pardon again," Jacob said, looking out to the Algiers neighborhood across the river, "didn't realize you were the captain." The mist was getting heavier. The cluster of squat building crowding upon the opposite bank were almost completely obscured.

"No harm," the captain said with a shrug. "Didn't introduce myself as such, did I?" He followed Jacob's gaze out to the river. The fog drifted in their direction from across the river. "Strange time of day for fog to be rolling in." Jacob watched the captain look up at the mast where the colors, their flags, flew out towards Algiers. "Odd that," the captain said, going back to work.

Jacob was about to ask what was odd about the flags when Christopher elbowed him and pointed at the figure walking out of the *Isabella's* cabin.

Gibson was beautiful, and no one would have described her as a mister. She was petite and young, but glided through the bustle of the ship with the determination and gravitas of a battlefield general. She wore a cream-colored blouse and a full, dark-green skirt that matched her eyes. Her curly, red hair piled on top of her head, and she wore a fine top hat cocked to the side. Jacob couldn't tear his eyes from her.

She stopped at the gangplank.

"Howdy, gents," she said, wearing an easy grin. "Y'all must be the two fine gentlemen Abbot Oullet sent to meet me."

Christopher took off his hat. Jacob, stunned for a moment, followed suit.

"We are," Christopher said. "The abbot didn't mention—"

"That I was a woman?" Miss Gibson interjected. "Doesn't in the least surprise me. Priests are a bit shady when it comes to dealing with the fairer sex. Capt. Abel, they been granted permission to come aboard yet?"

Capt. Abel turned, looked the Templars up and down.

"Permission granted," the captain said, nodding. "Make sure it's quick, though, gentlemen. And try to stay out of the way. We still have plenty of work."

Jacob and Christopher replaced their hats and crossed the gangplank to the ship.

"Miss Charlotte Marie Gibson," the young woman said, offering her hand to Christopher, "official head of the Pinkerton Detective Agency department of Occultism, Supernatural, and Witchery."

"Christopher Freeman." He shook her hand. "Apologies for our shock."

"No need, Mr. Freeman. I understand being a Pinkerton detective is a peculiar line of work for a lady."

"Jacob Smith."

"Pleasure to meet you, Mr. Smith." Charlotte and Jacob shook hands.

Charlotte turned and led the way to the nearest hold, threading in and out of crewmen at work. "Have your higher-ups told you what exactly I brought back?"

"No," Christopher said. "You see one relic, might as well seen them all. We just carry them back to the vault for safekeeping."

"Not curious at all?"

"Not particularly."

"Safer that way," Jacob said.

Charlotte gave them a queer look as she stopped in front of the stairs leading down into the hold.

"Watch your head," she said, heading down the steps first. Christopher went next. Jacob looked across at the quickly thickening fog as his head came level with the deck. He paused for a moment, the hair on his arms raising into gooseflesh. He shook his head, told himself it was just fog, and followed after Christopher and Charlotte.

The hold smelled of stale sweat and vegetable matter mixed with the salty damp of the open sea. Charlotte navigated the wooden structure like a second home.

"So, " Jacob asked as the trio walked aft past hammocks slung from the low ceiling, "what exactly does the Department of Occultism do?"

"Department of Occultism, Supernatural, and Witchery, Mr. Smith," Charlotte corrected. They continued through the hold as she spoke, passing by crates of foreign goods, and barrels of preserved food. "We investigate items of import, like your relic here, and find ways to secure them. We spot supernatural actors on American soil. Finally, we aid the Templars and the federal government."

They stopped in front of a padlocked, steel-grated door. An unassuming wooden crate sat on the floor of the cell. Charlotte pulled a necklace from beneath her collar and went to unclasp it.

There was a gunshot, followed rapidly by three more, from on deck.

"Wait," Jacob said, placing his left hand on Charlotte's shoulder. His right went to the pistol on his hip.

"What was that?" Charlotte asked. The sound of three more rapid fire shots came from the bow of the ship. "Gunfire?"

"I'm going to go check it out," Christopher said, pistol already drawn. He headed back through the hold, out the way they'd came.

"I'll come with you. Miss Gibson, you stay put."

"But, what about the—"

"Relic can wait," Jacob said, turning to follow after Christopher.

The Templars raced through the hold and back to the stairs. The sound of gunfire, a mix of calibres, came faster now. The rhythmic *crack crack crack* of shots from one weapon in particular underlined the battle-noise on deck. They stopped at the foot of the stairs and peered up into the heavy fog covering the deck.

"Dammit," Christopher said over the din of gunfire. "Can't see a lick out there."

"How many do you think?"

"No telling," Christopher said. "Hear that gun?"

"Sounds like a Gatling," Jacob said.

Bullets whizzed over the stairwell's opening. Bullets bit into the ship with thunks and the sound of splintering wood. A man punctuated it all with a scream.

"What do you want to do?" Jacob asked.

"We need to get up there. Men are dying."

Jacob nodded. Christopher took a deep breath, pushed down his hat with his left hand, and rushed up the steps. He crouched on the deck at the top of the stairs and went left. Jacob followed suit, but went right.

The fog almost had a tangible consistency to it, like it was coating Jacob's skin in an oil. Bullets whizzed overhead. He groped with his free hand for a crate or a barrel. Something, anything to hunker down behind.

He grabbed the boot of a prone sailor's corpse instead. Jacob felt farther, putting his hand in a pool of warm blood. He grit his teeth and kept searching, finally coming across a stack of thick, heavy crates and boxes. He crouched and slid behind them, whiping his hand clean on his pants.

Bullets kept coming. Two whizzed over his head. Two more impacted with his makeshift cover, sending splinters past his face. A man, Capt. Abel from the sound of it, wailed and cursed somewhere on the ship's foredeck.

The fog began to thin. The stream of bullets from the Gatling gun slowed. Jacob popped out from behind the cargo. The mist had diffused enough that Jacob could see Christopher up ahead. He sat with his back to one of the more forward masts, the surrounding deck splintered and riddled with bulletholes. Two sailors' corpses lay beside him. Another sailor, this one clutching at his bleeding throat, was just beyond.

Christopher saw Jacob peering out. Jacob put a finger to his lips.

The clumping and heavy thuds of booted heels resonated throughout the ship. Jacob glanced right and saw a figure moving in the greyish-white fog. He ducked back around the crates.

He'd seen a man wearing a white robe.

Jacob muttered a curse. Kukluxers. He popped his head out again. Where did they come from? Shit.

Christopher still crouched with his back to the mast. The fog was dissipating. Five figures moved amongst the crates near the bow. They must have boarded from there and begun moving sternward. They'd reached mid-ship already.

"Christopher," Jacob hissed. He pointed to himself and then to the bow, then pointed at Christopher and back at the stairs.

Christopher nodded.

Jacob cocked his revolver.

Christopher, staying low to the ground, scrambled down into the hold.

Jacob took Christopher's place, crouching down with his back to the mast. Behind him the deck creaked. Someone gave a muffled cry. Jacob cringed, waiting. A gunshot followed. The Kukluxers were finishing off the wounded. Jacob stood, his back still to the mast.

He switched his pistol from his right hand to his left and drew his broadsword. The deck creaked to his right. The Templar took a deep breath and brought his sword up to his chest. He mumbled a swift prayer and spun away from the mast, striking at head-height with his sword.

The Kukluxer's eyes went wide before his muffled cry was cut short by Jacob's sword. The Kukluxer's hooded head fell to the deck with a thud. Jacob grimaced as blood pumped from his opponent's open neck. It ran in waves down the front of the white robe, coating it in crimson. The body stayed standing for a moment, the stump still pumping gore, before collapsing to the ground in an uncerimonious heap. Least these bastards bled. That was a nice change of pace from the last time Jacob had fought them.

Beyond and to the left of the corpse, another Kukluxer crouched down with his left hand over a wounded sailor's mouth and a knife in his right. Jacob strode over the fresh corpse, pistol raised. The Kukluxer dragged his knife's edge across the sailor's throat. Blood gushed.

"Cowards," Jacob said. The pistol jumped and boomed in his hand as he fired. The bullet entered the back left side of the Kukluxer's hood and exited with a spray of blood and bone. The white-robed body slumped over its victim.

The Templar looked right, down the length of the ship, beyond the bow, and to the dock. A wagon was there, the Gatling gun mounted on a swivel turret in its bed. A Kukluxer manned it, looking out over the *Isabella*. Jacob couldn't do much on the ship with the Gatling surveying it. He had to put it, or its operator, out of commission.

Jacob raised his pistol and took a line on the gunner. He fired, but the bullet only winged the man. He cursed as the Kukluxer hollered and swung the gun around his way. Peaked hoods all over the deck turned Jacob's way. The Kukluxer cranked the gun, and its multiple gun-barrels spun into motion. Jacob fired another shot as the Gatling spat bullets his direction, but his aim was off. The bullet went wide of the frantic gunner.

Jacob retreated to the thick mast under a hail of bullets. The wood at his back trembled and shuddered as the Gatling gunner concentrated his fire on the Templar's cover. Splinters and sawdust filled the air. Jacob figured they'd have to change out the ammo hopper on the gun soon, then he'd make his move.

"Hold, boys," someone bellowed from the bow, "hold your fire."

The gunshots tapered off and the bullets from the Gatling slowed to a stop.

"You one of them Templars what killed my boys in Grace?" shouted the same voice.

Jacob thought about not answering. He reconsidered.

"I am," Jacob hollered back.

"You ain't a nigger, so my presumption is that you are the one-and-only Jacob Smith."

"I am."

"Listen, Jacob," continued the voice, closer this time, "I am Cyclops Potestas. I give you my word that you men can walk away if you just give us the relic. This deal cannot reach greater simplicity."

Jacob weighed his options. Footsteps came from all around him, just outside his field of vision. He could stay and fight, or he could run to a better position. But where would that be? The aft of the ship just put his back to the water, and left Christopher and Charlotte between him and the Kukluxers. As for just walking away in peace?

Jacob had smelled manure before.

"Jacob," Christopher whispered. He looked down at the hatch leading to the hold. Christopher and Charlotte were both crouched on the stairs. Just their vehemently shaking heads were visible. "No," Christopher mouthed.

"Gonna have to take a pass on that offer," Jacob called back.

"I had imagined that would be the case," Potestas said from the other side of the mast.

Jacob spun around the mast to his left. Potestas had beat him to it. Jacob ground to a halt. There was the owner of the voice. The two men eyed each other.

Potestas stood a few inches taller than Jacob, with straw-blonde hair and a thick set of muttonchops that met on his upper lip. He'd smeared blood like warpaint between his mausoleum-grey eyes and wore a grey greatcoat instead of white robes. He wielded a cavalry saber in his right hand.

Jacob went into action. He swung his broadsword for the other man's belly, but Potestas deflected the strike easily and struck out with his left hand. His fist stopped short of Jacob's sternum. An unyielding, powerful force collided with his chest and thrust him into the air. Jacob was launched backwards, up and over the stairs to the hold.

He landed on his back nearly ten paces away, the wind knocked from him, and slid another five before coming to a halt. Somehow he'd held onto both his sword and pistol. He gasped for breath, struggling to rise from the deck. He looked down the length of his body at Potestas as he walked calmly to Christopher, who had, sword drawn, positioned himself in front of Charlotte.

Potestas waved his hand from right to left. The same invisible force struck out at Christopher, launching him into the air and over the railing of the ship. The other Templar splashed into the Mississippi with a shout of surprise. Jacob groaned, praying Christopher was alright.

Jacob got to his feet, still gasping for air. Charlotte screamed for Jacob and turned, the crate containing the relic clutched to her chest. Potestas rushed forward and grabbed a handful of Charlotte's hair. Her hat went tumbling as the blonde man yanked her back to him. She screamed, flinging the crate at Jacob's feet.

Jacob, swearing, holstered his pistol and raced forward. He bent down and scooped the crate into his arms.

"Run, Jacob," Charlotte yelled.

She screamed again as Potestas, his hand still gripping her hair, wrenched her upwards. She stood on her tiptoes, eyes wide with pain, hands behind her head as she struggled to disentangle the man's hands. She kicked at him, clobbering his shins and knees, but Potestas didn't seem to notice.

Jacob glanced to the left and right of Cyclops Potestas. Two white-robed Kukluxers advanced from either side. They trained their shotguns and rifles on Jacob. Potestas brought his saber up and laid the edge across Charlotte's bare throat.

"Run!" Charlotte yelled again.

Potestas pressed the blade to her ivory neck. Blood welled.

"Though I feel your position at the bargaining table has changed for the worse, I will offer the same terms as before, but sweeten it a touch. I will throw this young lady's life into the bargain. Do not entwine the fate of this dear, young lady's fate with that of the crew's, Templar. I will kill her. I will open her throat here and now, so that you have the unique pleasure of watching the life leave her eyes, knowing your obstinance is the sole cause of her untimely death. Now, give me that for which I came."

Charlotte kept struggling even as Potestas lifted her farther from the deck and pressed his saber's edge deeper into her skin. Jacob, his mouth drier than the Great American Desert, swallowed hard.

"Give me your answer."

Jacob dropped the crate on the deck.

He kicked it to Potestas. It slid to a stop in front of the cyclops. Potestas withdrew his saber and released Charlotte. He pushed her away. She stumbled forward, a hand at her throat and another on the back of her head. The Kukluxers lowered their guns. Jacob sheathed his broadsword and went to her.

"Are you okay?" he asked, pulling a kerchief from his pocket and offering it to her.

"Why'd you give him the damn relic?" she asked in turn, ignoring Jacob's offer. She slugged him in the arm and, swearing, hit him in the chest. Jacob shrugged.

"Was that so difficult?" asked Potestas. He waved one of his men forward. The man came up, shotgun resting over his shoulder, and scooped up the crate with his free hand. He handed it to the cyclops and returned to where he had been, shouldering his shotgun again and training it on Jacob and Charlotte.

"Get the kegs," Potestas said to the man on his right.

"Yessir," The Kukluxer said in a muffled voice and retreated to the bow of the boat. Potestas turned and followed.

"Goddammit, Jacob Smith," Charlotte said.

"You're an innocent. Couldn't let him just kill you."

"Do you even know what you did? No, of course not, because you and your partner were all, 'seen one, seen 'em all.' Those are the teeth of Francois Mackandal."

"What are those?" Jacob asked. Barrels thudded on the deck. He looked past Charlotte. "Shit."

"What now?" Charlotte asked, spinning around. Three barrels rolled down the deck towards them. A steadily burning fuse protruded from the end of the center one.

"We gotta get," Jacob said, grabbing Charlotte's hand and turning to the stern of the ship.

"What about Christopher?" Charlotte asked as Jacob pulled her along .

"If he survived, he's fine."

They ran up the stairs. They made it atop the deck and sprinted for the aft railing. Almost there. Almost safe.

The barrels of gunpowder exploded. The shock wave from the explosion smacked into their backs and lifted them off their feet. Jacob felt the tremor shoot through him, from his feet all the way to his head, rattling his teeth and quaking his insides.

They flew over the railing and into the air, carried by the force. Jacob, despite his brain echoing and shaking from the force, registered the chunk of bannister that flew past his head.

It must have been blown free by the explosion, and was as thick as his arm and twice as long. For a moment, a picture formed in Jacob's head of what he'd look like with that piece of lumber sticking through his shoulder. Or his chest. Or his neck.

Jacob, arms pinwheeling, looked below him at the approaching water. He straightened his body into a line before splashing into the river, just like he was back at the old swimming hole of his youth.

His sword was a lead weight on his hip, and the boots didn't help none. He sank deep and had to struggle to swim back to the top.

He broke through the harbor's surface and took a deep breath. His ears were ringing like a fifty-pound cannon had fired next to his head.

He looked around, searching for Charlotte. She was treading water a few feet away, looking at the burning hulk of the *Isabella*. There was a creaking groan of wood behind them, the sound of an old woman giving up on life, the ship's death rattle.

"You alright?" Jacob asked, shouting as he splashed around and looked for his hat. He couldn't find it. Damn.

"Capt. Abel loved that ship like a wife."

"Come on," Jacob said, turning towards the dock, "swim ashore."

They swam down the river to put some distance between them and the *Isabella*. If the police hadn't shown up already, they soon would. A raid on a ship was one thing, they'd probably been paid to ignore that. An explosion of this size, followed by a burning, sinking ship in the middle of one of the world's busiest ports? No amount of coin could buy such ignorance.

Charlotte and Jacob swam down a couple piers till they could find a ladder.

"Dammit," Charlotte said, collapsing onto the dock when she'd reached the top of the ladder. "All that work for nothing."

"What do you mean 'nothing'?" Jacob asked as he climbed up after Charlotte. He stood and looked down at her. She looked like a soaked through red-headed muskrat. He probably did too, though. Except the red-headed part, of course.

"I spent six months in Haiti looking for those teeth, and now that goddamn Potestas has them."

"Yup," Jacob said, shrugging. "But we're alive."

"Do you even know what the relic does?" Charlotte asked. "No, that's right, you don't. You and your partner's cavalier attitudes. You didn't even want to know what it did."

"Well?"

"Well what?"

"What do the teeth do?"

"They infect people with zombie-ism."

Jacob remembered the term, had heard it somewhere before. He shook his head when it didn't come to him. "What's that?"

"Zombies are nigh-invulnerable, mindless killers," Charlotte said. She sighed, looking around. "They pass the infection to others, and whoever has the teeth controls the zombies. They'll tear apart anyone or anything with no regard for themselves or others."

Jacob flared his nostrils and took a sharp breath. He looked around before settling his eyes once again on the soaked-through Charlotte Gibson.

"Yup," he said again, hands on his hips, "but, like I said, we're alive. That's something."

"Oh, that's something, Mr. Smith? That's your great victory for the day?"

"We just narrowly avoided being blown to smithereens by a couple hundred pounds of blasting powder. Yeah, I'd call that a victory."

"But what about Mr. Freeman? Do you think he made it? And those sailors? Capt. Abel?"

"Christopher? He's tougher than new nails. Ain't too worried about him. He'll be along soon enough. As to the sailors, we were blind-sided. How'd Potestas even know your ship was coming in?"

"Must be a leak in one of our organizations. Someone tipped them off. Where do we go from here?"

Jacob peered out onto the docks, one hand shading his eyes. "We? That's cute."

"I'm the head of the OSW, and until I hear different, my assignment is to see the teeth of Francois Mackandal delivered into the hands of the Knights Templar. So, yes, 'we' may be cute, but it's certainly apt."

Jacob turned and looked down at her. He sighed.

109

"Guess our next step, then," he said, offering her a hand, "is getting some dry clothes on you." She took it and Jacob pulled her to her feet. "And, look," he said, pointing down the dock at a soaked through and grim-faced black man leaving a trail of water behind him, "there's Christopher now." Jacob grinned despite his weariness. "Told you. Tough as new nails."

"Sorry, but my room is the best we can do," Jacob said, opening the door to the room he'd rented for his stay in New Orleans. "I'll be sleeping in Christopher's."

"The order must keep you on a tight expense leash," Charlotte said, surveying the small, dank room from where they stood in the doorway. Wooden walls, wooden floors, no rugs, and a mattress likely chock full of bed bugs.

"No. New Orleans is boiling over. Colored men, even Creoles, can't stay in the same hotels anymore, so I'm staying where Christopher can."

"But why do I have to stay here? I'm white."

"Kukluxers know who the three of us are. Till this blows over, we all stick close."

"I'll concede that," Charlotte said, walking into the room. She turned and said, "I need to send a telegram. I need to inform the agency of my predicament and request funds to be wired."

"Can't do that," Jacob said, shaking his head. "Potestas knew everything. Can't tip our hand."

"What do you suggest then, oh wise Templar?" Charlotte asked, putting her hands on her hips. "I need new clothes, supplies, and a host of other things."

"The order will pay. Potestas blew up your friend's ship, not our hotel."

"Fine. If you'll excuse me, I'd like to dry my clothes."

Jacob nodded and went to tip his hat. He realized he wasn't wearing one and touched his finger tips to his brow instead.

He needed a new hat.

He closed the door and looked down over the saloon floor. He wanted a drink, but it'd have to wait. He walked next door to Christopher's room and went inside without knocking.

"Need more ammunition," Christopher said without looking up from where he sat cleaning his Colts on the room's only bed.

He wore just his long johns. His wet clothes hung over the sill of the open window.

"Need a new hat, too," Jacob said, stripping off his gunbelt and sword and laying them on the bed.

The room was small, hot, and muggy, but clean. The headboard of the only bed was pushed against the wall on the right, and a steamer trunk sat at its foot. The Templars brought the trunk with them from the monastery in Chicago. In the left corner of the room was a lone wooden chair. It may have been unvarnished and crude-looking, but it was sturdy.

"Yep. That too," Christopher said. He stayed focused on his guns. "Think we can trust her?"

"Who? Miss Gibson?" Jacob replied, unbuttoning his shirt.

"She could have told them about where we were meeting."

"Doubt it. Potestas tried to kill her," Jacob said, stripping out of his shirt and hanging it next to Christopher's. He sat down in the corner chair and began pulling off his boots.

"Could have been a double-cross. Could have been working with them and they cut her loose. She's Southern after all."

Jacob shook his head.

"That make her a Kukluxer?" Jacob tugged at his boot. "No, she spent too much time getting those teeth." He pried it loose with a grunt.

"Says she did," Christopher said, looking up briefly from his revolvers. "Besides, you shouldn't trust these Pinkertons. They're mercenaries. They only work for us and Washington because we're the highest bidders."

"I believe her."

Christopher grunted. "Just cause she's a pretty face."

Jacob grunted back. "Looks don't figure into this."

Christopher grunted again.

"They don't," Jacob said.

"All I'm saying is, the attack on the *Isabella* would make a good cover. Keep us off balance."

"She ain't the leak."

"Fine."

"What should we do next?"

"Wait for our clothes to dry, then grab chow and more ammo," Christopher said, slapping shut the cylinder of his revolver.

111

"Then we start looking for Potestas. And I know just the Voodoo Queen to help us find him."

"I still don't know why we're even going to see her," Charlotte said as she walked down the sidewalk sandwiched between the two Templars. "I can tell you everything you need to know about the teeth." The buildings of Dumaine Street crowded in around and over them and people of all nationalities pressed in. Jacob couldn't stand it.

"Ain't about just that, Miss Gibson," Christopher said, eyes ahead. "My auntie always said Madame Laveau keeps her fingers in everything. Auntie Patrice said all her seemingly magical power came from her exceptional hearing. If there's been any shaking and moving going on, she'll know. With the power that Potestas showed, and that Gattling he brought to bear while he did it, Mme. Laveau will know about him."

"Oh, alright," Charlotte breathed. "I still need to buy clothes."

"You look fine," Jacob said, glancing down at her.

"My hair is a mess. My dress is wrinkled, and my luggage was exploded all over the Mississippi. I do not look fine."

"Might could convince Mme. Laveau to do your hair while we're there," Christopher said.

Charlotte snorted. "What doesn't this woman do?"

"Take lip."

They crossed over Dauphine and kept walking. Two blocks later they came to Rampart and the end of the French Quarter. They turned left at St. Ann's in front of the wide expanse of impacted dirt called Congo Square. It had gotten its name for being the meeting place of slaves early in New Orleans's life. They'd ceased the meetings decades before, and there weren't slaves anymore, but the name stuck.

They stopped at the front entrance of the third home down on the right, a small adobe building that, like the other homes in the quarter, pushed against the sidewalk. A wooden fence constructed of tightly pressed-together boards extended from either side at about the height of the roof, restricting access to the rear yard. Christopher knocked without hesitation.

A few moments later a beautiful, tall, full-figured woman opened the door. Jacob could tell she was an octoroon, a woman of one-eighth colored heritage, from the look of her cafe-au-lait skin.

"Mme. Laveau?" Christopher asked.

"I am," she replied in a thick creole accent. "And who are you?"

"Christoper Freeman, ma'am. You don't know me, but I know your mother. I'm here because my Aunt Patrice said to come see her if I ever needed something out of the ordinary."

"My mother?" the woman asked, looking up to the ceiling. "Many apologies, but she's not taking visitors," Laveau the younger said, going to push the door closed.

"It's important I see her, ma'am," Christopher said, taking a step forward and putting his hand on the door. "Very important. I don't reckon you've ever heard of the teeth of Mackandal, have you?"

The woman's eyes flashed. "How come you be saying that?" she demanded in a hiss. She made a sign of warding with her right hand. "Don't mention that man, lest you call up his spirit."

"Not worried about his spirit, ma'am," Jacob said. "Worried about his damned teeth. They're loose in the city."

"Who was fool enough to bring them here, then?"

"We were," Jacob said. "And now we need help to get them away from the city."

Laveau sighed and opened the door all the way for the trio. "Come in with you, then. I'll ask mama if she's willing to visit."

Christopher stepped inside, followed by Charlotte and Jacob. The sitting room was small, with rug-covered wooden floors and stucco walls that held up a low ceiling. Chairs and a small table were arranged for meeting guests. Paintings of Catholic saints hung on the walls and candles of all colors and sizes burned throughout the room. Incense filled the air, adding to the oppressiveness of the heat.

The younger Marie Laveau told them to sit, and she left into the interior of the house. She went out into the backyard, leaving them alone in the house.

Christopher began pacing.

Jacob and Charlotte sat in silence, watching Christopher. After a minute, Charlotte closed her eyes and sighed. "This place feels good," she said. She sighed again. "Welcoming even."

"Be nice if I could breathe," Jacob said.

The rear door opened again and Laveau the younger returned. She walked back into the sitting room.

"She'll see you," she said.

Jacob and Charlotte stood. Their little band followed after Laveau. They walked into the next room, a larger area where the air reeked more strongly of incense and spices. The room looked much like the first, but with a table setup in the center.

Laveau pulled aside a heavy curtain in the back, revealing a windowed back door. She opened it for them. She touched Christopher's arm as he stepped through. "Please," she said in a lowered voice, "she's old now. Be quick about your talk, eh?"

Christopher nodded and went outside. Jacob and Charlotte followed him.

Mme. Marie Laveau knelt in one of her small herb gardens off from the patio, humming to herself as she pulled weeds. It was hard to tell her exact age, but the hair at her temples had gone to grey already, so Jacob guessed at late forties. Even at that age, she was a stunning woman, with creamy, brown skin and striking features. A colorful silk scarf wrapped up her dark hair and kept it out of her face.

The backyard was like a little piece of Eden crammed into the city, and more spacious than Jacob had imagined. Strange plants grew everywhere, vines climbed the walls and support beams of the roof that stretched over the flagstone patio and the wicker chairs sitting in the center of it all. It was cooler back here, almost pleasant, and the air felt fresher. The smell of woodsmoke from cooking fires filled the air, but the pungent odors of frankincense and sandalwood were thankfully absent. Jacob took a deep breath, a smile tugging at his lips.

At the sound of footsteps on the flagstone porch, Mme. Laveau turned her head towards them and called, "Christopher Freeman? That you?"

"It is, Mme. Laveau."

"Come here then. I'm not young no more, and my knees won't take this kneeling and standing up all afternoon like they used to," she said, laughing. Christopher walked down next to her. "Come here, then, sweet boy." She pointed a finger to her cheek and Christopher leaned down and gave her a kiss. "My little girl came out here and said, 'some man's at the door, saying you know a Patrice, and he knows you.' So, I thought, 'that must be Christopher. I ain't seen him in a good long year.' How's your Auntie Patrice?"

"She's fine last I heard, thank you."

"Did she go home like she said she wanted?"

"She did."

"Your wife and the children? What of them? Patrice worried so much after all you while she was here."

Christopher shook his head.

Marie Laveau patted the side of Christopher's leg. "The Good Lord keeps and protects his children, and doesn't give us more than our shoulders can bear, sweet boy. Now, why don't you help me up and introduce me to your companions?"

Jacob and Charlotte walked over as Christopher helped Laveau to her feet. Christopher began the introductions. "This," he said pointing to Jacob, "is Jacob Smith, my partner in the Templars."

"Templar, huh?" Mme. Laveau asked, turning to Christopher with a wide-eyed expression. "When did you join?"

"A couple years back," Christopher said.

"How do you know about the Templars?" Jacob asked.

"In this wide world, young man, there's not much I haven't heard of," Laveau replied with a nod. She turned to Charlotte. "Now, who is this young lady?"

"Miss Charlotte Gibson," Charlotte said, stepping forward and extending her hand.

"Dear girl," Laveau said, taking Charlotte's hand, "you're sensitive ain't you?"

Jacob glanced down at Charlotte and saw her eyes go wide. "How did you . . .?"

"Might say I can feel it, dear. Alright, Christopher, bring one of those chairs over. It'll be good to sit a spell while you tell me about what you came for."

Laveau the senior, had them sit in the wicker chairs. She sat and listened to the trio. They told their story from beginning to end. Mme. Laveau, after arranging her skirts, began hers.

"You came about the teeth, so we start with the man who owned them originally. Francois Mackandal was one of the greatest doctors Haiti has ever known. A Voodoo doctor, mind you, ain't like your surgeon on the battlefield. They're something else. They walk with spirits, make potions, and cast spells and curses.

"Story goes, he poisoned plantation owners and the other whites, made their lives a living Hell. He had his own army of zombies at his beck and call, and knew the secrets of a thousand recipes, rituals, and spells. Stories say he summoned Papa Legba and bargained for eternal life. Now, you say you found his teeth, so that story must not be true."

"Why not?" Jacob asked.

"Can you imagine the greatest Voodoo doctor ever going through eternal life with no teeth?"

"Right."

"Doc Mackandal's zombies, though, they were the old ways. They were abominations, possessions of corpses and the dead."

"The old ways?" Charlotte asked. "Not like the new ones?"

"No, no, no," Mme. Laveau said, waving her hand, "that old spell was refined over time. Zombies now, they're from the living. They are under your control and can do work and labor. Whole fields out on the islands are still harvested that way."

Charlotte made a face, wrinkling her nose. "How is that any better?"

"Mackandal's zombies were only good for one thing, and one thing only: killing. A bite from the creature or a drop of its blood mixed with your own would spread the disease into you. You'd become one of them and come under the spell of the doctor or queen," Laveau said. She shrugged and added, "At the least, the newer ones are productive."

"I still don't see how that's any better," Charlotte said.

Christopher waved off Charlotte's comment. "Is there any way to stop these zombies?" Christopher asked, leaning forward, resting his elbows on knees.

"The new ones, you give them a taste of salt. Brings the soul right back. The old ones, though . . ."

"Yes?"

"A stroke to the head. Well, that's the way we used to do it. A bullet, a club."

"How bad is this?" Jacob asked.

"Very," Charlotte and Mme. Laveau said in unison.

"Whole villages disappeared, plantations emptied and burned while Mackandal waged his war," Charlotte said.

Laveau nodded, sighing. She looked off and out of the garden.

"What about Potestas? To pull off an attack like that, he must have been here for a while," Christopher said.

Laveau shook her head. "I don't know. There's always white folks coming through, asking around about magic and spells. That's nothing new. No man fitting that description has come to my home, though, I can assure you of that. The power he uses, too, that's beyond my charms. He sounds to be a dangerous man, Christopher. You three had best be careful."

Jacob leaned back in his chair with a deep sigh. He looked up through the slatted wood of the porch roof. Sunlight filtered through the vines climbing and covering it. "So, we're no closer to finding this bastard." He rubbed a hand down his face.

"Not yet, no," Mme. Laveau said. "But," she said, heaving herself up with a groan, "I can help you in another way. I know what *gris gris* can help you if you are infected with the curse. It's an old charm, but it be powerful. Wait here, children."

Mme Laveau went inside. The trio sat quietly, staring at the garden.

"What's a sensitive?" Jacob asked after a long while.

"I feel things," Charlotte replied. She sunk back into her chair and seemed to hide her face. "That's all. Laveau's one too, I think. I see things as well."

"Things? What do you see?"

"Ghosts, vampires, spirits, demons, the future. Things. They have to be powerful, though."

Jacob nodded.

They stayed silent till Laveau returned from the house. She held three small leather pouches attached to sinew thongs.

"Here," she said, handing one to each of them. "You eat the peppers in here if anything happens. It will cure you of your ills. These peppers are rare, grown only by a group of monks in Mexico. Wish I could give more, but those are my last."

Mme. Laveau the younger came outside and stood in the doorway. "Mama, a messenger came by. Some folks are calling for your help."

"What is it, girl?"

"Yellow fever. It's bad and getting worse."

117

The elder Laveau made the sign of the cross. "We'd best get to moving, then. Now, you children be safe. Potestas sounds a danger already, and those teeth make him that much worse. Hear me?"

"Yes, ma'am," Christopher said. He pulled the pouch over his head and tucked it beneath his collar. Jacob and Charlotte did the same. They all stood and took turns kissing Mme. Laveau's cheek. They headed inside, but the old woman called for Charlotte to stay and have a word with her.

"What do you think?" Jacob asked when Christopher and he stepped out the door to the street.

"That we're deep in trouble."

Jacob nodded. He looked up and down the street and at the wagons rolling by. "One needle in a haystack this big."

"And that needle can raise an army from the straw around it," said Christopher.

Jacob nodded and spat in the street.

"What do you think the ladies talking about?"

"Don't know. If Laveau trusts her, though, I retract my previous statements. Laveau's never wrong, not leastwise when it comes to people."

Charlotte walked out of the house.

"What was that about?" Jacob asked.

"A lady doesn't divulge secrets, Mr. Smith. It's part of our mystique. Don't worry, it wasn't about Potestas or the zombies. Shall we be going? The day's fading and I still need a new dress. And, I believe, you still need a new hat, too."

July 27th

Jacob played out the deck on his game of solitaire. He tossed his cards on the bed with a sigh. "Goddammit."

"Mme. Laveau'll find something," Christopher said. He stood looking out the window of their small hotel room.

"Hope so," Jacob said. "I just hate the idea of waiting for Potestas to make his move. Hate sitting."

"Can't go stumbling around like blind men."

"Know that too. But sitting here on our hands don't help neither."

"No. It don't. But patience, you know. That's a virtue same as bravery and all the others."

Jacob grunted.

"Also, we can't be traipsing around in the daytime. Potestas has more men than us, and that means he's more eyes, too."

Jacob grunted again. He got up and began pacing the room.

"Why don't you go grab some chow downstairs? Get out of my hair for a minute."

"Fine. You want anything?"

Christopher shook his head and kept staring out the window.

Jacob went down to the dining area. He sat at the counter and ordered gumbo from the little Creole proprietor. He shook his head at the offer of coffee. Jacob asked for the daily broadsheet and the man brought him a copy of the *Picayune*.

The paper's headline read "Friends of Freedom Rally Tonight." Some of the delegates to the Constitutional Convention promised to come together and drum up awareness and support for their gathering, according to the article, even though the legality of the convention itself was still in dispute.

Jacob flipped through the paper. He found a mention of the sinking of the *Isabella* the day before. The police and newspaper blamed a boiler explosion as the culprit. Jacob grunted again. The yellow fever had returned, read another article. The previous two seasons hadn't been bad, but the rich folk were still leaving for the country. Of course, there weren't too many rich anymore. Most of their assets had been emancipated by President Lincoln.

The little creole man came back bearing a big, steaming bowl of sausage gumbo and a loaf of french-styled bread. The proprietor was a small, neatly dressed man.

"Y'all men gonna be staying much longer?" he asked as he set the plate down.

"Maybe. Don't know for sure. Still have business in the city. Staying till it's done."

"I see that girl you brought in. She's a pretty thing now."

"Reckon so. Hey, mister?"

"Yah?"

"Keep your eyes to yourself. We'll tell you when we're leaving."

The little proprietor wandered off, to propriet or something. Jacob didn't know and didn't care. He ate the steaming gumbo and continued to search the paper for signs of Potestas.

"I'm going to take a stroll," Christopher said. Jacob looked up at him from his game of solitaire. Dusk was falling. Jacob had brought the copy of the *Picayune* upstairs with him. Christopher had devoured the broadsheet, not saying a word the whole time, only making non-committal grunts and hmphs.

"Mind if I come with you? I need to get out of this place."

"Reckon I need some time alone."

Jacob glanced out the window at the darkening New Orleans street. "Think that's safe?" he asked, a frown tugging at the corners of his lips.

"Should be fine. Us Colored folks all look the same to Kukluxers," Christopher said, pulling his boots on. "Keep an eye on Miss Gibson, will ya?" He strapped on his weapons and walked over to the door. He stopped, put his hat on, and stepped out into the hallway.

Jacob grunted to the empty room. After a moment, he stood and strapped on his sword and pistol. He walked out into the hallway and over to the railing. Christopher left the hotel, turning right. Jacob knocked on Charlotte's door.

"Yes? Who is it?" Charlotte asked.

"Jacob Smith, ma'am."

"Just a moment." Jacob heard the old bed creaking and the sound of small footfalls padding across the hardwood floor. She opened the door. "Yes?"

"Going out for a minute. No time to explain."

"Is it about Mr. Freeman?"

"How'd you know?"

"I'd say these walls were thin as newsprint, but that'd be giving them too much credit."

"Yup. Stay inside. I'll be back."

"Be careful, Mr. Smith."

Jacob nodded before turning to run down the hallway.

Christopher was the type of man who walked with determination and long strides, which meant he could make pretty good time even when he didn't mean to. Jacob took the stairs two at a time and hit the door to the street at damn near a sprint. He looked both ways, catching sight of Christopher down the street. His big Boss of the Plains hat and confident, military-style pacing made him easy to spot.

Jacob began to shadow him.

They twisted through the streets in a meandering path, heading in the general direction of Canal. Christopher never looked back or checked over his shoulder, only occasionally taking out his pocket watch and checking the time. Jacob picked up his pace a little, not wanting to lose sight of Christopher in the quickly darkening streets.

Christopher turned right on Canal, heading away from the river. By this time most of the lamplighters had been out and about. The streets were cast in yellow, giving the passersby a scurvied tinge. Jacob followed after him as they walked over the blocks.

Up ahead, far beyond Christopher, Jacob could see the street was packed with a throng of people surrounding a makeshift wooden stage that blocked the thoroughfare. Some of the crowd carried torches, others carried candles. They weren't milling about, but instead stood in rapt silence, their attention focused on the stage.

A rich, baritone washed over the crowd. Jacob could hear the orator's voice even from a block away. ". . . The ideal that 'all men are created equal' shalt apply to all men, rather than a select few white landowners. This is the ideal for which so much valiant blood was spilled on the soil of Shiloh, Gettysburg, Antietam, Sharpsburg, Manassas, and too many other battlefields across this great land. This blood was not spilled so that, instead, treasonous and seditious men could pretend and demand subservience from other, more loyal men based solely on the color of their skin necessary for the . . ."

Jacob looked around, taking in the scene. The main crowd consisted of freedmen and women, a few white men, and a mass of mulattoes and creoles. When the speaker made a rousing point, they hollered and clapped for him. Around the edges stood a few white men Jacob decided were emphatically nonsympathetic to the cause of universal suffrage. It may have been their sneering gaze, their grey coats, or the Confederate hats perched atop their heads. Jacob couldn't decide which, there were just too many options.

Jacob saw Christopher near the back of the crowd, standing with his arms crossed and listening along with the others. Jacob took up a spot a dozen or so yards away, keeping an eye on the other Templar.

One of the Confederates, a short, wiry man with a mass of red hair and freckles covering his face, leaned over and nudged his friend. He whispered something to him before taking off his cap and making his way over to Christopher. Jacob watched as he "accidentally" bumped into Christopher from behind. Christopher turned around and looked at the little man square in the face. The ex-Confederate bumbled out an apology and continued around the edge of the crowd. Jacob kept his eyes on the man as the speaker continued.

"And we shall meet these threats to promises of freedom and equality with vim and vigor, my friends. The spirit of Mr. Lincoln shall stand with us on the battlefield of ideas and politics, giving his strength and guidance to us in our time of peril." The little man looked back at Christopher. Christopher didn't even register the man's presence. The ex-Confederate made his way through the crowd and headed riverward down Canal, walking by Jacob. Jacob waited a moment before turning and following.

Christopher wasn't the traitor. He'd just come out to hear a speech. But, then, Jacob thought, who in the hell was?

After a block or so, the man stopped for a moment. Jacob, hoping he was fast enough to not be seen, jumped aside into a nearby shop's doorway. It's easy to follow a man that's not suspicious or of unsteady humor. This little Rebel, though? He was neither. Jacob counted to five and stepped back out on the street. The man was farther along, but still moving at the same pace.

Jacob followed him for the next few blocks. The Rebel crossed over Canal. Jacob did the same a hundred feet behind. Jacob walked faster, closing the gap between them. They walked another block. The other man turned left into an alleyway. Jacob broke into a jog to catch up. He rounded the corner.

The man was already about to turn the corner at the end of the alley. Jacob's footfalls echoed from the brick walls. The Rebel, a startled look on his face, stopped and looked straight at Jacob.

Jacob picked up his pace.

The ex-Confederate bolted around the corner.

It's difficult to outrun a man half-a-foot taller that's already got the drop on you. Jacob came around the turn on the heels of the little red-headed man. Jacob caught up in a few long strides. Jacob kicked out the Rebel's legs from beneath him. Jacob's victim screeched in terror as he went face-first into the alley's slick cobblestones. He skid a foot as Jacob came to a stomping halt beside him.

The Rebel groaned, a gurgling sound. Jacob kicked him in the ribs. "Who are you?" Jacob asked.

Only a groan in reply.

Jacob kicked him again, lifting his body off the ground. "Who sent you?"

"Can't tell that." The man coughed and spat. Jacob reached down and grabbed the man by the back of his shirt and lifted him from the alley-stones. Jacob spun him around and threw him against the wall.

"Gonna ask," Jacob said, breathing hard, "just one more time. Then this gets nasty." The Templar slugged him in the face.

To his credit, the Rebel just grinned through the blood pouring from his nose. He spat a big blood and snot filled wad to the side.

"Fuck you," the Rebel said.

Jacob punched him again, stepping in closer this time and really following through. Something broke in the Rebel's face, likely his cheekbone. The Rebel grunted. Jacob punched him again. The Rebel's head snapped back into the wall, cracking like a watermelon landing in a throwing contest. He leaned down to the side, one hand covering his eye, the other beside him and out of Jacob's view.

"Alright," Jacob said through grit teeth, "you wanted it."

The man came up from his hunched posture in a surprise flash of speed. Dull brass gleamed on his knuckle. Jacob brought his hands up in defense and tried to step out of reach, but he was too late. The little Rebel slugged him hard in the gut, knocking the breath from him. Jacob bent at the waist, sucking in air.

"That's what you get, you fucking Templar," the Rebel said. He stayed for a moment as Jacob struggled to stand upright.

Damn, that was a lucky shot. If the Rebel was smart, he knew it too. Jacob put his hand on his revolver, still gasping. That little red-headed bastard was going to get his.

The Rebel looked at him, uncertain of what to do. He eyed first Jacob's revolver, then his face. The two men's eyes locked. Jacob gasped for breath, trying to right himself. He drew his pistol. The little Rebel darted from the alley.

After what seemed an eternity, Jacob felt somewhat right again.

"Damn it." Jacob said, grabbing his hat from the filthy alley's ground. He dusted it off and put it back on his head. He coughed and spat to the side. By now the little Rebel was probably mingling with the New Orleans crowd and hightailing it to Potestas. He could be anywhere.

Jacob sighed and gingerly touched his ribs. Not much to do for it now, but get back to the hotel before Christopher did.

July 28th

The day passed quietly for Charlotte and the Templars. The papers said yellow fever was working its way through the city. More folks were leaving.

Laveau still hadn't contacted them, neither. Jacob didn't ask Christopher where he'd gone the night before, and Christopher didn't offer to say.

Now, lamp lighters passed through the city as darkness descended.

A colored boy arrived at the door and knocked tentatively. He bore a telegram for the two Templars. Jacob took the telegram and tipped the boy a nickel. Jacob shut the door and opened the envelope with his knife. The monastery had sent it. He took out the message and read it. Jacob reread the telegram twice to make sure he'd read it right.

"It's from Col. Winnie. Says there's a possession in the city," Jacob said, handing the telegram to Christopher. "Wants us to visit the archdiocese at their offices on Chartres. Got a Father Cavey for a contact."

Christopher read it. He looked at Jacob over the telegram, eyebrow raised. "What do we do with Ms. Gibson?" he asked, scratching his chin.

"Take her with us?" Jacob offered.

"Reckon so. Can't leave her here. We're still too exposed."

"Armor?"

"Yep."

"Potestas?" Jacob asked.

"Not much to be done for it. Potestas'll have to wait."

Jacob grunted.

Christopher opened the steam trunk at the foot of the bed and began pulling their armor out while Jacob went next door. He rapped on Charlotte's door. "It's Jacob, Miss Gibson."

"Just a minute," she said.

"Come to our room when you've a moment."

Jacob walked back into his and Christopher's room. Christopher was pulling his chain shirt down over his head. "Think the breastplate will be awkward on the streets?" Jacob asked.

"It'll be night. 'Sides, this is New Orleans. Bet my poke people seen queerer."

Jacob squired for Christopher, helping him don his breastplate. Christopher turned while Jacob pulled the leather straps tight and secured them. Afterward, Chrstopher did the same for Jacob. Charlotte knocked on the door as Christopher was helping Jacob into his own armor. Christopher opened the door for her. She came inside and shut the door behind her.

"Message just arrived from the order," Christopher said. "Been a possession. You're gonna have to come with us to the office of the archdiocese. Ever dealt with a demon?"

"Not directly," she said, sitting in the corner chair, "but I have studied extensively about them."

"That's good," Jacob said. "Should be simple. Handle these all the time." He turned and looked at her. "That one of your new dresses?"

"Yes," she said, standing. "Like it?" She spread the skirt and curtsied. The dress was simple and functional, like you'd see around the campfire or riding shotgun on a covered wagon headed out West. She sat back down in the chair, smoothing her skirt.

Jacob nodded. "Glad you didn't go with something fancy." Charlotte pulled a frown. "That was a compliment," Jacob said. He went over to the trunk. It held more than their armor, it also held their weapons. He removed a heavy leather case and set it on the bed. "Do you know how to shoot?" he asked, opening it.

"I was raised in Texas," Charlotte said.

"Then pick out something."

Plush velvet lined the interior of the case to support and protect the array of firearms and accessories inside. There were two derringers, a snub-nosed pocket revolver, and a big, sixteen-inch-long pistol. A stock extended from the back of the big pistol so the shooter could brace its recoil against their forearm. Beside the guns, a powder horn was fit snugly into the velvet.

"Are they loaded?" Charlotte asked. Jacob shook his head. Charlotte picked up one of the derringers. Each miniature pistol was double-barreled in an over-under style. She checked the alignment of the stubby iron sights. She set it aside and picked up the pocket revolver. She hefted its weight first, then checked the sights just as she had with the first gun. She discarded the revolver with a shake of her head, and retrieved the derringer.

"Knife?"

"Wouldn't fit in my purse," Charlotte said. Jacob grunted and pulled out the big pistol. He handed the gun to Christopher. "That wouldn't either," she said, watching Christopher set the big gun to the side.

Christopher went into the case and removed a smaller box crafted from oiled leather. He opened the box. Inside were an array of different cartridges. He flipped the gun's frame forward, cracking it at the top and revealing the back end of the cylinder. The cylinder only had three cartridge chambers. Each of the three looked like it would hold one of the "big 50" Sharps bullets used by the buffalo hunters out on the plains.

"Man in Connecticut makes these for us," Christopher explained, holding up a bullet the length and width of his index finger. "They use a mercury fulminate in the tip. He tried selling them to the Union during the war, but the Gardiner won out. These cost a mite more, but they do the trick better."

"What's it for?"

"Trolls and demons mostly. Anything bigger than a bear."

"Why the powder horn?" Charlotte asked, pointing to the horn in the first leather case. "You don't use muzzleloaders."

"We don't have powder in it," Jacob replied, taking it out and slinging it over his head. "Salt."

"Salt?"

"An unbroken line of salt'll stop a demon. Stops a lot of other things too."

"Like slugs?" Charlotte asked.

Jacob smiled. "We really keep it for the demons, though."

"I'll get my purse."

July 29th

It was past midnight.

They walked through the streets quickly. Jacob and Christopher, both wearing their great coats from the war, flanked Charlotte.

At the opposite corner of the next intersection, five men stood in a ring beneath a gas lamp. All five wore pistols on their hips, and were hooting and hollering loud enough to wake the dead. One of the men staggered backwards and forwards. His friend steadied him with a hand on his shoulder, but the man still couldn't keep his feet in one place.

The trio walked past. The five men stopped talking. They turned and glared at the Templars and Charlotte.

Charlotte started to turn and look, but Jacob touched her arm and said, "Eyes ahead, ma'am." She looked up at him as they kept walking. She shifted her gaze forward.

They turned the corner at the next block. Up ahead, a crowd of forty or so people stretched in a ragged rabble across the entirety of the road. It was made up of colored and white folks.

"What's this?" Charlotte asked.

"Dunno," Christopher replied. "Doesn't look good, though."

"I'll check it out," Jacob said. He left Christopher and Charlotte standing on the sidewalk and pushed into the crowd.

"Ladies and gentlemen," said a man from the head of the rabble, "I will kindly ask you to step back. In an effort to forgo the spread of the infectious yellow fever, this area has been cordoned by order of Maj. Gen. Absalom Baird." The man shuffled the orders in his hands.

Jacob made his way through to the front of the crowd.

Half-a-dozen Union infantry stood in a crescent, bayoneted rifles held at the ready in case the crowd surged. Their commanding officer, a lieutenant by the look of his shoulder straps, stood on an overturned crate. Behind him, the soldiers had positioned wagons across the road and both sidewalks, blocking access except through the central corridor they controlled.

"This is a matter of public safety," the officer read aloud from his papers in a thin, nasal voice, "and, pursuant to the power invested in Maj. Gen. Baird by the president of the United States and the governor of the State of Louisiana, he has effectively closed this quarter to civilian access. If you are a resident of this area, respect our authority in this matter and please understand that this restriction is neither wanton, nor ill-tempered. This new disease is similar to yellow fever, albeit more deadly. The delirium and resulting uncontrollable rage which results from the infection is unprecedented. This decision has not been taken lightly. It is, I say again, for your safety." The lieutenant folded the papers and stepped down from his crate.

The crowd roared its disapproval.

"Please," the lieutenant shouted, hands in the air, "control yourselves."

Jacob ducked back through the shouting and downright ornery crowd. He'd be damned if he got shot for being in the wrong place at the wrong time. Plenty of other ways for that to happen already. He walked back to Charlotte and Christopher.

"Get an earful of that?" Jacob asked, jerking his thumb back over his shoulder.

"Delirious rage, huh?" Christopher asked.

"Yup. Doesn't sound good, does it?"

"Regardless of how it sounds, we'll have to find another way around, gentlemen," Charlotte said. They turned to leave.

A window shattered somewhere inside the quarantine, beyond the barricade. A scream like bloody murder, or worse, followed. Christopher and Jacob spun, flipping their coats back, hands on their pistols. The crowd surge towards the barricade.

Three Springfields discharged in rapid succession. Jacob couldn't tell if the soldiers at the barricade had fired into the civilians, but that didn't matter much. The crowd broke, terror on their faces, and stampeded away from the barricade like cattle in a lightning storm.

Jacob and Christopher looked at each other and grabbed Charlotte. They ducked into a side alley as the crowd went rushing past.

A colored man was pushed to the ground and trampled underfoot by the others. Another man, this one white, came back to aid him. Luckily, the victim looked more or less intact as the good Samaritan dragged him to his feet.

"Things fall apart," Christopher said, shifting around in the alley. His feet crunched on broken bottles and refuse.

"People let them," Charlotte said. Her face stricken, she looked down at the alley. "Look at all this glass." She gestured at the ground.

Jacob looked down the length of the alley. She was right. Shards of glass covered the ground, even more than you'd think to normally find in a city this dirty. "Just glass, Miss Gibson," he said, touching her arm. She looked up at him.

"Just feels a bit different. I must confess, this all has me a bit unsettled."

"You get used to it," Christopher said as they walked out of the alley and onto the street.

They continued on their way to the offices of the bishop. Outbreak of yellow fever, or not, they had a job to do.

They used the knocker on the Chartres Street gate, a small black door in a small, white gatehouse that broke up the monotony of the ten-foot-high plastered wall surrounding the small estate. The entirety of the offices, formerly the home of the Ursuline nuns, took up a city block on the upriver side of the French Quarter.

A small, middle-aged man came to the gate and asked their business. Christopher and Jacob introduced themselves and Charlotte.

"We have an appointment with," Christopher said, pulling the telegram from inside his coat to read again in the dim gaslight, "Father Pierre Cavey."

"Yes," the man said, stepping aside for them. "We were told to expect you, sirs. We will accept Miss Gibson as well, based on your word. Father Pierre is praying in the chapel. My name is Dorset. I will take you to him."

They walked into the gardens which covered the area between the gatehouse and the main building. Even in the darkness, the main building impressed. It was three stories and, unlike the rest of the French Quarter, was actually French in style. Symmetrical in design, the main offices stretched to the left and right, joining the small, newer looking chapel on the left hand side. A small balcony rose over the entryway. A man was leaning against the railing having a smoke. He looked down at them as they approached.

"You know," Christopher said, a grim smile on his face, as they walked between the statues of the Ursuline saints in the center of the garden, "supposedly there are vampires locked in that upper floor. Rumor is that the bishop had them sealed in with nails blessed in Rome."

"Actually," said Dorset, looking back over his shoulder, "we used screws. But this has nothing do with them, does it?" They turned to the left, in the direction of the chapel. A small exterior door was set in the side. Dorset led them within.

They followed him through the sacristy, the preparation area behind the altar, and out into the nave, the main space of the chapel. There, at the side altar in front of the statue of Mary and all its lit candles, knelt a priest. No other light illuminated the chapel.

"Father Cavey," said Dorset, walking up next to the kneeling priest, "I apologize for the disturbance, but the men from Chicago have arrived." Dorset excused himself and turned to leave. Father Cavey raised his head from his hands. He blinked rapidly and looked at the three newcomers with bloodshot eyes.

"Thank you for coming," he said, still kneeling.

Cavey was young, Jacob thought, young and tired. His accent was decidedly French, but not near as thick as Abbot Oulett's. The priest stood shakily and walked to them, hand extended in greeting. Christopher and Jacob shook his hand. The priest looked at Charlotte questioningly.

"This is our associate, Charlotte Gibson," Jacob said. "She works with the order on occasion."

"If she offers her assistance, I'll accept it. I know I said thank you already, but I truly mean it." Father Cavey gestured to the front pew. "Please, sit."

"We'll stand if it's all the same," Jacob said.

Father Cavey nodded absently, sighing. "I will tell you of why you've been called, then." He walked over to the pew and sat. Jacob, Christopher, and Charlotte followed in his wake.

131

Charlotte sat next to the priest. Jacob and Christopher remained standing, arms crossed. Father Cavey looked up at them.

"Earlier today, a number of our Ursuline sisters were possessed."

"A number?" Jacob asked. "How many is a number?"

"Seven."

Jacob and Christopher looked at each other, then back to the priest.

"Seven?" Christopher asked. "Are you sure it's possession?"

"They each have recoiled at the touch of holy water on their skin, and two have screamed at the presence of the crucifix. Their eyes show the appropriate level of whiteness."

Jacob grunted. "Yup. Sounds like a possession."

"Have you performed an exorcism before?" Christopher asked.

"No," Father Cavey said, shaking his head and sighing again. "I will only be supporting, though. We have an exorcist in New Orleans, one appointed by the bishop."

"And he's experienced?" Charlotte asked.

"Yes, rather so in fact," said a voice behind Jacob.

"Jacques?" Christopher Freeman said, turning on a heel. "Is that you?"

A giant of a man stepped out of the shadows of the sacristy and into the nave. Christopher and he embraced and clapped each other on the back, Rousseau saying, "Very much so, my little friend." He'd passed middle-aged and moved into his twilight years. His hair had long gone white, but his eyes still had a youthful brightness as they twinkled in the dim light from the altar votive candles.

They broke the embrace. "I thought you were still in St. Louis. When did they ship you down here?" Christopher asked, shaking his hand.

"I was just visiting my friend Pierre here," Rousseau said, waving his hand to encompass the whole world and all its troubles, "when all this happened. So I offered my services."

"Jacques," Christopher said, turning to Jacob, "is the best man you could hope to have on your side in this kind of fight. This is my protege, Jacob Smith." Jacob and the priest shook hands. "This is Charlotte Gibson, head of the Pinkerton division on this kind of thing."

"We're acquainted," Charlotte said, rising from her seat and smoothing her dress. She and the priest shook hands. "It's good to see you again, Father Rousseau."

"And you as well, Mlle. Gibson," Father Jacques said. He put a hand on Christopher's shoulder. "It pained me to hear of Henry's death. He was a good man." He turned to Jacob and said, "You were with him?"

Jacob nodded. "Yup. He went down fighting."

Father Jacques nodded and said, "That is good. He would have had it no other way." He clapped his hands together. "Shall we go to the main hall? On the way, I will tell you of what I have found, yes?"

The Templars nodded. Father Jacques led the small group back through the sacristy and into the garden. He reached into his black coat and removed a cheroot case. He pulled one out and produced a match from his pocket. He struck the match on the side of the church. He inhaled deep and blew out the smoke. "Pierre," he said, turning to Father Cavey and saying something in French. Father Cavey nodded and walked ahead to the main building. "I sent him up to prepare the instruments of the Sacrament. Come, I will enjoy a smoke and we can talk."

They walked down the path together. "You've picked up a few more demons, Christopher. I see them trailing after you like hungry ducklings with razor teeth."

Christopher shrugged. "Sure they ain't Jacob's you see?"

"Oh, no, no," Cavey said, laughing and looking back over his shoulder at Charlotte and Jacob. He kept smiling and said, "These are definitely yours."

"Wait? Demons?" Jacob asked.

They stopped in the central area, back with all the Ursuline Order's saintly women surrounding them and praying to the Heavens. "Father Jacques sees the demons that follow people. Everyone has them. Tempters, creatures that feed off your emotions. I don't think they're demons in the same way he does, but they're still others. Things. How many does Jacob have?"

"Five or six. I say that because one of them isn't always there."

"What kind of demons? Avarice or . . .?" Jacob asked.

"The funny thing about demons," Father Jacques said, taking a drag off his cheroot, "is that we are all aware of what demons

133

perch on our shoulder. We just do not want to be, no? You know, M. Smith."

"What about Ms. Gibson?" Jacob asked, turning to look at her.

"I'd wager that's not a polite inquiry, Mr. Smith," Charlotte said, raising an eyebrow at Jacob.

Father Jacques laughed out loud, coughing afterward. "She makes such a fuss, because she can sometimes see yours. She is like me, sensitive to such things. Or has your malady passed as you'd once hoped, Mlle. Gibson?"

"Still malaised," Charlotte said, her lips pressed into a thin line.

Father Jacques nodded. "It is a burden," he said, exhaling smoke sharply through his nose. He turned to Christopher, saying, "But now we have other matters to discuss, no?"

"Yep. What do we know about these possessions?"

"There are seven, as Father Cavey said before. They are powerful demons as well, very powerful. Our brief investigations of the nuns' lives gave us nothing to indicate this possession would be likely: no contact with the occult, no unclean or lewd acts, habits, and so on."

"Do you believe them capable of manifestation?"

"I am confident of it, hence the message to your abbot. We are lucky you were here."

"Don't reckon luck has much to do with it," Christopher said.

"This may be tied to us," Jacob said.

"What?" Father Jacques said, dropping his cheroot on the ground. He rubbed it out with the toe of his shoe. "How can that be?"

"We were attacked earlier," Christopher replied. He sighed. "There's a relic that's fallen into the wrong hands. The power the attackers had, they might be able to summon demons like this. We've seen the like from them in the past."

Jacques exhaled sharply again, stuffing his hands into his pockets. "How do you wish to proceed, then?"

"Well," Christopher said, spitting to the side, "not like we can ignore the nuns. If it's not a trap, then we're abandoning them. If it is one, of course, we're walking right into it. But, regardless, they are innocents. It's our duty to defend them."

"Can't help but agree," Jacob said. "If it's the same bastards, then they just upped the ante by taking hostages. We can't leave them sisters by the wayside, can we?"

Father Jacques shook his head slowly. "No," he said, looking at the three of them, "you are correct. There is no way to just leave it. Shall we go then? *Oui*?"

He turned and walked up the middle path towards the front entrance to the old convent. The four of them entered through the double doors beneath the balcony. The doors opened on an unimpressive antechamber. A set of stairs led up to the second floor landing. The landing wrapped around in a railed balcony and overlooked the entryway.

"The sisters are upstairs in the old dining hall," Father Jacques said, walking up the stairs. "It was the only room large enough to hold everything. We moved them earlier when we sent for you." They followed the priest up the stairs to the landing. He turned left at the top.

Three closed doors stood on their right. At the end of the landing a set of french doors with shutters opened onto the balcony over the front entrance. Father Jacques stopped at the first door. "We have created a sanctuary here for our vestments, a prayer space of sorts. The next door, that is where the sisters lay. Is there anything you need before we begin?"

Christopher looked back at Jacob and Charlotte. Jacob shook his head. Charlotte stood, just staring off into the distance, but responded when Jacob touched her arm.

"No," Charlotte said, shaking her head, "I'm alright."

"*Bon*," Father Jacques said. "If you'll excuse me." He walked into the first door, the sanctuary. It was a cramped room lit by a flurry of candles. Father Cavey knelt within, his eyes closed in prayer. He wore his prayer stole already. Father Jacques shut the door behind him.

Jacob and Christopher walked down to the next door and stopped in front. They both drew their firearms and checked the cartridges. Jacob adjusted the straps on his armor, glancing occasionally at Charlotte. Charlotte, hugging herself, walked down the landing and looked out through the doors.

"There are fires in the city," she said. She walked back to the two men and stopped next to Jacob. "So, what will you two be doing?"

"Waiting for the priests to complete their exorcism," Jacob said, looking down at her. "Waiting till the creatures manifest." He shifted on his feet and holstered his pistol.

"And when they manifest?"

"Send 'em back to Hell," answered Christopher.

Fathers Jacques and Cavey opened the door and came out onto the landing. The smell of incense preceded them. Father Jacques led, a Bible open to Psalms. Father Cavey followed, a holy water bucket and sprinkler in his hands. The items were called an aspergillum and aspersorium, but Jacob always thought of them as the bucket and sprinkler. The priests wore their clerical vestments: black cassocks, shoulder cowls, and purple stoles around their necks. Father Jacques nodded to Christopher before opening the center door, then the two men walked through. Christopher, Jacob, and Charlotte followed.

The room beyond was large enough to hold a banquet table and all the guests that would accompany one. The priest had closed and shuttered the windows and, between these and the ones on the floor above being closed, the heat was stifling. Jacob pulled at his collar. Sweat trickled down the back of his neck.

He looked at the nuns as the priests processioned to the big, staff-like crucifix in the center of the room. Each had their own small bed. Four nuns lay on the left side of the room, and three on the right. Their hands and feet were shackled. They wore heavy nightgowns and sheets pulled up to their waistlines. They did not move. Despite the heat, they didn't sweat. Jacob gritted his teeth as a chill went up his spine. He followed Christopher farther into the room, his hand on the hilt of his sword.

Father Jacques began speaking in a loud, clear voice, reciting the *Rituale Romanum* from memory: *"Exorcizamus te, omnis immundus spiritus omnis satanica potestas, omnis incursio."* A faint gust of wind flickered the bedside lamps. The nuns remained motionless. *"Infernalis adversarii, omnis legio, omnis congregatio et secta diabolica."*

Father Jacques continued walking, stopping beside the central cross. The wind continued rising ever so slightly with each syllable of Latin. Christopher and Jacob stood on the outer edges of the room, not wanting to break Father Jacques's concentration. The father continued to chant as Christopher walked over to Jacob and touched his arm. Jacob looked at him. Christopher pointed to his eye with an index finger, then gestured at the nearest nun.

She had awakened. She stared at Jacob with wholly white, pupil-free eyes. Something touched Jacob's arm, startling him.

It was just Charlotte. Jacob pointed to the nun for Charlotte. She looked from Jacob to the nun and back again, her own eyes wide. The wind became more severe now.

"Ab insidiis diaboli, libera nos, Domine," Father Jacques said, turning from the cross and making a circuit around it. He nodded to Father Cavey, who followed after him with his bucket and sprinkler. Father Cavey began sprinkling the women with holy water.

Steam and smoke rose from where the blessed water touched their skin. The possessed women did not scream or whimper. They made no noise at all.

The lamps flickered violently, throwing shadows across the ceiling and walls, as the wind continued to rise.

Father Jacques walked to the first nun on the left, the one on which Charlotte, Christopher, and Jacob all focused. He stopped beside her bed. He took the end of his stole into his hand, his mantle of sacred office, and sketched a cross on the woman as he finished the ritual in a full, confident voice. *"Benedictus deus. Gloria patri."*

This time, the nun did recoil.

She writhed on the bed screaming, her voice like a wailing mountain lion, big and terrifying and full of agony. The wind howled now, blowing out half of the hurricane lamps in the room. The nun, her teeth bared, broke her gaze from Jacob and fixed her focus entirely on Father Jacques.

She lunged against her chains, her hands twisted into claws. Father Jacques, to his credit, didn't flinch one bit. "By the dominion and strength of Christ, I compel you to leave this body," he said, making the sign of the cross with his stole again.

The nun recoiled again, crying out in pain.

"I say again," he shouted above the wind, crossing her with his stole again, "by the dominion and strength of Christ the Almighty, I compel you to leave this body."

As the nun writhed on the bed, Father Jacques moved to the next. Christopher walked out into the room to relight the lamps.

Something clamped on Jacob's arm. He looked down.

It was Charlotte. He hadn't even noticed before, but her petite hand gripped through his overcoat and the chainmail sleeve beneath. He could feel her digging into him like the '49ers going into the Sierra Madres. He turned his head forward, his lips pressed thin, and watched Father Jacques restart the rite, this time over the second nun.

"Exorcizamus te, omnis immundus spiritus."

They stepped out of the room hours later. Father Jacques had made three passes over the nuns.

Now, sitting in a rickety wooden chair on the landing while having a cup of coffee, he looked like he'd just finished swimming the Mississippi all the way to St. Louis and back again. Father Cavey sat next to him, eyes at half-mast.

"Hard work, *oui*?" Father Jacques said to Father Cavey.

"Unrewarding," Cavey replied. "But, *oui*, hard also."

Christopher and Jacob leaned against the railing together.

"I can't understand why they're not manifesting." Charlotte said as she paced the landing between the Templars and the balcony doors.

"Some rites take longer than others," Father Jacques said. "That's all. Patience, my child."

"But they aren't cursing or taunting you, either. No temptations, no sacrilegious speech."

"She's got a point," Jacob said. "This don't feel like a normal exorcism."

"Of course it doesn't," Christopher said, turning to Jacob. "There's seven sisters in there, and all possessed at the same time."

Charlotte walked out onto the balcony. Jacob followed after her. The muggy, still air touched his skin. Dawn was a ways off, but not too far.

"Look," Charlotte said, pointing out to the city beyond the white walls, "there's still fires in the city. Is that an everyday occurrence?"

Fires burned at intersections throughout the gridded streets of the French Quarter. They were giant, and many, but controlled.

Jacob leaned forward onto the railing. "You doing alright?"

"Yes," Charlotte said. "No." She shook her head. "No. No, I'm not. Are you?"

"Don't feel right. We're in here. Potestas is out there doing God knows what."

"I agree. This is all a distraction. How do you do this? These exorcisms?"

"Was told I had to," he said, sighing. "It's my penance. You could probably see that, though, with your sensitiveness and all."

Behind them, the balcony door opened. A lucifer struck on the rail and flared. Father Jacques had joined them. He stepped up next to Charlotte. *"Merde,"* he said, looking out at the city. He looked down at Charlotte, saying, "Apologies, my child. What are those fires?"

"Likely has something to do with the new yellow fever going round," Jacob said.

They stood in silence broken only by the crackle of Father Jacques's cheroot. A rider approached on Chartres Street, beyond the white wall that separated them from the rest of New Orleans. He reined up his horse at the gatehouse and jumped down at a run. He went to the door.

"Don't tell me that's about another possession," Jacob said.

Father Jacques breathed a sharp, nasal sigh and snubbed out his cheroot on the railing. He went back inside.

"Is that why you have the little girl following you?" Charlotte asked.

"What?"

"Your penance. You have a faded little girl that follows after you."

Jacob turned around and leaned back, his arms folded. "Likely."

"Don't worry. She smiles. She doesn't blame you, I think."

"No," Jacob said, pushing off the railing, "she told me a couple years back that she didn't." He walked back inside and stood with the other men.

Father Cavey slept upright in his chair. Father Jacques and Christopher were talking. "No," Christopher said, raising his voice a little, "we're staying."

"Look, Christopher," Father Jacques said, "I believe I understand why you choose to stay. But, you must realize that there are greater wheels in motion here. Blindness, and staying here to fight that which does not wish to fight, does no service to the greater good. You and Jacob must find this Potestas."

"I ain't leaving those nuns," Christopher said.

The front door opened. Dorset, the gatekeeper, came walking up the stairs. In his hand he held an envelope sealed with a dollop of wax. "This came for Father Cavey," he said, holding the message out to the men for inspection.

"From whom?" Father Jacques asked.

"A soldier."

"Give it here then." He took the letter from Dorset and broke the seal. "Pierre needs his slumber. Sleepy man," he said, smiling. He opened the handwritten letter and held it up in the light, his lips moving slowly as he read. "It's from Maj. Gen. Baird. He requests that the diocese open its churches for the sick. The yellow fever spreads, jumping from block to block. Here, read," he said, holding out the letter to the Templars. Christopher took it and began reading. Finished, he handed it to Jacob.

The letter was short and to the point. The military struggled to control the infection. They'd set up clinics around the city, but had reached their limit. They requested nuns and priests and any other clerical staff to aid the troops in caring for the sick.

"You can't send any of your people," Jacob said.

"Nonsense," Father Jacques said. "We will not hide, curse or no curse. We will care for the sick, as the Lord said to do on the Mount."

"Then let us go first," Jacob said. "We can get down into the districts and look around before you and your folks stick your necks out. Chris and I can go right now while you prepare."

"What about if the demons manifest?" Christopher asked. "We'll be leaving the priests here as sitting ducks."

"I'll go by myself, then," Jacob said.

"What? Send you down into that beehive? I don't know who would kill you first, the zombies or the people on the street."

"Well, dammit," Jacob said, "what else do you want me to do? I can't sit here on my damn hands."

"Can't let you go alone," Christopher said.

"I'll go with him," Charlotte said. She'd snuck back in while they argued over the letter.

"*Quoi?*" Father Cavey asked as he awoke with a jerk. "What is this?"

"I'll go," Charlotte repeated.

"Well, how the hell do you suppose you'll get past the guards?" Christopher asked.

"I'm a university educated woman, Mr. Freeman. I'll come up with something."

"Father Jacob Smith," the lieutenant said, folding the letter and handing it back up to Jacob in the driver's seat of the wagon. They were stopped at a barricade leading into one of the quarantine areas closer to the Mississippi.

"Thank you," Jacob said, taking the letter and putting it back inside his black suit-jacket.

"The bishop requested we assess the needs of the city before coming to a decision on which churches and facilities to open for aid," Charlotte said.

"Sister Charlotte Gibson, was it?" the soldier asked.

"Yes."

"Well, needs are high as the river in spring, and the bridge is washed out. But that's the way, innit?"

"Quite."

"I'll send one of my troopers with you to light the way," the lieutenant said. "This area isn't safe to travel through unarmed."

Jacob, not for the first time since leaving the diocesan offices, felt naked. The rest of the streets seemed safe enough while they wore these get-ups. But the quarantine areas? No telling what all kinds of trouble they could get into here, and he would've liked to at least have his pistol. He looked at Charlotte in her nun habit, then back to the lieutenant.

"Locals restless, Lieutenant?" Charlotte asked.

"No, Sister. The afflicted." The lieutenant turned and shouted, "Bradley. Report." A young man not nearly eighteen came rushing to a halt in front of his commanding officer. Jacob could see the telling red welts of acne on his forehead and chin in the crackling firelight. "Pvt. Bradley, guide these clergy to the clinic and wherever else within reason they wish to go."

The private saluted and ran to retrieve a firebrand. "He's a good sort, if a bit young," the lieutenant said to them in passing. He slapped a mosquito on his neck, cursing. "Dammit. Pardon

141

my language, Sister," he said, looking at his palm. He removed a handkerchief from his pocket and wiped his hand clean, saying, "Thought we'd licked these buggers when Gen. Butler was commander."

Pvt. Bradley returned. Jacob drove the wagon up a ways and left it on the side of the road. The lieutenant posted a guard for them. The horses knickered softly as Jacob, Charlotte, and Bradley headed up the road to the tavern the military had converted to a clinic. Bradley walked out in front, but not too far, his rifle slung over his shoulder and his torch held out high.

Groups of soldiers and small cadres of soldiers escorting civilians walked by Jacob and Charlotte. Most carried torches or lanterns. The soldiers' faces were stern by the firelight. The civilians, though, the civilians' faces were awash with horror.

"Name was Bradley, right?"

"Yes, sir. I mean Father."

"How bad?"

Bradley bit his lip and shook his head. "I don't look it, but I was in the war. I've seen worse, seen far and away worse, sir. But not by much. The lieutenant, he seems to think it'll all blow over. The lieutenant, he's one of the good ones too. Got us out of plenty of scrapes, kept me alive during the war, and he seems to know what he's doing and where he's going. So it can't be all that bad if Lt. Grimes thinks it'll be fine. We was at Shiloh together, you know, and Gettysburg, too. So I trust him. He says we'll be fine, I believe him."

"What about the other soldiers?" Charlotte asked. "What do they think?"

"They think we're fucked," Pvt. Bradley said, then swore again at his slip. "Sorry about that, Sister."

Charlotte rolled her eyes. Luckily, Bradley was walking out in front and couldn't see her.

Ahead, at the next intersection, they turned left. In the center of the street, the troops had built a great bonfire. Soldiers with bandannas tied round their faces threw couches, sheets, blankets, chairs, carpets, stuffed animals, a crib, clothing, curtains, and all manner of other things onto the fire from a great pile of goods they'd built up in the street. The paint on the buildings nearby pealed from the heat.

"What are they burning?" Charlotte asked Pvt. Bradley.

"The belongings of the infected, Sister, per Dr. Becket's instruction."

A brace of guns roared a few blocks over, followed by a scream of pain and terror. Jacob's right hand went to his pistol, which just made him feel foolish all over again for not being armed.

Charlotte gripped Jacob's arm. A smaller caliber shot, likely a pistol, followed.

Bradley didn't flinch. He turned around and shrugged. "Must've got another," he said. "Want to see the clinic?"

"Yup," Jacob said.

They walked the short distance to the clinic. It was in a saloon named St. Nicholas. A line of the sick snaked in through the front doors. They all, to a man and woman, looked much worse for the wear. The rusty red of blood infection traced their veins beneath green, flabby skin. Bradley pushed forward, shouting for them to make way.

At the sight of Jacob and Charlotte, weak, sweaty hands reached out for blessings. They groped for his face and tugged at his roman collar. Charlotte's eyes widened as she backed away respectfully, an outstretched hand trying to keep her measured distance.

"Uh, bless you," Jacob said awkwardly, eying their fingernails and dry lips flecked with bits of what might be curse-riddled foam. "The Church is doing all in its power." Which had a bit of truth to it, so Jacob felt he wasn't truly lying. "Um, have faith," he added as they finally made it through the soldiers and into relative safety.

Jacob looked around them, taking in the scene. The St. Nicholas had been turned into a clinic, alright. The once spacious dance floor had been overtaken by beds from nearby homes and standard army cots. Straw mattresses had been thrown onto the tops of tables and were being used as makeshift beds for the sick. Jacob recognized the scene from his own short stint in a medical tent during the war.

Civilians and doctors paced, tending to the sick, which filled every bed available. Jacob watched as newcomers were guided up the stairs by the staff. Armed soldiers were everywhere, posted on the landings and between the beds. They stood at ease against the walls. Not a man lounged, though. A potent cocktail of determination and resignation mixed in their eyes. They had seen war, and lived. They were going to make it through this, their faces said, even if the civilians didn't.

"Stay here, Father," Pvt. Bradley said, walking away. "I'll find Dr. Becket."

Charlotte touched Jacob's arm. "I've never seen anything like this."

"You weren't in the war," Jacob said. "Seems right familiar to me."

"No, not the sick. Those other things I see. There's a man here, a tall, colored man in a top hat."

"A man in a top hat?" Jacob asked, looking around. He considered squinting his eyes, to try and peer into that other realm, if just for a second, but he knew he'd just look a fool for the effort. "What do you mean?"

"He's shackling them, Mr. Smith. He's chaining all these sick around the neck like they used to do to slaves at auction," she said, despair creeping into her voice. She gripped his arm tighter. "Oh God," she said, her voice raw and scratchy. "Oh God, no."

"One turned," shouted a soldier on the far side of the room. A general, screaming roar went up, and people burst into activity as one of the patients, a middle-aged black woman, began clamoring from her sickbed.

The soldier who had sent up the alarm shouldered his rifle with practiced ease and sighted the patient before she'd untangled herself from the bedsheets. He fired, the blast from his Springfield shaking the nearby glassware and spraying the contents of the woman's brain over her pillow.

He removed the spent cartridge and began packing his rifle again as the rest of the clinicians began cleaning up the mess, scraping it into a bedpan and stripping the bed for the next patient.

"God," Jacob said. "Goddamn."

"Father Jacob Smith?" a voice asked. Jacob turned to the speaker, a short, thin man with dirty blonde hair and a drooping, untrimmed mustache. He wore a filthy, blood-covered, white coat that stretched almost to his kneees. "Thank you for coming. I'm Dr. Lawrence Becket." The doctor wiped his hand clean on his coat and offered it to Jacob. The two men shook hands.

144

"This is Charlotte Gibson," Jacob said. "Sister. Sister Charlotte Gibson."

"The habit gives her title away," Dr. Becket said. "Come up to my office? We can speak there."

"Your office?" Charlotte asked.

"A room of ill-repute, I'm afraid, in a house of equal fame. But, an office nonetheless, Sister. Didn't the progenitor of your particular creed spend time with such as the former owner of my room? Come."

They followed him up the stairs. The doctor walked with a stiff leg. They walked around the balcony, through the last door available, and into a spacious room.

"The madame's room," Dr. Becket said, walking into the room and taking a seat at a big roll top desk. "It was the biggest, but, honestly, had the unique peculiarity of being the only one of the sleeping quarters with a writing desk. I use the term 'sleeping' lightly, of course."

He reached into the vest beneath his white coat and produced a cigarette case. He opened the case and, after offering cigarettes to both Charlotte and Jacob, took one out and lit the tip with a match he struck on the desktop. He took a drag and leaned back in his chair, crossing the right leg over the left with help from his hands.

"Thank you again for coming," Dr. Becket said.

"City's sick," Jacob said. "The Church aims to help."

"Yes," Dr. Beckett said, nodding, "it most certainly is." He began to count off with his fingers as he spoke. "Whatever the church is able to provide, whether it be as simple as lint and bandages for the bitten, or quinine, calomel, sugar of lead for those with the fever, will gladly be accepted by the city and Maj. Gen. Baird. Clean sheets and water as well would leave me humbly appreciative."

"Are you certain it's yellow fever, Doctor?" Charlotte asked.

"What else could it be, Sister? It's the summer, and we are within the influence of the gulf. Fever struck horribly only a few years ago. The people made it through then, and run the risk again."

"What about the afflicted attacking others and infecting them?"

"Simple delirium," Dr. Becket replied, a forced smile on his face. "As to the bites being infectious, there is no definitive proof as of yet that this action spreads the disease." He took a final drag from his cigarette and stubbed it out in the overflowing ashtray on the desk.

"That letter from Baird," Jacob said, looking from Charlotte to Dr. Becket, "Maj. Gen. Baird, I mean, mentioned opening up some churches."

"Yes," Dr. Beckett said, "but I am not affiliated with the higher functions of the containment strategy. My responsibility lies solely with the treatment of this district, Father."

Charlotte seemed pensive within the white coif surrounding her face. "Father Smith," she said after a moment, "did you still wish to look at a home of the infected?"

"What?" both Jacob and Dr. Beckett said in unison.

"You mentioned on the ride over that you had some experience with diseases of the tropical nature while you were at seminary, and you had a theory on infections and communicable diseases you wished to investigate further."

"Oh," Jacob said, clearing his throat. "Yes. I did." He pulled and tugged at his roman collar, trying to adjust it. Damn things were scratchy.

"Would that be possible, Dr. Becket? We would take our escort, Pvt. Bradley, with us, of course, to be certain of our safety."

Dr. Becket leaned farther back in his chair, stroking his nicotine-stained mustache.

"Normally, I would be inclined to the negative in such a decision. But, seeing that you are a man of the cloth and are only looking to fulfill scientific curiosity," he said, shrugging. "I can't see any obstacle provided that you take Bradley with you. And, of course, that you supply me with any notes or findings you may come across, Father. Though, I doubt you will find much new, of course."

"Yup," Jacob said with determination. "I can do that."

Dr. Becket looked at Jacob, eying him carefully, then at Charlotte. "Excellent," he said after a moment. He slapped the armrests of his chair and, again with the help of his hands, uncrossed his legs. He stood and took turns shaking hands with Jacob and Charlotte. He escorted them back downstairs.

The situation hadn't changed. The line of new patients still stretched out the door and into the street. "Pvt. Bradley," Charlotte said to the pimpled soldier as he approached, "Dr. Becket has given his consent so that Father Smith and I might investigate the home of one of the infected."

Pvt. Bradley looked from Charlotte to Jacob, worrying away at his lip with his teeth. "Well, sure, I guess, ma'am. I mean Sister. I mean, are you *sure*? There's no telling what's in any of those houses. Some of the people, they're fevered. They're attacking people on the street, you know."

"You're armed, son," Jacob said. "Reckon we'll be fine."

"Fine. But anything happens, it ain't my fault."

"Deal," Charlotte said.

They walked back out into the street. Jacob looked east. The sun was on the move from behind the horizon. The smoke from the fires rose, mixing with the yellowish-orange sky, painting it all maners of blue and purples. It would have been beautiful under other circumstances.

"Wonder how Christopher is doing," he said to Charlotte. She didn't respond. They followed Pvt. Bradley, who headed north through the cramped streets.

"So, you two want to see one of the infected houses?"

"One of the early ones, Private," Charlotte replied.

"Those are all locked up, I think. Dunno if we'll be able to get you two in there."

"Let's try at least," Jacob said. He pulled the hat from his head and slicked back his hair. Throngs of soldiers walked the streets. More guns fired a block over.

"Sometimes," Pvt. Bradley said, looking back, "the people . . ." He refocused ahead of him. "Well, the delirium takes over 'fore we have a chance to get to them and they're just out in the streets wandering. Or we go to clear a house, or an apartment, and they're inside scratching at the doors. Them folks we find, they go wilder than a fighting dog at the sight of us."

Bradley lapsed into silence.

"We've gotta just put 'em down in those cases . . ."

"You do what you gotta, son," Jacob said after a moment. "It's alright."

"Thanks, Father."

They walked another block. Here, silence hung over the deserted street. A stray dog ran across their path and down an alleyway.

"Stop," Charlotte said, her hand on Jacob's arm. She closed her eyes and pointing at a two-story red-plaster home with its windows shuttered and its door shut, said, "That house."

There was a large red "X" painted on the front door. A sign beside the door identified the building as a boarding house.

"That one, Sister?" Pvt. Bradley asked.

"Yes," she said, "this one. It feels right."

They crossed the street. Pvt. Bradley tried the door. The knob wouldn't turn.

"Back up a step, there," Jacob said. Pvt. Bradley and Charlotte backed up. Jacob reared back and kicked the door near the knob, wrenching the door back in its frame.

"Hey," Pvt. Bradley shouted.

"This is in the name of intellectual curiosity, Private," Charlotte said as Jacob kicked again, sending the door flying open and slamming against an interior wall. Jacob walked in first, followed by Pvt. Bradley and Charlotte.

Noxious smells greeted them in the front entryway. A set of stairs connected them to the second floor. An arched doorway led right into an empty parlor. All the furniture had probably been disinfected and burned when the soldiers had emptied the house of afflicted. The wallpaper looked new, the chair rail pristine and devoid of scuff marks. Dust bunnies huddled together in the corners of the room. Dead mosquitoes lay in a mass grave on the window sills.

Silence filled the building.

Charlotte walked into the parlor and closed her eyes. "It's here."

"What is?" Jacob asked.

"Something," replied Charlotte as she opened her eyes and walked further into the parlor. She turned and walked through an open doorway at the back of the room and into what had likely been a dining area.

Jacob and Pvt. Bradley followed after her. Two doors led off from the room. One in the back, and one to the left.

Jacob felt Bradley turn and size him up. "You two aren't with the Church, are you?" Bradley asked, scratching the back of his head.

"We are," Jacob replied, turning to Bradley. "Just ain't a priest, is all."

"And Sister Gibson? She's not a nun neither, is she?"

"Nope," Jacob said. "Sure ain't."

Charlotte opened the door at the back and walked into the kitchen. Skillets and pots filled with half-rotting, half-cooked food sat on the range. Just beyond Charlotte, Jacob saw that one of the windows was shuttered. Brown butcher paper covered a hole in two of the glass panes.

Charlotte looked around and, her mouth shaping a silent "oh," went left and disappeared around the corner. "Here, Mr. Smith," she called from within the kitchen, "I found something."

Jacob walked in quickly and ducked his head around the corner to look at her. A small table stood in the corner, away from the stove. A closed door led from the kitchen and another opened out into the alleyway. Charlotte stood in the middle of the small room holding a large, curved shard of glass. She gazed down at it, her mouth agape. The piece looked to have come from an oversized jar of some sort. "What is it?" Jacob asked.

"I have no idea," she said, turning the object in her hands, "but I think it's a clue to what's going on."

"Be careful with it then."

"Is there anything to put it in?" she asked.

Jacob looked around, but anything that was cloth had been removed with the rest of the home's furnishings. He stripped off his jacket and handed it to Charlotte. She wrapped the shard in the black cloth.

"Often," she said, closing her eyes, "I can get a feel for an object."

"Feel for an object?" Pvt. Bradley asked.

"Yes, Private. Feel where it came from and what it really is."

"Can you backtrack it?" Jacob asked, shifting his weight from one foot to another. "To its source, I mean?"

"Sometimes. This is wrapped up with so much negative feeling and emotion, raw hate, that it's probably left a bright, shining path to its origin."

"Who's the owner?" Jacob asked. He already knew the answer, but he wanted it spoken aloud. It would give him something to hunt.

149

Something thudded against the pantry door. Jacob's instincts took over.

He stepped past Charlotte, shoving her back towards Bradley. Another thud, this one shaking the door in its frame. He cursed again as his hand went to his empty hip.

"Thought y'all cleared this place, Private?" Jacob asked, sidling backwards against Charlotte. Dammit. He knew he should have come armed.

"We did! The red 'X' says we did. You saw it on the door."

The latch on the door broke.

An afflicted spilled out.

It was big, and, from the look of his clothing, had once been a sailor. The creature stood at least six-and-a-half feet tall. Muscles, big enough that Jacob couldn't really discern a neck, bulged under its torn shirt. Vague tattoos crisscrossed Sailor's arms and shoulders, blending with its grey, dying skin. Its skin sagged with the sickness.

If Sailor was powerful enough to beat the door open, Jacob sure didn't want to get in its way.

The afflicted trudged towards Jacob, its milky-white eyes staring into nothing. "Here," Charlotte yelled, handing the skillet off the stove to Jacob. He looked from Sailor down to the cast iron pan. Maggots crawled in the rotten meat. The Templar hefted the sturdy weight in his hand.

"I can't get a clear shot," Pvt. Bradley said from the rear. "You gotta move."

"Don't worry," Jacob said, "I got this."

He shuffled forward, pan reared back like it was his broadsword. He swung at the afflicted, hitting it in the side of the head and sending rotten food and maggots across the kitchen. Reverberations from the iron shot up Jacob's arm. The force of the blow knocked Sailor back, but didn't kill it.

Jacob cursed as Sailor, unfazed, straightened and came at him. Jacob wanted to sidestep the creature, but between the cramped quarters and the need to protect Charlotte, he was cornered. The afflicted came at him, a low groan rumbling in its chest.

It was on him.

Charlotte screamed as Jacob and the afflicted locked in a grapple. Jacob dropped the skillet as he tried to fight off Sailor.

The creature's superior weight and strength bore down on Jacob, forcing him to his knees.

Sailor's dripping jaws crept closer to the Templar's face. Panic welled in Jacob as the afflicted's hot, rank breath blew across his throat.

"Private!" Jacob hollered. Sailor weighed down on his locked arms, knocking him backwards onto the kitchen floor. "Miss Gibson?" he shouted. Sailor's gnashing teeth were coming closer and closer to his throat. He looked up as he frantically shoved at his attacker.

Charlotte had pulled her habit up around her waist on her right side, exposing long, black stocking-covered legs. She was fiddling with the garter on her thigh.

"What in the Hell are you two doing?" Jacob shouted, unable to, despite the overwhelming smell of grave breath, take his eyes from Charlotte's calves and thigh.

"Saving your life," Charlotte said. She pulled out the small, two-barreled derringer Jacob had given her in the hotel room. "Hold still," she said, putting the muzzle of the tiny pistol to Sailor's animated head.

She fired crosswise, keeping Jacob from the bullet's trajectory. Greyish-white brain matter sprayed over the kitchen wall. Sailor slumped down atop Jacob, releasing rot gas from every orifice. Blood began to pour from Sailor's mouth as Jacob twisted away, shoving the newly minted corpse off him.

Jacob stood and dusted himself off. He touched his face, feeling for any fluid. None of the blood had gotten on him. That was better than a Christmas miracle in his book.

"Thank you kindly, Miss Gibson," Jacob said, smiling wanly.

"At least one of us had the presence of mind to come armed, Mr. Smith," Charlotte said, returning the smile. "And the owner is Potestas."

"Figured that," Jacob replied, leaning back against the stove and looking down at Sailor's rotting corpse.

"You two done with your investigating?" Pvt. Bradley asked from the living room. He sounded out of breath. "Or can I go back to the barricade already?"

*   *   *

The trio stood on the street. The sun had risen fully above the buildings now. Jacob stifled a yawn and shook his head.

"Well, we should get you two back to your wagon."

"Yes, Private, you're absolutely right," Charlotte said. She cradled the wrapped glass shard against her chest like a swaddled newborn. They started down the street.

"Think you'll be able to stop this?" the private asked.

"Reckon so," Jacob said, hoping the lie stuck. If Charlotte could backtrack that glass to Potestas, they could likely stop the infection from spreading. From where he stood, though, that "if" looked almost too tall to leap.

They walked in silence.

On other blocks, the city had come awake. Carts made their way onto the street, people left for work, shop owners swept their front porches and opened the doors for customers, ships loaded and unloaded goods. Business and life went on for the time being. Here, though? A crumpled newspaper blew across the baked pavement.

More Springfields fired ahead, just up the street. A pistol fired off three shots. Silence, then a scream, followed by howls. Another Springfield fired. Pvt. Bradley looked back at Charlotte and Jacob, his hand on the rifle slung over his shoulder. His eyes frantically danced back and forth between the two imposters. His gaze settled on Charlotte for a moment.

They heard another rifle shot from near the brothel-cum-clinic. The boy looked back at Jacob.

"Go on, son," Jacob said. "Reckon we can find our way back to the wagon."

The young private nodded. Another scream, followed by a rifle's shot and report. Bradley took off running down the street.

"Where do you suggest we go from here?" Charlotte asked.

"Get back to the wagon and follow where that glass leads us."

They started off down the street. Pvt. Bradley was twenty or so feet ahead of them. Gutteral cries came from the intersection. The soldier unslung his rifle and turned the corner ahead, disappearing from view. Another series of rifle shots followed.

Charlotte and Jacob picked up their pace.

Jacob held out a hand to Charlotte when they neared the corner. He walked up and peeked his head around.

Bodies lay scattered on the street. Some were soldiers, their blue uniforms torn irreparably, their faces mauled by bite marks and claws, their stomachs torn and their entrails collecting dust and dirt on the street.

Others were civilians.

Most had been put down with bullets to the head, or been clubbed till their faces were beyond recognition. The black blood drenching their clothes looked like some foreign tar.

One boy who couldn't have been older than sixteen, sat against a street lamp not far from the entrance to the St. Nicholas saloon. His legs stretched out into the street. He held his thick, white, ropy intestines. Jacob thought the boy must be dead, but then he blinked and looked down at his fistful of organs. He tried to stand, but fell back against the lamp. He began trying to put his guts back into the open cavity of his stomach, mewing quietly from the effort and pain.

Jacob looked away, searching for the private.

Pvt. Bradley, in the middle of it all, stood over a corpse. He stabbed it with his bayonetted rifle, sliding the thin blade into the brain through the eye socket.

"They're dead," yelled Pvt. Bradley, waving his left hand in the air. "All the afflicted are dead."

Soldiers came out of the saloon, rifles pressed against their shoulders. Jacob looked back at Charlotte and waved her forward with his hand. They went around the corner together.

"Don't look too hard, Miss Gibson."

"I – I'll try not to."

"We're going to the wagon and we're going to get. Hear me?"

"Yes."

Jacob ushered her down the street. She still cradled the shard. Some men from the barricade through which they'd entered advanced up the road towards them. There were three soldiers, two enlisted men and the lieutenant from earlier. They'd missed the fight, but that didn't matter.

The enlisted men supported their commanding officer between them. His skin had gone green. They debated whether they should put him down now or wait for another trooper to do it. The lieutenant barked orders for the other two men to get it over with.

Jacob and Charlotte stopped and watched them pass.

"Cock my revolver for me," the lieutenant slurred out through cracked lips, "if you're yellow."

"Was he bitten?" Charlotte asked as they passed by.

"No ma'am," the one supporting the lieutenant on his left side said, "he just come down with it. Seen it happen before."

"It ain't my business, Father," the soldier on the lieutenant's right said, "but they'd shoot me for desertion were I to leave. You two, though, you folks got a chance. I'd leave this city to burn for its sins."

Jacob put his hand on Charlotte's shoulder and turned her back to the wagon. They walked down to it and Jacob helped Charlotte climb up on the passenger side.

They turned the wagon around and drove out past the undermanned barricade.

Charlotte had Jacob turn riverward at the next intersection.

They had come back to the docks near where the *Isabella*'s berth had been. Jacob had been wrong about the city coming awake. Instead, New Orleans felt deserted.

Ships were here, sitting in their berths, empty of sailors and deck hands. Jacob, shielding his eyes against the glare, looked out west, downriver to the Gulf of Mexico. More ships anchored out there, waiting for word of an all-clear in the city. Jacob imagined that's what the Union blockade had looked like just three years earlier. Ships just waiting.

"It's just ahead," said Charlotte.

"Where?"

"I'll say," she replied.

Jacob drove the wagon about two blocks farther up New Levee. Still no one in sight.

"Here."

They got down from the wagon.

"I'm not armed," Jacob said.

"Remember?" Charlotte asked, patting her thigh. "I am."

Jacob grunted.

They walked up the street. A pack of dogs ran across their path. One stopped and looked at Jacob and Charlotte, seeming to take their measure. They held sand in the dog's mind, Jacob guessed. The pack turned and ran upriver in the direction of the square.

"The diocesean office ain't far away," Jacob said.

"Let's just take a look. Alright? If anything feels wrong, we leave."

"Fine. Just feel like I'm in my birthday suit without my gear, that's all."

They walked a little farther along, Charlotte with her eyes closed and lips parted.

"There," Charlotte said, almost gasping. She pointed at one of the little warehouse buildings on their left. "That's it."

Jacob took off his hat and ran a hand through his hair. He looked up and down the street, out at the ships anchored and waiting in their berths. He turned out to the ships down the Mississippi. He spun and looked at Charlotte in her nun habit. Black stockings flashed in his mind. He took a deep breath and sighed.

Charlotte opened her eyes and looked at him. "You haven't the affliction, have you?"

"What?" Jacob asked. "Hell no. Sorry. No, I mean."

"What's the matter, then?"

"Just thinking. Just thinking, that's all."

"That's it, Jacob," Charlotte repeated, pointing again to the warehouse. "That right there."

"I know. Let's go."

They crossed the street to the opposite side. They skirted around refuse and debris from broken crates. All the smells of the city assaulted them: rotten vegetables, wood smoke, brackish water, urine. They stopped in front of the warehouse.

"It's deserted, I think," Charlotte said, her voice a whisper.

"How do you know?"

"Feelings, like everything else. I can't see through walls, if that's what you mean, but I have a good sense of most places. Our destination is empty of people."

"Anything else?"

"Whatever has been left behind is evil. But we already knew that, didn't we?"

They went down around the edge of the building. It was only about twenty feet wide, but stretched almost a hundred long. They followed the alley that ran along the warehouse's edge, coming to a wooden door on their right.

The door opened inward, but looked sturdy.

Jacob gently pushed Charlotte back. He looked back at her, eyebrow raised. She didn't respond. Jacob reared back and kicked the door. He kicked it again, clearing the way.

Jacob went inside.

The first room had once been an office. Two boarded-up windows looked out onto the mud-alley Jacob and Charlotte had just walked in from. An open door to their right led off into the warehouse. The remnants of a chair that looked to have been kicked to splinters sat piled in the corner. A layer of dust lay over everything. Boot scuffs in the dust on the ground led deeper into the warehouse.

"Need to find a light," Jacob said over his shoulder, grinning, "lest you can see in the dark, too."

"No," Charlotte said. "We certainly need a light."

They walked through the door. Jacob felt along the wall on his left. A lantern hung there. Jacob pulled it down. He took a lucifer from his pocket and struck it on the wall. He lit the lantern and held it out in front of them as they walked farther into the room.

The warehouse's beams stretched onward like the ribs of some great beast. To the left of the door was a space large enough for a wagon. Wooden doors big enough to allow a cart were set on rollers. From the looks of it, the doors led outside. Boxes and boxes of large caliber cartridges had been stacked nearby.

Ten sets of unmade bunk beds ran down the length of the building on their right. Footlockers sat at the foot of each. Three tables with chairs surrounding them stood on the left, dirty dishes piled on two of them. Four large bottles sat on the third. They were curious looking, dome-shaped pieces of glassware with short necks and large, capped-off mouths. Green and brown water filled the bottom inch of each bottle.

Jacob and Charlotte walked closer to the bottles, Jacob holding his lantern up high. He leaned in close and looked within the nearest. Something covered the top of the water. He reached out to the top of the bottle and, careful to not lift it from the table, shook.

The inside of the dome came alive with mosquitoes. Hundreds of them flitted and buzzed in a black swarm. A shiver went down Jacob's spine and his hair stood on end as Charlotte gasped beside him. He left the bottle where it was and walked farther into the room.

Two doors at the end of the room led out. Between them, pinned to the wall, was a hooded corpse. A sign hung from its chest. The sign read: "Remember that Secrecy is Paramount. Don't Wear a Confederate Hat on the Street." Someone had driven the sign into the body's sternum with a railroad spike. Jacob didn't have to look beneath the hood to know that the corpse had red hair and freckles covering its face.

"Who is that, do you think?" Charlotte asked, shuddering.

"Someone who couldn't remember to not wear his goddamn hat."

They walked over to the door on the right. Charlotte put a hand on it. She breathed deeply and put an ear to the wood. Charlotte squinted her eyes and made a face. She looked back at Jacob, her lips pressed into a thin line.

"There's something there," she said in a lowered voice, "but I can't tell what it might be."

"Thought you said this place was empty. Is it Kukluxers?" he asked. She shook her head. "Afflicted?" She shrugged.

Jacob touched her shoulder and gently moved her behind him. He pushed the door open and stepped back. The darkness was thick enough to spread on cornbread. But nothing went for Jacob's jugular, so that was something. He brandished the lantern and stepped into the room.

Thick or not, the dark still retreated from the light. As soon as Jacob walked into the next room, though, he wished it had shown some grit and stood its ground.

The room measured only about fifteen feet in length. In the right corner, directly across from them, sat crates neatly stacked nearly up to the ceiling. One of the crates at the base of the stack had been pried open. Straw packing hung over the top. Inside were two glass bottles almost identical to the ones on the table in the bunk area. The crate had enough space for two more.

A cell of some sort, constructed of thick glass and reinforced with metal bars running around it, had been built in the left corner of the room. An opening was cut into the glass, with a rubber sphincter of some sort installed as a seal. One of the dome-shaped bottles had been filled with swamp water and pushed through the seal. Flanking the bottle were two sets of rubber gloves so someone could reach inside the cell and manipulate objects.

Jacob stepped closer, lantern raised.

The afflicted inside lunged into the light and against the cell, rocking the framework at its foundation. Charlotte jumped back, shrieking. It pawed at the slick glass, its grey face smashed against the interior wall, its unseeing eyes lolling around like a dying calf's. Nostrils flared. It sniffed for them.

Jacob heard the buzzing now.

Mosquitoes flew around the afflicted. Thousands of them swarmed around it in a thick cloud. The afflicted settled back down and began pacing again. The creature ignored the insects as they crawled over its unseeing eyes, into its slack mouth, and inside its nose.

Jacob approached the glass, peering closer at the afflicted. The creature didn't slap at the bites. Mosquitoes stabbed their needled noses into its skin, filling themselves with its blood. And the curse.

Charlotte wretched. She groaned and gagged again. Jacob put his hand to the glass. The mosquitoes continued to buzz.

"Is that shard we found earlier," Jacob asked, turning and looking at Charlotte, "from a bottle like these?"

Charlotte mumbled a reply. Jacob turned his head forward and watched the trapped afflicted. Its back to Jacob, it fell against the glass and slid to the ground in a heap. The afflicted tried to crawl upright. Charlotte spit on the ground.

"Yes," Charlotte said, coughing. "Yes, I think it was." She wiped the back of her hand across her mouth.

"They must wait for there to be enough mosquitoes in each bottle," Jacob said, taking a closer look at the rubber gloves set into the glass, "then use these gloves to cap it off."

"He's using the mosquitoes to spread the disease," Charlotte said. "He's using them like bombs."

"They could throw them into buildings, or just leave them sitting open in back alleys. These jars could be anywhere in the city."

"What do you think?" Charlotte asked.

"Go look through the rest of the bunkhouse." Jacob said. "Gotta find something that tells us where he is. I'll poke around here a bit. Holler if you hear something."

Charlotte, her face paler than normal, gave a weak nod and went back into the main room.

Jacob turned and looked at the stack of crates in the corner. All were full of bottles except for the open one on the floor. But how many had they loaded with mosquitoes and already used throughout the city? And how many were still hidden or with the Kukluxers?

Jacob went back to the workbench near the door.

Clippings from the *Crescent*, *Picayune*, and *Bee* had been cut out and pinned to the wall over the bench. Jacob recognized one of them as the article he'd been reading before he and Christopher had headed to the *Isabella*. More than a dozen others were around it, each one dated sometime during the previous months. They detailed the calling of the Constitutional Convention by the governor, the fight between the mayor and federal forces, and President Johnson's orders to not interfere. The board displayed the whole political saga in newsprint.

"Dammit," Jacob muttered.

Charlotte came back in. "Jacob," she said, "I believe I found something."

Jacob followed her out into the bunkhouse and through the door on the left.

The room beyond was the same dimensions as the one with the caged afflicted. Someone had drawn a six-foot-diameter circle in dark ink on the floor. Within it was sketched a pentacle. Burned down stubs of candles were at each of the five points of the star. Some kind of foreign writing ringed the whole thing.

"It's a summoning circle," Charlotte said.

"How do you know for sure? They could've done all manners of things with this. Cast curses, done some scrying. Who knows?"

"I'm the head of OSW, that's how. See these characters here?" she asked, walking around the edge and pointing down to a set of sigils. "Enochian keys. This?" She pointed to another set. "This is from the *Clavis Salomonis*, the *Book of Solomon*. They summoned demons with this circle."

"Any clue what they summoned?"

Charlotte shook her head. "No," she said, coming back over to stand by him, "but I think it has to do with the possessed nuns." She crossed her arms. "And from the looks of some of these characters, its real focus is you and Christopher."

"Right," Jacob said, rubbing a hand down his face. "Dammit."

"What do we do?"

"Burn it," Jacob said, walking out of the room. "Burn the whole damn thing to the ground."

They found a barrel of coal oil in the main room. Jacob tapped it and poured the contents over the bunks and boxes of cartridges. He saved a portion for the mosquito breeding room with its afflicted prisoner.

He ushered Charlotte out of the small warehouse when he'd finished. Fumes from the oil filled the air. The war had taught him those fumes could ignite with a simple spark. He stood in the office and scratched a lucifer into life. He watched it burn for a moment, wondering if any of this would be worth it.

Jacob threw the lit match into the main room.

Hot air blew past him as the room combusted in reds and yellows.

He stepped out into the alleyway. "We need to get moving," he said as he shut the warehouse door behind him. "Those Gatling cartridges are gonna start firing off soon."

They walked back to the wagon. Jacob helped Charlotte up into the shotgun seat. He looked at the warehouse. Smoke was coming out through the walls and ceiling. The rapid, uneven staccato of firing Gatling bullets began as Jacob climbed up and drove the wagon away.

Jacob and Charlotte marched up the stairs together. Christopher was leaned back on the rear legs of his chair, his feet kicked up on the railing. He rested his chin on his chest and had pulled his hat down low. He looked up as Jacob and Charlotte came around onto the landing.

"Took y'all long enough," Christopher said. "What's it like out there?"

"Dreadful," Charlotte said.

"And about to get a mite worse," Jacob said.

They led Christopher out onto the balcony and told him what all had happened in the last few hours. As they told their story, the sun and the plumes of smoke continued to rise over New Orleans. By the time they'd finished, the day had reached nearly noon. Jacob could tell the city was awake. Screams, gunshots, and bugle calls sounded in the distance.

Still, the police had yet to step up.

"Can you find Potestas?" Christopher asked.

"Nothing there had any resonance to him," Charlotte said. "If I could find something important, then I might be able to. But without that, my sense won't do us any good." She bit her lip uncertainly.

"What?" Jacob asked her.

"Just something that's worrying me."

"And, that is?" Christopher asked.

"Well," Charlotte said, teeth still grinding away on her lower lip. "It just feels like he purposely didn't leave anything. Like he knew you had a sensitive with you."

"Shit," Christopher said.

"So," Jacob said, looking from one to the other, "it was an inside job."

Charlotte and Christopher both nodded.

"What else do we have then?" Christopher asked.

"Well, the convention starts at noon tomorrow," Jacob said. "From the newspapers' talk, Baird ain't gonna move to protect or stop them. He might, but he's playing his cards close to his chest."

"We need to warn them," Charlotte said. "If we can stop the convention, then we can stop Potestas's plan."

"We also need to stop Potestas," Jacob said. "Stopping the convention is part of his plan."

"And there's the nuns," Christopher said. "Don't get me wrong, I want the convention to continue. Likely, more so than either of you."

"Potestas flanked us," Charlotte said. "They're a ruse to keep you two occupied, Mr. Freeman."

"But we still need to save them," Christopher said.

"Listen," Charlotte said, throwing her arms in the air. "Have either of the priests been able to manifest the demons? We all know they're strong enough to manifest, don't we? Then why in the hell don't they?"

"Back off," Christopher said, leaning down into her face. "This is what we do. We're Templars, not Pinkertons or the

Union. We don't protect cities and kill Kukluxers, alright? We free people from goddamn possession." He wagged a finger in her face. "So, if you want to try and save the city, go right ahead. But doing that ain't my orders. My orders are to free them nuns. They ain't to go and follow my personal politics. Get me?"

"Woah there," Jacob said as he, arms outstretched, forcibly inserted himself between the pair. "We don't need this. Not now."

"You're right," Christopher said, looking hard at Charlotte over Jacob's shoulder, "we don't." The other Templar turned from Jacob and went inside, slamming the balcony door behind him. Jacob didn't follow.

"Are you going to help me?" Charlotte asked Jacob's back.

Jacob turned. "I don't know," he said, rubbing a hand over his face. "I just don't know."

"You don't know?" she asked, crossing her arms. She leaned forward, looking into Jacob's eyes. "You don't know, Jacob? You saw what Potestas has, and you saw how well the Union's containing it." Charlotte advanced on him, fiery eyes narrowed. "You know he'll bring this city to its knees. What next? St. Louis? Chicago? He could have an entire army by this time next week, or even sooner. What then? Still going to worry about your damned nuns?"

Jacob, teeth clenched, exhaled sharply through his nose. Charlotte, sensing his rage, took a step back. Jacob took a deep breath like Hatsuto, the Buddhist Templar, had taught him. He kept his hand by his side and looked away, still breathing deep.

"I – I'm sorry," Charlotte said.

"I'm sorry," Jacob said. He took another breath. "You don't need to be. We need your help. And I reckon you need ours just as much. Our orders say one thing, your orders say another cause you ain't been sent new ones. I'll try one more time to convince Christopher. He and I can go through the exorcism with the priests again. If we can't shake these demons loose, then I'll go with you. We'll stop this, and we'll stop it together. Deal?"

Charlotte kept her arms crossed. She looked at Jacob. She looked at the garden. She looked out at the city, with all its clouds of smoke and soot hanging in the air.

"Fine," she said, turning back to Jacob and sticking out her hand. "Deal."

They shook on it.

"I'm going to help her find Potestas when this is over," Jacob said to Christopher as the older black man helped him don his armor in preparation for another rite of exorcism.

"I am too," Christopher replied.

"No, you ain't understanding me," Jacob said, fixing his breastplate into place and tightening his leather straps. "Reckon what I mean to say is: Whether or not we get the demons to manifest in the next hour or so, I'm gonna help her."

"That's your choice," Christopher said. "But I ain't until we save them nuns."

"I know."

"So, you telling me you're going to disobey the order to save this sorry city? Even after these people fought against us in the war?"

"Doing it because of the war. Remember what you told me when I came back to the monastery? After Mr. Bennett had passed?"

"Not really, no."

"You said I may have been a boy in blue before, but I weren't now."

"Don't recall saying that."

"Well you did. So I'm going to help Charlotte try and save New Orleans."

"Charlotte now, huh? Was Miss Gibson before. Told you before about them pretty faces, Jacob. Shouldn't have sent you out with her."

"Hand me my gunbelt."

They waited on the landing as before. Fathers Jacques and Pierre processed from their staging area and into the banquet hall. Jacob and Christopher followed the two men. Charlotte trailed after. She'd kept her word.

The city already baked from the summer heat, but the priests still kept the windows shut tight. Light filtered in through the shutters. The nuns lay on their beds, their faces untarnished by sweat and devoid of marring. Some people couldn't stand against the inhuman invasion of a demonic presence. Some people's skin turned, their countenance broke and fell. These young women, though, they stood to the test. Jacob could feel that they went toe-to-toe with the creatures. They were putting in their twenty rounds, mayhaps more.

The fragrance of new incense piled atop old as the priests continued to the formal crucifix that still stood in the center. The fragrance of Jacob's sweat mingled with the burning myrrh. It unsettled him.

Jacob thought he heard a mosquito for the briefest of moments, just a buzzing of wings breaking the New Orleans air. But, for all he knew, that noise came from the demons. They played tricks on your mind. They felt your fears, dug them up from the cold, dark places in your mind. They chewed them up and spat them back at you.

Father Jacques began his rounds. This time didn't change from the first. The hissing, the wailing, the steam and smoke. The demons still wouldn't speak.

Father Jacques walked over to Christopher, Jacob, and Charlotte. He simply sighed and shrugged. He shook his great, grey head. "I do not know anymore," he said. He took a kerchief from his pocket and wiped it across his brow, sopping away the sweat. "These are not normal demons."

Jacob and Christopher stood with crossed arms. Jacob looked to Christopher.

"Alright," he said, "that's it. Told you I was going after this go-round."

Christopher pursed his lips.

Father Jacques looked from Jacob to Christopher, then back again to Jacob. "You are leaving?" he asked.

"Charlotte and I found the source of the afflicted, and we found the summoning circle for these creatures. We were right. They're all tied together. We stop this bastard from destroying the city, we might just stop the demons possessing the nuns."

"Jacques?" Father Cavey called from the center of the room.

"But, why did you not speaker sooner?" Father Jacques asked.

"Jacques?"

164

Jacob shrugged.

"Father," Charlotte said, resting a hand on Father Jacques's arm, "Jacob and I wanted to give you one last chance."

"Jacques?" Father Cavey asked again, his voice raised.

"What, Pierre?" Father Jacques asked, spinning around.

Jacob, Christopher, and Charlotte all looked past Father Jacques at the nuns hovering in the center of the room. They were only floating a few yards above the ground, but Jacob had to admit that floating even a few inches impressed in its own way.

Father Cavey walked backwards towards the group from the center of the room, staring up at the seven sisters. They floated in a wedge, with one in the lead and three spreading out behind and to either side.

"*Merde*," said Father Jacques.

Christopher walked up quickly and grabbed Father Cavey by the shoulders. The priest jumped.

"Everyone out," Christopher said, pulling Father Cavey backwards and pushing him out the door. Father Jacques followed him.

"THE OTHERS," the nuns said in unison, "MAY LEAVE." They raised their right hand and pointed at the Templars. "FREEMAN AND SMITH, YOU MAY NOT." Smoke began drifting out of the hems and sleeves of their gowns. Jacob watched as it curled down to the ground and spread out to the corners of the room, settling on the floor. Smoke poured from their luminescent eyes.

Christopher ushered the others out, saying, "Get out of the building and into the chapel."

The priests went willingly.

"I want to stay," Charlotte said.

"No," Christopher said, shoving her out of the room with one hand and slamming the door closed with the other, "you just think you do."

Christopher joined Jacob. The smoke began filling the room, rising to their waists now. "What's the plan?" Jacob asked.

"Kill as many as we can."

"Not much of a plan."

"Guess not."

Jacob drew his sword. The smoke obscured the other side of the room. Soon the beds would be hidden, too. Next, the nuns would be out of sight.

Jacob saw and felt movement near the center of the room. Hulking, hunched-over shapes shook the hardwood floor with each step. Jacob gripped his blade in both hands and brought the sword up to guard his chest. The smoke began to thin.

Seven demons in all stood across from the Templars.

"Well," Christopher said. He licked his upper lip. "That's something."

Jacob sucked his top front teeth and said, "Yup. Sure is."

Three were purplish, imp-like creatures about the size of small dogs. Their arms were thin and long, hanging past their knees. Bat-like wings with claws at the end sprouted from their backs, and scorpion-stringered tails grew from the base of their spines. If it weren't for their shark-like rows and rows of razor sharp teeth, Jacob thought, they'd almost be cute. In a Hellish kind of way, of course.

The other four demons couldn't have been more opposite. They stood as tall as Jacob, but their chests were as broad as a grizzly and almost as hairy. Black, metallic bull horns sprouted from their foreheads. Their faces were a distorted mockery of a man's, their steam snorting noses snubbed, but their brows and jaws protruding and obscene. Blackened teeth pressed against their lips. Their cloven hooves buckled the wooden flooring wherever they stepped. They held halberds with blades made from great chunks of volcanic glass.

Christopher Freeman drew his big, three-shot revolver casually. He cracked the gun forward at the cylinder, checked the load, and closed it. He thumbed back the over-sized hammer. Most demons the Templars encountered had never seen a gun, let alone the big three-shot. He raised the pistol and took a bead on the lead demon. He braced for the recoil, putting his free hand over the stock that extended over his forearm. Jacob figured the demons were in for a surprise.

The gunshot shook the window-panes and set the chandelier to trembling. The recoil kicked the gun high, even with the extra support Christopher had given it.

The bullet hit the lead grizzly-demon in the throat, disintegrating its neck and most of its left shoulder in the explosion. The impact sent it reeling back into the center of the room, its arms flailing and halberd swinging in a wide arc. The demon stumbled backwards into the crucifix, knocking the church ornament from its stand. Obsidian blood pumped down the grizzly-demons chest and arm, gushing down onto the hardwood. The creature burbled, still standing, trying to suck in air through what remained of its throat. Fine wisps of smoke rose from singed fur and exposed sinew. Jacob had heard one of those exploding bullets could take down a buffalo. He hadn't believed the stories before. He did now.

The creature sank to its knees, sending tremors through the floor and up the walls. The other demons, almost curious it seemed, watched as the grizzly-beast fell face first, embedding its horns in the hardwood and shaking the building. They stared at their fellow's prone form for a long moment.

Jacob felt a cold drop of sweat trickle down his side. This was going to get ugly.

Almost as one, six heads swiveled to Christopher and Jacob. The demons charged.

"Salt," Christopher said as he aimed at the next target. Jacob grabbed the powder horn from his belt and ripped off the cap with his teeth. He began pouring a fine border of salt between them and the charging demons. The line of salt would stop them for the time being. At least he hoped it would.

Ducking, Jacob cut in front of Christopher. Christopher fired another shot over his head.

"Goddammit," hollered Jacob as another of the grizzly-demons fell and the building quaked, "not in my goddamn ear."

He finished the semi-circle and drew his pistol. He fell in beside Christopher as the demons came to a skidding halt. One of the grizzlies came close to the salt. Sparks flashed and the smell of sulfur filled the air as the grizzly-demon, its flank scorched and smoking, recoiled with a howl. Jacob said a silent word of thanks for that.

Christopher fired another booming shot into the creature, cutting off its cries.

The seven sisters still floated where they had before. More smoke filled the room. The silhouettes of more horns appeared in the cloud.

"Shit," Jacob said.

"SHIT IS RIGHT," growled one of the grizzlies, chortling.

"Well," Christopher said, cracking open his big gun and reloading, "that ain't exactly what I'd call fair."

"WE ARE LEGION," said one of the imps, cackling and flying up to the ceiling. Jacob shot through its wing. The imp, shrieking, fell to the floor.

"Plan B," Christopher said.

"Plan B?"

"Plan B."

"Ready?"

"Ready."

They turned on their heels, opened the door, and ran into the hallway. They slammed shut the door behind them. A great howl from within the room shook the floorboards and the balcony doors.

Braced on the railing for support, the Templars took the stairs two steps at a time. Wood splintered above and behind them as the grizzlies attacked the walls to either side of the salt barrier. Christopher, out in front, hit the front door at a sprint and charged out into the garden. He veered right onto the grass and headed towards the chapel. Jacob's boot landed on the lawn just as the windows on the second floor shattered. Plan B wasn't working out the way it was supposed to.

Jacob threw up a protective arm as glass rained down on him. Up ahead were the flowerbeds closest to the main building. Waist-high shrubs surrounded the colorful blooms. Christopher leapt the small hedge and kept going. Jacob followed. As his feet left the ground, a heavy weight slammed into his right side, driving him across the grass. No, Plan B definitely wasn't working out.

Jacob felt the stinger first. He looked down as it stabbed ineffectually at his breastplate-covered collarbone and heart. A little imp was clamoring up his body. It must have been what broke the glass.

The Templar rolled over on his back and pushed at the creature. The imp, all teeth, rows and rows of teeth, and slimy purple skin, bit into his left forearm, tearing through the sleeve of his greatcoat and grinding into his chainmail.

Jacob lifted the creature off his body. He drew his revolver, cocked back the hammer, and put the business end to the imp's head. The creature stopped writhing and fighting. Its eyes rolled up and looked at the pistol barrel pressed to its forehead.

Jacob pulled the trigger. Yellow-green blood and brain matter sprayed across the grass. Jacob climbed back to his feet and looked for Christopher.

Christopher, bloody sword drawn, stood over the corpse of one of the grizzly-demons. The blade of its halberd protruded from its gut. The corpse bled from half-a-dozen other cuts. Christopher wiped his sword clean on the creature's fur. He sheathed his sword as Jacob ran up to meet him.

"You okay?" Christopher asked.

"Yup."

More glass tinkled above them. Jacob looked up. A mixture of ten or more grizzlies and imps were coming through the window. Jacob and Christopher turned and ran for the chapel.

They hit the door at a run. The priests and Charlotte had locked the door behind them. Christopher turned and stood guard, drawing his big three-shot revolver. Jacob pounded on the door with his fist, the knocks drowned by the booming of the big pistol.

"Hey," Jacob hollered, still pounding. Christopher holstered his gun. He took out his two smaller caliber pistols and began firing into the crowd.

"Jacob," Christopher yelled.

Jacob spun and drew his pistol. Only ten or fifteen feet separated the Templars and the demons. Three of the big grizzlies kept charging, and six of the imps dove through the air. Jacob fired at the lead grizzly, unloading all five shells as fast as his off-hand could cock the hammer. The bullets didn't even slow the demon down.

Someone grabbed Jacob by the shoulder and yanked him backward inside the sanctuary. They slammed the door shut. Jacob blinked as his eyes adjusted to the abrupt dimness. The demons roared just beyond the door. He realized someone was shaking him. He blinked again and looked around.

"Jacob," someone said. Who was shaking him? He looked down at the little hands on his jacket's lapels. He looked down into Charlotte's eyes. "Jacob?" she asked again. "Are you okay? Are you hurt?"

"What?" Jacob asked. "Where's Christopher?"

"Christopher's fine. We pulled him in already," Charlotte said, shaking him again. "I asked if you were hurt."

"No," he replied, shaking his head. "No, I'm fine."

169

"What's going on? What happened out there?"

"There was more than a dozen of them. More than we could handle."

"Are we safe here?"

"I think so."

"You think so?"

"I mean, likely we're fine."

"Give me a straight answer, Mr. Smith."

"Demons can't enter consecrated ground," Jacob said, heading to the nave. "As long as we stay put, they can't come in." He flexed his left forearm and rubbed it. The imp had bruised it through the mail, but thankfully hadn't broken the skin. Jacob didn't want to consider what he would have caught if it had. Would probably make zombieism look like a cold.

"You said you were fine."

"Yup, I did. Mail stopped the teeth."

"I still want to look it over."

Jacob sighed. "Fine."

They went into the sacristy and Jacob stripped off his coat and shirt. He stripped out of his breastplate and chainshirt. He put his arm out for inspection. A multitude of minute pinpricks marked where the imp had bit him on the forearm. Black and blue and red bruises invaded his skin. Charlotte sucked in air through her teeth.

"Not that bad," Jacob said, yawning. "Get some of the holy water from over there."

"Water?" Charlotte asked, almost in shock.

"Blessed water. Important difference. Bring it here."

Charlotte went over and took the holy water from the sacramental cabinet. She handed it to him.

"Would've been worse if one of them grizzlies did the biting."

"Grizzlies?"

"We make up names for the demons sometimes, if we've never seen them before," Jacob said, uncorking the jug of holy water. "The big ones? I call 'em grizzly-demons, 'cause they sorta look like the way my granddad described grizzlies."

"They look more like gorillas crossed with longhorns to me."

"Never seen a gorilla," Jacob said, pouring some of the holy water onto his arm. The wound smoked and sizzled and steamed.

"Jacob!"

"What? This?" he asked, raising his smoking forearm to Charlotte. "Don't hurt. Just the saliva from the imps getting washed out by the holy water."

"Imps? Those are the small ones right? Why are they imps?"

"'Cause that's their name. Imps are imps. If it's small, spindly, got a tail and wings and lots of teeth, you generally got an imp on your hands."

Jacob reached down and picked up his great coat. He looked down at the tattered left sleeve. The imp bite had shredded the sleeve from the elbow down. He drew his knife from his belt and began cutting at the left shoulder seam.

"Read in one of our books at the monastery's library that demons ain't like people in the way they're classified. People, we've got white folks, colored folks, Injuns, and Celestials. Demons? There are more types than you, or I, or any other person could count. Angels are the same way, too."

"What about God?"

"The same. Every god's different."

Charlotte sat up straight. "What?" she asked, cocking her head to the side. "I meant, could God count them?"

"There's more than one god," Jacob said, tearing the sleeve from his great coat, "so you gotta be specific with your question." A seamstress would have done a better job, but his butchering would keep the tatters from getting in his way. "Lots of gods, in fact. Minor gods, greater gods, demigods. That's just the way of the world and all those beyond. Some of 'em could likely get an accurate count."

"But what about Jehovah?"

"Jehovah?" Jacob asked, shrugging. "He could, I reckon. Jehovah's pretty tough. Miracles get done in his name, and priests force demons back using his power. But, he ain't the only one that strong. The Bible says there's more than one god. And there's myths from all over, from everywhere around the world. Read some of them when I joined the order."

"I've read much of them as well."

Jacob nodded absently. "See?" he asked, holding out his forearm. "Told you it weren't bad. Let's go see the others." He began putting his armor back on.

Charlotte sat quietly, staring at nothing as Jacob pulled on his jacket.

"What do you believe in, Jacob?"

"Huh?"

Charlotte pursed her lips together. She seemed pensive. "I mean," she began, mulling her words, "do you believe in a Christian god? That there's a heaven, and all that the bible teaches?"

"Heaven? Met an angel once, so I reckon I believe in a heaven. What about you? You believe in the hereafter?"

"I don't know for sure. I think it has something to do with faith, though. I falter on that part, though. It's difficult seeing the things we see. And you?"

"Faith, huh? Some days I have faith in Jehovah, others I don't."

"What about the other days?"

"Reckon it's just myself."

Charlotte stood, sighing. "I believe that's the best we can hope for in this world. Are you ready?"

"And willing," Jacob said.

They left the sacristy and went into the chapel.

Christopher, Father Jacques, and Father Cavey spoke together in hushed tones. Christopher shook his head at Father Jacques.

"What's the plan?" Jacob asked.

"Don't exist," Christopher said.

"Untrue," Father Jacques said. He seemed upset. "Christopher will not heed me, that is all."

"It's a shit idea, that's why."

"Let us put it to Jacob, then."

"Fine," Jacob said. "Shoot."

"There's a ritual," Father Jacques said, hands held out, pleading. "I know it. If successful, we can stop the demons for the time being."

"Great," Jacob said. "Why ain't we done it yet?"

"'Cause there's a catch," Christopher said.

"Always is. What is it?"

"One of us," Father Jacques said, "must be the subject of the rirutal."

"Oh. Like we gotta kill him?"

Christopher shook his head. "No human sacrifice. But the person's gonna wish we had."

"How does it work?" Jacob asked, going over to the front pew and taking a seat.

"One of you perform the ritual on me," Father Jacques said. "And I become a vessel of sorts, absorbing the demons into my being. I contain them."

"So you force a possession?" Jacob asked, eyebrow raised.

"Exactly," the priest said, nodding.

"Demons ain't gonna be happy," Jacob said. "Gonna wreak all kinds of havoc while they're inside."

"Which is why I don't wanna have the priest do it. We can fight our way out," Christopher said, crossing his arms and leaning back against the altar rail.

"No we can't," Charlotte said. "There's too many of them. How many bullets do you have left, Christopher?"

"Plenty."

"For your three-shot?"

Christopher paused for a long moment, lips pursed. "Three."

"And your normal guns aren't slowing the grizzly-demons down."

"But we can still—"

"Get yourselves killed?" Charlotte interjected in a low voice. "There's still a city falling apart out there, remember? Who's going to save it if you've been torn apart by a hundred demons in the garden?"

"And those nuns, too," Jacob said. "Can't save 'em if we're dead. Will this pull the demons from them?"

Father Jacques scratched his chin. "I believe so. I believe it was the original intention when it was created."

"And you," Jacob asked, leaning forward and resting his elbows on his knees, "you're willing to do this?" He looked up at the older priest. "It's a tall order, Father."

"I am willing. I have faith the Lord will give me the strength needed for this."

There was that word again, Jacob thought. Faith. He turned his eyes to Christopher. "It's your call."

Christopher closed his eyes and leaned his head back. "Fine. Don't suppose there's another way."

Jacob sighed. "Reckon not. How do we do this?"

"I'll need Miss Gibson's help," Father Jacques said. "She's the only one with experience in this matter."

July 30th

Jacob rubbed his eyes. Midnight had come and gone and they were well into early morning. The sun would be rising soon.

"Doesn't feel right to be doing this in the church," said Christopher.

"I agree," Father Cavey said.

"Don't matter what it feels like, I reckon," Jacob said, "long as it does the trick."

"Feels sacrilegious, is all."

Father Pierre, Christopher, and Jacob stood in the sacristy, arms crossed. Jacob and Christopher had grabbed a few hours of sleep earlier, which would have to do. Father Cavey shifted from leg to leg, his eyes wide, his scant hair askew on his head. Charlotte and Father Jacques worked on preparing the ritual out in the chapel. Charlotte had taken Jacob's knife and some of the extra candles from storage.

"Look," Jacob said, "the father says there's nothing evil about the ritual. It's just pre-Christ."

"Still feels bad," said Christopher.

"Magic is magic, whether it be black or white," Father Cavey said.

"If Father Jacques thinks this can help us," Jacob said, sighing, "then maybe it can. Maybe this is the path we're supposed to take."

"Why's that?"

"'Cause it's the only one we see, that's why."

Charlotte knocked on the wall outside the door. "Gentlemen?" she asked. The three men looked at her. "We're starting," she said and went back into the chapel.

The trio followed her.

Father Jacques lay in the center of the chapel floor, spread eagle. He had stripped down to the waist, his flesh white as a cuttlefish bone. Charlotte had drawn a circle of salt around him. Three candles formed a triangle, one at the fingertips of each

175

outstretched hand and a third at a point drawn straight down from his groin.

Charlotte stood a few feet from him, her long tangle of orange-red hair falling loose around her head. In her right hand, she held Jacob's knife in a reverse grip. She had bunched up her dress around her waist, exposing pale, unstockinged legs and bare feet. Her sleeves were rolled back, showing pale, freckled arms.

Jacob tried not to look at her, but his eyes kept drifting back.

Charlotte had been practicing all evening. She had spread out her practice papers on one of the nearby pews. A variety of figures and runes covered them.

She turned to the three men. "Are you ready?"

"How long will this take?" Christopher asked.

"Just a few minutes."

She began the ritual.

Charlotte walked the perimeter of the circle, speaking in what sounded like Latin with too many consonants to Jacob. She finished making the round and, having returned to her original spot, raised the knife over her head in both hands. She spoke a few more lines, her voice rising as she came to the end.

Charlotte joined Father Jacques in the circle, showing care to not step in the salt. She bent down over him and began carving into his skin, speaking the same foreign lines over and over. Blood welled up under the tip of the blade. Father Jacques's face twisted in pain.

Charlotte sliced a rune over the priests heart, a simple triangle and circle. She cut into his shoulders, carving more runes, before moving onto the left side of the priest's chest. Father Jacques inhaled sharply as another symbol was cut into him. The blood ran in rivulets down his chest and flanks, collecting in dark pools where his back met the flagstone. Charlotte, sweat beading on her forehead, continued the litany as she stepped out of the circle.

She bent down over the little saucer of chrism at her feet and ran a finger down the blade, forcing the blood into the mixture of oil and incense. She set the blade on the flagstone and picked up the dish.

Charlotte smeared everything together and stepped back into the circle, taking position over Father Jacques. She dipped her thumb in the chrism-blood compound and bent over, smudging Father Jacques's lips. She smudged a spot between his eyebrows, then stood. She pronounced another line of the twisted tongue.

Father Jacques arched up, his back rising off the tiled floor.

Jacob felt a ripple pass over him, like the tone of the place had changed in some small way. The chapel retained its holiness, but another presence now lay over everything. It felt ancient, almost like the way the dusty books in Col. Winnie's bolthole of an office smelled. It emanated from the circle and permeated the chapel. Jacob felt almost peaceful for once.

Jacob glanced at Christopher and Father Cavey. Their brows were furrowed. They could sense it, too. What was this spell? Where had it come from?

Charlotte stayed standing over Father Jacques, looking down on him, her hair covering her face. Bending at the waist again, she leaned in close to the priest's face, hiding them both from the Templars' and Father Cavey's view. She blew gently.

She straightened and stepped from the circle, sweat running down her face and arms.

"It's complete," she said, sighing. She collapsed into the pew. "Help him stand, please. You can break the circle."

Christopher and Jacob helped Father Jacques to his feet. Father Cavey handed him his shirt.

"Did it work?"

"We will know soon enough," Father Jacques said, wincing as he pulled on his shirt. He bled and sweat through the front, the cloth clinging to the open wounds on his skin. Jacob cocked his head to the side and looked at the smudges of blood and chrism on the priest's forehead and lips. "Are you alright, my son?"

Jacob shook his head. "Nothing," he said. "Just reckoned for a moment there that I'd seen them smudges before. Probably nothing."

"Likely saw it in one of Col. Winnie's books?" Christopher asked.

"Likely," Jacob said, nodding. "How do we try this thing?"

"There will be no trying," Father Jacques said. "It will work. I feel it. I have faith."

"Alright," Jacob said.

"I still do not like this," Father Cavey said. "Not at all."

"Well, it's done," Charlotte said from the pew. "And, despite your misgivings, it's our best course."

"Pierre," Father Jacques said, clapping the other priest on the shoulder, "have faith. God would not allow this ritual to take place within these hallowed walls if He did not wish to allow it. Is that not correct?"

"No," Father Cavey said, shaking his head and sighing, "you are correct. We've seen many things today, have we not? This will work, if it is His will."

Father Jacques nodded roughly and winced again. "Arm yourself, friends. We face the enemy."

Christopher and Jacob left the priests and Charlotte, and returned to the sacristy. "What's the plan after this?" Jacob asked.

"Charlotte and I try to protect the convention," replied Christopher as he shrugged into his great coat, "and you call up the cavalry to meet us there."

"Thought we was the cavalry," Jacob said.

"Sincerely hope that ain't the case," Christopher said, frowning.

"What about Potestas? He's got the teeth still. He's the threat."

"We'll find him. From what you say, he'll be at the convention. If you can get the blue coats there, we can put him between us and them."

"Alright. What if they won't come?"

"Then we're up a creek," Christopher said, grabbing Jacob's shoulder. He walked out into the hall.

Charlotte and the priests were already waiting near the exit to the garden.

"Are you ready?" Christopher asked Father Jacques.

The priest nodded. "*Oui.*"

"Let's get this show on the road, then." Jacob and Christopher stepped up and flanked the priest.

Father Jacques opened the door.

The demons seemed to have multiplied. They writhed in the garden like they'd sprung from the pages of some demented bestiary. They crawled over the statuary, trampled the flowers, ate the grass, stripped the bark from the trees, and fought each other over scraps of tapestry. The demons stopped and all looked at the small party of humans. Behind him, Cavey gasped.

Father Jacques stepped across the threshold of the chapel and out into the garden. New Orleans held its breath.

The priest opened his mouth. The air stirred as a breeze started on the far side of the garden and blew across the horde and towards the priest. He pushed his shoulders back and opened his mouth farther, causing the wind to rise sharply. The trees bent towards the chapel. Leaves tore from branches as the wind increased to a gale. A scream went up from the legion. The smarter demons turned and tried to run or fly away.

The imps were the first to be sucked in. They beat their wings against the tearing wind but were pulled back by Father Jacques's sucking mouth. Their bodies stretched and extended as they arched over the heads of the grizzly-demons, They disappeared down Father Jacques's gullet.

Next came the grizzly-demons. Some held onto the grass with their claws, others stabbed the poles of their halberds into the earth, and still more just stood or tried to run away. The unprepared went first. Like the imps, they tumbled head over hooves, stretching and twisting in the wind. Next came the ones that had clawed into the lawn. Finally, those who had anchored themselves with their halberds. The poles snapped under the force of the infernal sucking.

Finally, no demon remained. Just the sounds of bugles and sirens floating in from over the wall.

Jacob and Christopher rushed into the garden, weapons drawn, scanning the area. Father Jacques, holding his sides and groaning in pain, fell to his knees. Charlotte and Father Cavey rushed out and crouched next to him. Father Jacques waved them off and stood. His brow was furrowed, his face a mask of sweat-soaked agony. But he stood on his own.

"You alright?" Jacob asked.

Father Jacques groaned. "I need a place to lie. Rest will help. Please, forget me and see to the sisters."

"I'll help you to your bed, Father," Charlotte said. "Come with me."

"Father Cavey," Jacob said, "you're with us. We should check on the nuns like Father Jacques said."

The Templars and Father Cavey crossed the destroyed garden and went into the building. Charlotte and Father Jacques trailed behind them with Charlotte supporting the older man under his arm.

Jacob and Christopher walked up the stairs first, pistols drawn. They went around the landing and opened the doors to the banquet hall. Broken glass and overturned beds littered the ground. A layer of shredded straw, husks of corn, and mattress feathers covered everything. In the middle of it all lay the seven sisters, their eyes closed. Jacob and Christopher holstered their revolvers.

Father Cavey rushed past the Templars and into the center of the room. He knelt beside the nearest woman and touched her cheek with the back of his hand. He grabbed the edge of his stole and touched it to her forehead and nose. Nothing. No steam, no smoke, no cries of agony.

"Praise the Lord," Father Cavey said, crossing himself, "they're free."

"We'll be going, then, Father," Christopher said. "We still have work."

"Thank you," Father Cavey said, tears at the corners of his eyes. "Thank you for all of your help."

"Didn't do nothing," Jacob said. "Thank Father Jacques. 'Sides, we still gotta save him."

"Jacob's right. We need to leave now."

Father Cavey stood. "I'll contact the bishop and tell him the staff may return," he said. "This place must be cleansed. For the moment, I will take care of the nuns and allow them to convalesce."

Jacob and Christopher nodded and said their goodbyes. They clomped back downstairs. Charlotte waited for them in the entry hall.

"Are they safe?" she asked.

"For now. We need to stop Potestas and get them demons banished before Father Jacques splits at the seams, though," Christopher said. "No telling what'll happen down the line." The trio walked out into the garden.

"Cavey said the Union's made a temporary headquarters at Washington Square," Jacob said. "Reckon it's not too far."

"Why don't I go?" Charlotte asked.

"You're a woman," Christopher said.

"And Christopher's a Negro," Jacob added. "So I'm the one to go."

"Wouldn't I be better suited to diplomacy, though?" Charlotte asked.

"No. Don't want you wandering the city by yourself, anyhow," Jacob said. "That's final. You can stay or you can go with Christopher. Ain't gonna be worrying about you, too, not with Father Jacques laid up the way he is."

"Fine," Charlotte said, her face stony.

"Alright. We meet at the Mechanics Institute?"

"Alright," Christopher said.

"Agreed."

The sun rose and beat down on Jacob Smith, New Orleans, the white folk, the colored folk, the afflicted, Washington Square, and everything else with no discrimination. Jacob took off his hat and wiped sweat from his forehead. He slicked his hair back and looked over the scene from his spot on Dauphine.

The square was small, no larger than a city block. Royal Street bounded it on the riverward side. On the other, Dauphine. On the downriver side, a broad thoroughfare named Elysian Fields, and Frenchman on the upriver. Men in blue moved, milled, and marched about the miniature tent town in a beehive of activity. Occasionally, a spot of white appeared, a daring man who had stripped to his undershirt in the heat.

Jacob spat on the street. He'd loved serving in the Union, in his own way, but was glad to be rid of it. He slicked his hair back again and approached the guards, hands raised.

"Hullo the camp," he said to the soldiers when he was within earshot.

"Halt and come no closer," one of the soldiers called. He was a big man, thick in the shoulders and heavy in the beard, but still young in the face. He and his partner raised Springfield rifles and drew beads on Jacob. "We'll have none of your plague."

"I ain't infected," Jacob called back. He stayed where he stood. "Come to see Maj. Gen. Baird on behalf of the Catholic diocese."

"We'll have none of your Papacy, neither," called the other

soldier. He was thin as a fence post and just as tall. White whiskers covered his face. A hard wind would snap him like seasoned wood.

"Let your commanding officer decide, then."

"Baird's not seeing any man, woman, or child, Papist or not."

"He requested the Church's assistance," Jacob called. "Let me talk to your lieutenant. I'll stay right here and just wait a spell."

"Griffin," Big Beard said, slapping Fence Post across the chest with the back of his left hand, "go on and get Maj. Overman. Let him sort this shit out." Fence Post Griffin eyed Jacob and lowered his rifle. He went into the camp. "We'll see what the major says."

"That's right fine," Jacob hollered back. "Reckon I can approach? While we wait, I mean?"

"Fuck no, you can't." Big Beard spat to the side. "You keep your afflicted ass away from here, Papist."

Jacob sighed. He looked up at the sky. The dark haze settled lower over the French Quarter this morning. Soon, people would be wearing kerchiefs over their face just to walk the street.

Gunshots fired far off in the distance, up close, and in between. If the city hadn't completely fallen apart already, it soon would.

There was some commotion down the street from back the way Jacob'd come. He turned towards it.

A group of colored civilians rounded the corner. Two men and three women. One of the women held a child close to her breast. The men looked haggard and exhausted, the women uncombed and unkempt. All wore tattered clothes, and Jacob noticed one of the men favoring his left leg. They'd managed to arm themselves with some crude clubs, but they didn't carry any firearms.

The group made it about fifteen feet down the street before a dozen or so afflicted came around the corner behind them.

The creatures had decayed in varying amounts. One loped in some broken-leg cemetery dance, another dragged a foot behind him with each step. A woman, blonde-haired and wild, looked to have just turned. Her skin had hardly changed. Just the eyes. The wild, searching eyes marked the afflicted.

Big Beard fired from behind Jacob. The head of one of the afflicted, a snaggle-toothed old black man with curly grey and white hair snapped back. The force of Big Beard's bullet, even at the seventy-five feet of distance, knocked the creature backwards from its feet and into the air.

Jacob drew his revolver and advanced towards the rushing civilians. He raised his pistol and drew a bead on the afflicted. He saw the terrified eyes of the civilians as they slowed their approach.

"Y'all get clear," Jacob shouted, waving them out of the way as he advanced. The men and women bolted to the left and to the right, instinctively staying low and covering their heads with their hands. "Hey," Jacob yelled at the pursuing afflicted, trying to get their attention. He stood his ground, waiting for them to get inside of fifty feet or so. He opened fire, fanning the hammer on his pistol.

It reminded Jacob of shooting melons off posts.

Six bullets left his revolver's barrel. Six afflicted fell to the cobblestone in twisted lumps, their blood and brains leaking out in blackened puddles. Jacob holstered his pistol and drew his sword.

Big Beard fired again, felling another creature.

The afflicted converged on Jacob. In one swing he cleaved through the head of the lead creature, the blonde woman, and brought his blade down into the head of another. He spun to the left, elbowing another creature's face, flipping it off its feet. He wrenched the sword free and retreated a dozen steps, back-pedaling at a quick pace.

The creatures were strong, and took a beating well. But, they were slow with their feet and dim with their wits. They simply came at him in a malformed wave.

Big Beard fired again, but only knocked his target from its feet. The afflicted twitched and groaned and dragged itself back upright.

Jacob darted forward, the flat of his blade laid over his left forearm. He poked the blade forward, driving into his target's eye-socket. He withdrew the sword quickly and danced to the side as the creature collapsed in a heap. Only three remained.

His arms were loose and warmed up, the exhaustion having left them. Jacob grinned, moving in on the afflicteds's flank. He felt like Lee at Chancelorsville, like he'd outwitted them all.

He swung again, decapitating another, and swung at the one on his right. The creature, formerly a big, heavyset white man, groaned deep in its throat. Jacob's sword lodged in its collar bone. Thick sludge welled out of the cut and around the blade. The afflicted didn't go down, though.

It reached out with blackened nails, outstretched fingers grasping for his face and eyes. Jacob, arms outstretched, kept it at sword's length, a good five or six feet. It kept him from the afflicted's bite, but it also kept him from being able to get any leverage on the sword.

Out of the corner of his eye, Jacob saw the second-to-last afflicted coming at him, its clawed fingers outstretched. Jacob sidestepped to the right, just out of its reach. He kept his grip on the sword and spun Fat Man along with him. The Templar breathed heavily, trying to kick at Fat Man, but it was too far away.

He lunged in closer and tried again, connecting with Fat Man's belly. The other afflicted bulled into Jacob, knocking him to the cobblestones. Jacob held on to the sword to steady himself, but only managed to drag Fat Man down with him instead. He thudded onto his back, driving the wind from his lungs and knocking his hat from his head. Eyes wide, Jacob watched as the creatures bore down on him. What a waste, Jacob thought. All this, and no redemption to show for it.

All of a sudden he didn't feel too much like Lee. More like Rosecrans at Chickamauga.

The other, smaller one was coming at him, hands outstretched, its mouth full of rotting teeth and infectious foam. Fat Man was in a perpetual state of falling. Jacob's sword embedded in its collarbone was the only thing keeping it upright. The hilt of Jacob's sword shoved into his breastplate, pushing it down against his chest as he struggled vainly to get up and away from the afflicted.

"Damn," Jacob gasped out. He grunted, trying to beat the second afflicted away with a flailing fist. Definitely more like Rosecrans. He'd overplayed his hand, and now he was going to pay for his cocksureness.

A rifle fired. The second afflicted's nose exploded from its face as the bullet passed through. It crumpled to the cobblestones. Another shot, this one from a pistol. Fat Man lurched to its side, but kept coming. It still struggled against Jacob's grip, reaching down at his face, gurgling and groaning.

A blue-coated soldier wearing an officer's cap walked up behind Fat Man. He put the barrel of his revolver to the afflicted's ear and pulled the trigger. The creature slumped forward. Jacob continued to hold it, knowing that if he tried to move, the corpse would just fall on him. The pommel of his sword still pressed his breastplate into his chest.

The officer walked around into view, crouching down next to Jacob. "Well, as I live and breathe," he said. "Jacob? Jacob Smith?"

"Yes?"

"Maj. Joseph Overman. You were briefly attached to the Ninth Cavalry in Missouri, were you not?"

"I was," Jacob replied. He peered up at the officer's face. "Joey Overman?" Jacob asked. "How in the hell did you become major? All the qualified captains die in the war?" He grunted against the pain as the corpse resting on his chest shifted and wheezed with corpse gas. "Never mind, tell me when this thing's off me."

"Apologies. Just a moment," Maj. Overman said. He shouldered into the corpse, knocking it off to the side. The body fell to the street, thudding like a side of beef dropped on the floor. Jacob lay there for a moment, hand where the pommel of his sword had been, breathing deep breaths.

"You alright?" Overman asked, standing over him.

"Yup. Think so. Didn't get bit or bled on, thank God."

"That wouldn't be fortunate," said Overman, offering him a hand. Jacob accepted and Overman helped him to his feet. Jacob went over and looked down at Fat Man's corpse. He kicked it over and went to wrenching the sword from its collarbone. Jacob cursed himself for his brashness. Almost got himself killed this time.

"What in the hell are you doing in New Orleans? And working for the Church?"

"Long story. I need to see Maj. Gen. Baird, though," Jacob said. He wiped his sword clean on Fat Man's shirt and sheathed it. He leaned down and picked up his hat, placing it on his head. He drew his revolver and flipped open the cylinder. "Quick-like," he added. He ejected the spent shell casings from his revolver and reloaded it with fresh cartridges.

"Not a chance," Overman said. They turned and headed back to Washington Square. "The major general's come down with the fever."

"Dammit," Jacob said. "How long ago?"

"Just a few hours. He's not well. Surgeons are doing all they can, but, well . . ."

"Well?"

"Not a man or woman who's contracted this fever has come out the other side. Not a one. Talk is that President Johnson's going to continue the quarantine. All food and goods coming into and leaving have been curtailed. The place has gone wild, feral."

"Seems the case," Jacob said as they passed through the gates and into the camp. Big Beard and Fence Post glared at him as he passed.

"I myself am near recommending the city bombarded. We can't let this disease spread," Overman continued as they walked through the camp. Soldiers saluted Maj. Overman as they passed. He gave them the briefest of recognition and kept his focus on Jacob.

"This isn't yellow fever, you know."

"I know that. But what name would you use? A fever which makes a living man impervious to attacks unless they're shot in the head? I don't believe the president or our superiors would understand that. Care for a drink? Lord knows I need one." He took Jacob's elbow and led him off the path. "This is my tent. I have a bottle stashed away."

"Listen," Jacob said as he followed Overman through the tent flap, "Joey, reckon I need to come clean. I've dealt with more strangeness than most men. I can help you folks, but only if you can help me."

"What kind of strangeness?" Maj. Overman asked as he grabbed a bottle of whiskey and a tin cup from the small folding desk in the tent's corner.

"You wouldn't believe me."

"You'd be surprised." Overman poured a healthy cup of whiskey for Jacob. "I'm a God-fearing man, after all," he said, handing Jacob the tin cup.

Jacob took a sip of the whiskey. "Demons, mostly," he said, wincing at the taste of the firewater. He took another drink. God, it felt good. "But some like this. Living dead. There's an organization that's working against the Union. Call themselves the Kukluxers."

"Heard of them. Ex-Rebels," Overman said, taking a long pull from the bottle. He pulled up a canvas chair and sat. He gestured to another seat for Jacob. Jacob took it. "Demons, you say? Like fallen angels?"

"I know," Jacob said, shaking his head, "it sounds like I need to be in a sanitarium. But it's real. There are things out there I can't explain, and you wouldn't believe me even if I could."

"So what does this have to do with the fever? That's the thing, Jacob, demons are fine. We all have them, do we not? But demons don't turn people into lunatics. At least not whole cities-full."

"My partner and I had an object stolen from us," Jacob said, taking another sip. "It's the source of this. One of those Kukluxers took the relic. He used it to start the fever."

Overman took another long drink from the bottle. "Jacob," he said, exhaling sharply and setting the bottle aside, "let's suppose what you're saying is, on the outside spread, actually even possibly true. How can you stop it?"

"By destroying the object."

"And these Kukluxers have it?"

"A man named Potestas, yes."

"Potestas, you say?"

"I know where he is, Joey. He's at the convention at the Mechanics Institute."

Overman laughed, slapping his thigh. "What can you show me to prove your case?"

Jacob sat back. He chewed on his lip. He took a sip of whiskey. How could he prove this story of his?

Wait. Maybe there was something. He just hoped Fat Man's weight hadn't damaged it.

"I might have something," Jacob said as he began reaching inside his breastplate. "An old woman gave it to me."

Maj. Gen. Baird's tent smelled of warm alcohol and hot death. The surgeons had closed the flaps against the sun. The general, an old, bald man with a great salt-and-pepper beard, lay tucked under the sheets on his cot, alternately baking and freezing in the sepia-toned light. Surgeons wearing blood and pus-covered white coats milled about. One of them leaned over the major general, feeling his forehead. He looked to Maj. Overman and shook his head.

"Alright," Overman said, holding the tent flap open, "everyone out."

The surgeons looked at each other. "Fine," one said, with a shrug, "not much to be done anyway."

The surgeons left.

Overman looked at Jacob. "Are you certain this will work?"

"Never said that," replied Jacob. "Said I might have something to cure him."

"That's fine and dandy, then. Well, it won't hurt him any worse."

"Reckon not." Jacob walked over to Maj. Gen. Baird's bedside. He pulled up a canvas seat and sat next to him. "Major General?"

The old man's eyes opened. He tried to turn his head to look at Jacob. "No," Jacob said, taking the pouch from his pocket, "don't do that. I'm gonna give you something to eat. I want you to chew and swallow it. Alright? You hear me?"

Baird nodded as much as his weakness would allow. Jacob opened the drawstring on the pouch and shook the contents out into the palm of his hand. The little, dried pepper looked fiery beneath its crust of strange, pink salt. Some of the salt broke off in Jacob's hand as he handled it.

"Here," he said, feeling like a priest offering the Eucharist on Sunday. Baird opened his mouth and Jacob fed it to him. "Chew, Baird. Don't matter how hot it gets, you just keep on chewing."

The old man chewed. His lips seemed to lighten. A blue light shone out through his teeth, illuminating his jaw. He continued to chew, his nose lighting up the same way. The light crept into his eyes, shining like twin beacons from a lighthouse, and down into his throat. It pulsed with each grind of his teeth. Jacob leaned in close and looked at Baird's face. The sweat began changing color, changing to the amber color of tree sap. It ran more profusely as the old man continued chewing.

Jacob looked at Maj. Overman, eyes wide. "I think the pepper's actually working." He grinned from ear to ear. "First good news in days."

The old man swallowed. "This pepper," he croaked, exhaling black smoke, "tastes of embers and fire. Heat. I need milk. Is that smoke?"

"Not yet, Major General. You eat the whole damn thing, then we'll get you a glass. And, yup, it's smoke."

Overman left to get a glass of milk for the major general. The old man kept chewing.

"Who are you?" Baird asked. "And help me sit upright."

Jacob helped the old man sit up. He began the long explanation of how he'd arrived in the major general's tent. By the time Overman had returned, Baird had thrown off the bedsheets. He'd also heard most of Jacob's story.

"Who is this man you're after?" Maj. Gen. Baird asked.

"Name's Potestas."

The old soldier sucked in breath.

"Ring a bell then?"

"I received a letter from him three days ago. I decided it was a letter from a crazy man, the product of a mind addled by the war, and dismissed it out of hand."

"What did you do with it?"

"It should be on my desk with my other correspondence."

"May I read it?"

"You may."

Jacob walked over to the desk and sifted through the letters. He found the one from Potestas. He withdrew the letter from its envelope and began to read.

Dear Major General Baird,

I trust that though this letter may find you in good health, such good health shall be fleeting. Why will it be fleeting? you ask. Because I shall make it so. I have in my possession a powerful weapon. I will use it on this despicable city and all its cowardly denizens. I will cause them to rise in defense against the Northern and Negro aggressors, just as they should have originally done on that April day in 1862. You and your soldiers can not hope to stop me. But believe me when I say I truly hope to witness you try. Driving your army before mine will be one of the finer points in my life.

Cyclops Potestas had signed his name below the missive.

"Well," Jacob said, finishing the letter. "He's cocky ain't he?"

"Yes," Baird replied. "I would tend to agreement. Now, to the point, sir. How can we help?"

"We need to protect the Constitutional Convention."

"We'll have plenty of time, then," Baird replied. "Lord. Nearing noon on the 30th already? And the city falling around our ears?" He picked up his pocket watch from his table and looked at it. "We still have several hours. Plenty of time to mobilize the troops."

"Reckon you don't, sir," Jacob said. "It starts in just a few minutes."

"What?" Baird asked, his voice rising. "I was informed it started at six this evening."

"Don't know who told you that," Jacob said, "but I know it was scheduled to begin at noon."

Maj. Overman nodded and said, "Mr. Smith's correct, sir. We sent runners to try and stop them from proceeding, even before Mr. Smith arrived here."

"Their response?"

"That this was all," Overman said, taking out a piece of script-covered paper and unfolding it, "quote, 'nothing more than Rebel trickery meant to circumvent the democratic process,' unquote, sir."

"Help me up, young man," Baird said, swinging his legs off the bed. "Maj. Overman, go ready the troops. We march for the Mechanics Institute before the next tolling of the bells. God willing, our effort will not come too late and be in vain."

"Sir," Maj. Overman replied, snapping off a quick salute. He left the tent, barking orders as soon as he exited the canvas walls.

"And you, sir? Will you march with us?" Baird asked.

"Reckon I won't. I've got friends in the hall, and can make better time on my own."

Baird nodded, frowning resolutely beneath his salt-and-pepper beard.

"I could use a horse, though."

"Here," Baird said. He walked shakily over to his desk. He grabbed a quill and a loose leaf of paper. He scribbled down a quick note, signed it with a flourish, sanded the ink, and handed the letter to Jacob. "Give this to the quartermaster. He'll provide you a mount."

Jacob took the note. "Thank you, sir." Out of habit he went to salute, but stopped himself. He offered the major general a hand instead. They shook.

"No, Mr. Smith, thank you. I'd be out of my wits and trying to tear Overman's throat asunder, were it not for your assistance."

"Yup," Jacob said. "Reckon you're right." He jerked a thumb over his shoulder. "I'm gonna get now. Still got a city to save, and all."

Jacob rode down Rampart on an old nag, the only spare horse the Union had. Jacob didn't care much. He only needed to go a few blocks. He'd taken Rampart because he figured the wide thoroughfare would give attackers less cover from which to ambush.

No healthy person walked the street. What could be looted already had been. Shops were either boarded up, or empty and thrown open to the world. Glass littered the street. A newspaper floated through on the blast-furnace-hot wind. People stayed locked inside their homes. They were scared. Of course, they had cause to be.

Jacob stopped in front of one of the shops. A sign of warning had been painted on the outside wall. "Don't try. I am sleeping inside with a big dog, an ugly woman, two shotguns, and a claw hammer."

He shook his head, smiling. He rode on.

A pack of wild dogs fought in a butcher shop over scraps. A whitish mongrel flipped a grey mutt onto its back, its foamed muzzle close to the whipped dog's throat, teeth bared. The grey mutt whimpered loud enough for Jacob to hear it out on the street. The Templar nudged his horse with his knees, clucking his tongue. They continued on.

He rode past Congo Square. The Union had staked it out when they were still trying to maintain order. A makeshift tent city half-stood abandoned, the canvas fluttering in the boiler-hot breeze.

He reined his horse in at Common Street and dismounted. The din of gunfire rose up from just south. He went the rest of

the way on foot, poking his head around the old Spanish building at the corner of Rampart and Canal. Potestas's army spread
out in front of the Mechanics Institute a block south. Afflicted,
dead policemen, dead civilians, and the white, peaked hoods of
Kukluxers covered the breadth of Canal and reached almost to
Jacob's position. There must have been hundreds of them.

"Damn," Jacob muttered. He needed to get around behind
the building and find another way in. He retreated around the
corner and mounted his horse. He rode back to Common Street
and turned right. The empty road stretched before him. He rode
down the street towards Dryades. At Dryades he dismounted
and popped his head around the corner.

The institute was pushed up against Dryades street and stood
near center on the city block. The structure itself, a three-story
stonework building with a columned facade, took up most of
the space on its side. Its grounds kept it separated from the
other buildings on the Canal and Common Street sides. Jacob
couldn't see the back, the side of the block which butted up
against Baronne. He hoped that way would provide him an entrance.

Potestas stood in the back of the wagon sporting the Gatling.
His army swelled around him. His booming voice rolled down
Dryades. "You knights," Potestas yelled, pointing to a cadre of
white-robed Kukluxers, "up to the front with the ram. Break
down those damnable doors."

A sickening roar, something akin to a scratchy groan, went up
from the ramshackle army as the men charged forward over the
corpses decorating the front steps of the institute. They hoisted
an iron-bound tree trunk which had been turned into a battering ram. The men inside opened curtains on the second floor.
Rifles and pistols appeared from the windows, firing down on
the approaching Kukluxers.

Jacob didn't wait to see the outcome. He got back on his
horse and crossed Dryades, continuing down Common Street.
Baronne, ahead, looked to be empty. He took a right at the intersection. It was clear. Buildings lined either side, shops and
boutiques mostly. Alleyways led between some of the shops.
The Mechanics Institute peeked over the buildings to his right.

He dismounted, hitched his horse, and headed down the
nearest alley. From where he stood, he could tell it intersected

ahead with another back alley. It looked to be divided from the back part of the institute's grounds by a wooden fence. The barrier's slats were old, and the paint was peeling.

The smell of rotting flesh hit him as soon as he slipped between the buildings. He pulled his kerchief from his pocket and covered his mouth. A colored woman's corpse lay to the side, still cradling her dead baby. They'd been left next to a pile of decaying vegetables. The heat and humidity had bloated the bodies. Likely, they'd been dead since the day before. Jacob stopped next to them and knelt down.

The woman had been bludgeoned to death, her head caved in, her teeth knocked out. The baby's mouth hung open, like it'd died mid-cry. Jacob said a silent prayer, stood and walked past her, deeper into the alley. He heard movement ahead.

He stopped at the intersection and looked both ways. Three afflicted crowded to his left over the body of a dead dog. One of them was small and waifish with ragged, straight brown hair. It had been a small boy, a child. The second one was an old colored woman missing her left arm. The third was a younger, busty white woman wearing a torn dress. They ripped out the dog's white entrails and tore into its gut. Canine blood and filth covered all three. Jacob felt a momentary pang of sorrow for the mutt. Jacob cocked his pistol.

"Hey," he shouted down the alley at the trio. No response from the afflicted. "Hey," he shouted again. Waif-boy noticed first. He perked his head up like a prairie dog and looked around with dull eyes. Jacob raised his pistol, taking a moment to breathe. He pulled the trigger. Jacob's bullet knocked the boy backwards out of his crouch, splaying him out flat on his back.

Jacob took a bead on the other two and finished the work. He reloaded his pistol, clearing the old cartridges from their chambers and thumbing in fresh ones. He looked down at his belt and his dwindling ammunition. Jacob holstered his pistol with a grunt and tugged his belt up higher.

Probably should have just killed them with his sword. But, then again, look how well that went in front of Washington Square.

Jacob took a moment to look around. The fence wasn't too high. He could probably jump it, or go through it. But there was no telling what prowled the other side. He looked up at the institute's windows. They were close enough to touch, it seemed, just on the other side of the fence. They'd really been going for maximum use on their space.

He looked up at the back wall of the shops he stood behind. They were three-stories-tall. The bottom floor consisted of the shop itself, and the top two probably housed living quarters. Whatever was inside, whether it be afflicted or people, it'd probably be dangerous. He remembered the buildings all had balconies on their fronts. He walked back through the alley and looked up. A balcony for each floor stretched across the entirety of the street-facing side.

Yeah, he reckoned he could climb that. He went to it.

He unhitched his horse and brought her over. He climbed up and used her saddle as a stepping stone, climbing up to the second floor. She shifted uncertainly at first, but the Templar made it just fine.

As he stood on the railing of the second floor balcony, Jacob tried to remember why this was a good idea. He also tried to remember why he hadn't just stayed behind and ridden with the troops. They were on their way after all. He used an ornate, ironwork balcony support and finished climbing to the third floor, only catching his boot in the leaf-work once.

He looked up at the roof, heard movement inside the building, and continued the climb. He still couldn't figure why he'd done it. Goddamn, this had to be one of his stupider ideas.

He dragged himself over the edge of the roof and lay their for a moment, baking in the sun. At least no one was trying to kill him up here. That was a nice change of pace. He sighed and closed his eyes. He breathed deeply for a moment, listening to the gunshots and cries for help coming from inside the institute.

After what didn't feel like long enough, or, conversely, too damned long, he sat up. He stood and walked over to the alley-ward edge of the building. On the institute's grounds beyond the fence, a small group of afflicted milled around. Jacob guessed most of them had been called to the front by Potestas. Sounded like he was about ready to make his move.

Only fifteen or so feet separated Jacob from the institute's rear wall. He could see across into the third floor, and down into the second floor. He stuck out a raised thumb and measured the distance. He could make it.

He looked down at the alley, the institute's grounds, and the fence separating the two. While it was only fifteen feet straight across, it was probably over thirty feet to the earth. He breathed deeply. He really hoped this would work.

Jacob walked back to the other side of the building. God, this was stupid. He breathed deeply again. Really stupid. He sprinted alley-ward, his boots thudding on the tar and shingles, his coat flying out in his wake.

He stepped up on the edge of the roof and launched out into the seemingly vast expanse of space that stretched between the rooftop and the rear windows of the Mechanics Institute's second floor. Air rushed past his ears, his coat flapped around him, and the windows kept coming.

He tucked his head down, covering his neck with his chin, and pressed his hat to his head. Jacob realized he was grinning as he smashed through the panes of glass, splintering the grilles that kept everything together, and raising a hell of a racket. He tucked himself into a ball before he landed on the hardwood, rolling across the floor and hitting a decidedly solid meeting table.

He looked out from within his cocoon of armor and oiled wool.

He'd made the jump. He slapped the hardwood floor. He'd actually made it. Jacob started to laugh. How the hell had he made it? Truth be told, he didn't care all much about the how part, just that he had. Maybe he did just need to have a little faith?

He stood and shook the glass off his coat. He took his hat off, dusted off the felt, and stuck it back on his head with a wide grin. Hadn't even lost his hat. Goddamn!

"You there," said a voice behind him. A gun cocked. "You hold right there, monsieur." Jacob felt the pistol trained on his back. From the sound of the hammer mechanism, it probably belonged to a big Navy Colt. Jacob's grin faded.

Jacob sighed and raised his hands to the ceiling. He rolled his eyes and turned around. "Ya got me."

His captor was a small creole man, older, well-dressed, and well-groomed. Jacob guessed his race as quadroon, a quarter colored, from his cafe-au-lait complexion. He also guessed the man used a bucket of grease each day to get his hair to slick the way it did.

195

"Take that revolver out and put it on the floor." Jacob did as he said. "Kick it over here." Jacob kicked the revolver over. "What's your name, boy?"

"Jacob Smith."

"The other two told us about you."

"Yup. Christopher Freeman and Charlotte Gibson get here already, then?"

"Yes. Yes, they did."

"In that case, you mind pointing that pistol somewhere else?"

The man looked down at the big pistol, then back up at Jacob. "My apologies, friend." He pointed the barrel at the ceiling and carefully lowered the hammer of the revolver. Jacob walked over to where his revolver lay on the floor, gave the man a look, and retrieved it. He holstered it.

"Mind telling me what's going on?" Jacob asked as he walked out of the room and into a hallway. The report of gunfire came from inside the building. He turned right, following the sound of it.

"We're surrounded. What else is there to tell?"

"Are we armed?"

"Of course. Think we'd come here any other way with the city the way it's been?"

"Didn't think you'd come to begin with. Stupid of ya, you ask me."

"The convention was too important to abandon. We needed to make the call for suffrage."

"Gonna get the lot of you killed is all that'll happen."

They turned left at the end of the hallway and followed it. Jacob looked through the windows at the surrounding area. Beyond would be Common Street. He had to be sure and keep his bearings in this place.

"We'll serve as an example to the other coloreds throughout the South, and—"

"I guess being a martyr ain't too bad," Jacob interrupted. "Only I never went in much for it. Pa always said a dead man was one that wasn't much good at living life."

"Pardon my saying, but what in the hell does that even mean, Mr. Smith?"

"No idea. Pa got killed before he could explain it. Guess he wasn't much good at it, neither."

They walked out onto a landing that looked over the first floor's gigantic hall. The second floor landing wrapped as a balcony, encircling the whole of it. Across the way, Jacob saw men shooting down on the enemy from the upper windows.

He could see why they'd chosen this space for the Constitutional Convention. Simply put, it was gigantic, bigger than even the largest church Jacob had been inside. Tables and lecterns had been re-purposed for defense. Rather than using them as places of meeting, education, and governing, the delegates had thrown them against the windows as makeshift fortifications.

Easily two score men of all colors, shapes, and sizes, gathered below. Men pressed themselves to the doors, holding the barriers shut against the Kukluxers and afflicted. Christopher led the group from the center, his back pushed against the doors, hollering encouragement and cussing the quitters.

In one corner, away from the fighting, a miniature triage for a dozen or more wounded had been set up. Charlotte worked down there, wrapping bloody wounds in cloth strips made from various articles of thrown-off clothing. Two dozen or so corpses lay in another corner.

Desperation filled the air.

Jacob and his escort walked down the stairs and into the main hall. The battering ram boomed against the near-splintered door. Charlotte looked up from the man she'd been bandaging as Jacob stepped onto the floor of the main hall.

"Jacob?" she shouted.

"Howdy, Miss Gibson," Jacob hollered back as she threw her bandages aside and came running over. She slammed into him in her excitement, throwing her arms around him. She pulled back and, standing on tiptoes, threw her arms around his neck. Uncertain what to do, Jacob kept his arms by his side.

"Thank God, Jacob," she said, stepping back to look at him. "Thank God you're here. Did you bring aid? I almost thought the worst. How did you even get in?"

"Troopers are on their way. For now, though, we need to keep these folks safe." As an afterthought, he added, "And I jumped in through the second story."

"You what?"

Jacob turned to the quadroon man and asked, "What was your name, sir?"

"Montegut. Baudin Montegut."

"Where were you when you heard me come in?"

"Patrolling the rear windows."

"Alright. That door," Jacob said, pointing to where Christopher led the defense of the main door, "that ain't gonna hold much longer. We're gonna need a defensible position to fall back to. Can you collar some of your men and start building barricades on the second floor landing? I want every heavy table at the top of the stairs. You hear me?"

The man nodded. "What about—"

"Don't ask me every time you need to make a decision, Mr. Montegut. You're a grown man. Act it. Go to work." Montegut's face burned red. Jacob turned to Charlotte. "Miss Gibson, I want you to get the wounded upstairs. Those that can't move on their own, we'll have to leave behind."

"But, I—"

"Miss Gibson," Jacob said, grabbing her shoulders and looking down into her shocked face. "Look at me, Charlotte. There's an army out there. These men knew what they were doing when they came here. We won't be able to save everyone. You're a Pinkerton. Now do your job." He squeezed her shoulders. He'd called her Charlotte, he realized. "Do your job. I'll do mine." He turned back to Montegut, who still just stood there. "Mr. Montegut?" he asked.

Montegut sputtered and started, saying, "Mr. Smith, I—"

"—am not doing what I asked," Jacob said. "Now go get them barricades up, or go to the grave knowing you failed your comrades." He turned and walked towards Christopher at the front barricade. He spat to the side. The battering ram pounded again. The splintering door would only take a few more swings.

"Christopher?" Jacob called when he was about twenty feet from the door.

"Jacob?" Christopher asked, still pressed against the door. Strain showed on his face. "Come for one last stand?"

"Not if I can help it," Jacob said. The battering ram pounded against the door again, causing Christopher to lose his footing a little. Jacob rushed to Christopher's side and pressed his back against the door. "Got them building barricades on the second floor landing."

"Troops coming?"

"On their way."

"Here's hoping we make it."

"We've gotten out of worse," Jacob said, grunting as the Kukluxers rammed the door again. "Goddamn they pack a punch, don't they?"

"Reminds me of my time in the ring," Christopher said, grinning. "At least there's no mosquitoes."

"Not yet," Jacob replied. He looked up at the landing.

Montegut and some other men dragged a long table down the walkway. Charlotte led the last of the wounded up the stairs, hopefully out of harm's way. Christopher was probably right. This was a last stand.

A Kukluxer shoved his pistol in through the window fortifications on their right and shot one of the delegates through the eye. Jacob thanked God that, at least, the dead man wouldn't rise with the affliction.

"How much longer till we retreat?" Jacob asked.

The battering ram thundered on the door again. The door almost buckled this time around.

"Not much," Christopher said. "Alright," he hollered to the men manning the door and window barricades. "Mr. Smith here just informed me Maj. Gen. Baird's on his way with the troops. We can hold out in this building, but we can't hold this door." The battering ram collided with the door again, splintering open one of the wooden panels. "When I give the word," Christopher yelled, ducking from a grasping white-robed arm, "we make for them stairs. Y'all hear me?"

The men around them gave a general cry of acknowledgment. Jacob couldn't tell how much desperation filled their voice, but he could tell they all knew the situation was grim.

Jacob pushed off from the door and turned. He saw white-peaked hoods through the door's busted panel. He drew his revolver and fired two shots through it. One of the men fell, crimson soaking his peaked-hood from the inside out. The other bullet ricocheted off the stonework. The battering ram fell to the ground of the entry chamber on the other side of the double doors.

"Let's get a move on, men," Christopher shouted, pushing off from the door.

To a man, the delegates ran for the stairs, leaping and dodging overturned tables and chairs. Christopher and Jacob backpedaled at a jog, watching the door as they retreated across the expanse of the hall. The final boom from the battering ram sounded, throwing the doors wide as the Templars began to climb the stairs.

Gunfire erupted from the entry. Bullets flew through the air, whizzing around the Templars. Bullets ricocheted off the stone steps around and ahead of Jacob. They neared the top of the stairs and dove over the barricade. The delegates, their eyes determined, angry even, crowded behind the overturned tables, pistols clutched in steady hands. They wrapped around the balcony, extending out over the blockaded stairway. It would be a killing zone.

"Don't shoot," Christopher said breathlessly, "until you see the eyes in their hoods. You hear me?"

"And aim for the head if it's an afflicted," Jacob added.

Potestas was smart.

The afflicted came in first. They pushed through the broken front doors like a great herd of cattle being driven from a corral chute, spilling out across the hall's floor, becoming a sea of rotting, once-human flesh. They were all colors: white, black, brown, green, yellow, grey. Their mouths hung open, their arms groped at the air. They must have numbered a hundred, maybe more. The afflicted surged forward, shoving each other to the ground, trampling the already broken furniture, trampling each other.

Montegut came at a run and crouched next to Jacob. "Mr. Smith?"

"Fine work, Montegut," Jacob said without taking his eyes from the herd of afflicted. "We might live a while longer."

"Thank you, Mr. Smith. We found something."

"What?"

"Barrels of coal oil."

Jacob grinned. Then he heard it. A bugle call.

He grinned wider and clapped Montegut on the shoulder, saying, "Take the barrels around the landing. Douse the stairs from top to midway. We just gotta hold out a little while longer."

The barrel crew ran alongside the landing, rolling the barrels on the ground behind the barricade. The sounds of battle outside became louder. Baird's men had added their own guns to the ruckus.

Craig Gabrysch

Kukluxers began taking up positions in the antechamber, firing through the windows and the broken doors. The afflicted had closed the distance already and began to climb the stairs.

The delegates started to pour the oil. It flowed out, light and clear. It reeked, the smell of it filling the institute.

"Don't fire till they're finished with the oil, men," Christopher yelled to the delegates. "One spark and they're going up."

The afflicted came trudging and crawling up the steps, their eyes vacant, their mouths slack. They ignored the coal oil, coming up the steps in a wall of flesh and disease. The barrel men finished pouring and stepped back from the landing. When the mass of afflicted reached just fifteen feet away, Christopher stood and raised his gun. The delegates rose with him. He fired, leading off a salvo from the delegates.

Flames erupted at the back of the afflicted as the crawling wall near the barricades fell back under the hail of lead. The explosion launched flaming bodies into the air.

Jacob, losing himself in the moment, watched a body arch up and almost reach the ceiling. It landed with a dull thud on the upper landing to his left, its body still alight. Smoke, blistering heat, and the acrid smell of cooking, rotten flesh filled the room as the delegates continued to fire into the horde.

Jacob broke off from the barricade and ran down to the landing towards the way he'd come in. He stopped and looked over the spectacle on the stairs. The afflicted near the back had slowed, the muscle and skin cooking from their bones, their eyes bursting from their sockets.

He turned to continue on his way. A wave of heat flashed his torso. There was a raspy moan.

Jacob spun to meet the threat, his pistol raised. The smoldering afflicted who, moments before, had been launched onto the landing grabbed hold of his shooting arm. He looked into the creature's flame-blistered face with its tongue rolling out, saliva dripping from its maw, and the hair on its head burned away. This was as far from good as anything could get.

Waves of heat emanated from the afflicted's cooking bones. The creature's touch scorched Jacob's skin through his armor. Jacob roared and tried to yank his arm away from the afflicted. He kicked at it, but he couldn't break free. His finger jostled the

201

trigger as he struggled, discharging the pistol by accident. The bullet flew well wide of the afflicted's head.

Jacob stumbled backwards over a piece of debris and lost his footing. He fell on his back. The creature clamored on top of him, fighting to get at his face with what remained of its gnashing teeth. Jacob brought up his left arm and forced it against the creature's throat. If he could just get his gun up, he'd get another shot.

A long string of yellowish saliva dripped from the afflicted's slathering mouth. Jacob tried to turn his head away, but he was too late. The disease-ridden spit dropped onto his lips and front teeth. Jacob fought to free his shooting hand. He only managed to get the muzzle of his revolver redirected. But, he'd moved it just enough.

The barrel was pointed into the afflicted's jawline. Jacob pulled the trigger. The bullet, entering through the creature's chin, expanded on impact and exited through top of its skull in a shower of bone fragments and rotting brain-matter. The afflicted collapsed on top of him.

Jacob kicked off the smoldering body. He stood and spit to the side.

He thought about sticking a finger down his throat, but then wondered if his hand carried the disease. Sticking his hand in his mouth might just make it worse. He just had to hope he wouldn't get the sickness.

Pulling himself together, Jacob jogged back to where he'd first come in through the window. He looked into the room. Within, Charlotte administered to the wounded. He did a quick head count: Only three had had to be left behind. That was a small wonder, right there. She had them spread across the heavy conference table Jacob had first rolled into during his high-flying entrance.

"Jacob?" Charlotte asked. "Was that a bugle out there? What's going on? Are we safe?"

"Union's coming. Here, everyone that can, help me with this table. Got an idea."

Jacob, Charlotte, and five of the walking-wounded pushed the long conference table against the windowsill. With three to a side, they managed to lift it up and push it through the hole Jacob had left in the window. They guided it out and laid the outside edge on top of the institute's back fence. They had a slide to the back alley.

"This isn't going to work," Charlotte said.

"Oh, ye of little faith," Jacob replied, grinning at his own handiwork.

"Jacob?"

Jacob grunted.

"Are you feeling alright?" Charlotte asked. "You look a little piqued."

Jacob looked at Charlotte's throat. It was bare. There should have been, instead, a pouch with her pepper. "Your pepper," Jacob said.

"I used it already." A booming roar cut through the gunshots, making the rifles and pistols sound like kids' fireworks. Charlotte grabbed hold of Jacob to steady herself as the whole of the building shook from the top all the way down to its foundation.

"Jesus, don't he know civilians are in here?" Jacob yelled.

"What was that?" Charlotte asked.

"Cannon fire," Jacob said, going for the door. "Baird's bombarding the institute," he said over his shoulder. "I'm going to see how Christopher's doing. Start sliding them wounded down the table. Get 'em out, Charlotte."

He ran out the door and into the hallway.

Back at the stairs, the situation had deteriorated. Christopher had abandoned the barricades. Instead, he leaned over an injured white man. The man cradled a hurt arm. His face glowed with blue light.

"Pepper?" Jacob asked.

"Yeah. He's Judge Howell. Head of the convention, Jacob. Too important to my people down here. Couldn't let him go."

"Gave mine to Baird," Jacob replied, putting a hand on Christopher's shoulder. "I made an escape route. Go down the hall and take your first left. It'll get us out."

"I'm not leaving."

"Someone needs to protect the delegates on the other side, Christopher, and get them out of the city."

"I ain't leaving you here."

"I'm already infected," Jacob said. He put a hand on Christopher's shoulder. "Go."

Christopher didn't say anything. He went back to the barricade, eyes straight ahead. Jacob crouched down behind the banister to the left of the stairs and looked out over the entrance hall.

Union cannons had blown a six-foot-wide hole to the left of the double doors. Dead Kukluxers were scattered throughout the antechamber, their blood-soaked robes ragged and torn to shreds. Potestas tried to rally his troops in the center of the room. Jacob returned to the barricade and took up a position next to Christopher and Montegut. Jacob felt the fever creeping in and taking hold of his body.

"Start sending off the delegates," Jacob said to Christopher. "I'll stay and cover your retreat."

The afflicted had gained ground in the last few minutes since Jacob had left to deal with his escape plan. The fire on the stairs had gone out and most of the delegates had exhausted their ammunition. Jacob reloaded his revolver and handed it to Montegut.

Jacob drew his sword. If an afflicted came close enough, he struck its head from its shoulders, or cleaved its head in twain. They didn't stop coming, though. Soon, the bodies of the afflicted piled in front of the barricade. They kept on, crawling over their fallen comrades.

Soon, it was only Montegut and Jacob on the barricades. Jacob stripped off his gunbelt and handed it to the other man, saying, "Don't got much ammo, but you'll need it."

"Mr. Smith," Montegut said, taking the gunbelt and strapping it on, "thank you."

"Just go."

Montegut left Jacob on the barricade. He stood and struck down another afflicted, blood spraying onto his coat and shirt. Another took its place. There were just too damned many of them.

Jacob retreated from the barricade as they began to overrun him. The creatures swarmed down the landing, falling over each other as they followed after him in a tide of death.

"Templar," Potestas roared from the hall below. Jacob stopped and peered over the railing for a moment. Potestas, the damned cause of this all, stood down there at the foot of the stairs.

"Baird take care of your men yet?" Jacob hollered back.

"Baird may have stopped me for the time being, but I can feel the fever in you, Templar. It'll do for you, just wait and see."

"Go to hell," Jacob yelled.

He ran down the hall to the conference room exit. He looked inside. Only Christopher and two of the delegates remained.

Another cannonball rocked the building, almost knocking Jacob from his feet.

"Jacob," Christopher hollered, "come with us."

"Potestas is coming. I need to draw him off."

Christopher just looked at him. "It's been good," he said after a moment.

"Yup. Sure has," Jacob said, stepping back into the hallway and closing the door. "Sure has," he said to himself, jogging down the hall away from the landing. He needed to distact the Kukluxers long enough for the others to escape. He stopped at the stairs and waited for Potestas and the afflicted horde.

Potestas came around the corner, his great coat sweeping out behind him. Blood and gore slicked his cavalry saber. "It's only a matter of time," Potestas said, marching down the hallway at the front of his army. "You can run, Jacob, but that's only gonna make it work a sight faster."

"Maybe," Jacob said. "Probably." He ran up the stairs to the third floor, taking the steps two at a time. The upstairs was dark. The hallway stretched on.

What little light there was came in through the doors on his right, filtering in through the office windows. Jacob ran down the hall looking into the open offices, searching for a way out.

Nothing.

Ahead, the hall turned off to the left. Potestas and the afflicted army followed close behind. Jacob took the turn. About fifteen feet down on his right, a sign hung on a door: "Roof Access." He tried the door. It was locked. Seemed like every damn door he ran across had been locked.

He stepped back, hoping he had enough strength in his fevered body to bust it open. He threw his shoulder into it. The door budged a little. He slammed into it again. The door flung open. He ran inside, massaging his shoulder.

The room beyond was a small utility closet. Racks of cleaners and rags stood in one corner. A ladder on the far side of the

205

room led up to a wooden access door. He climbed the rungs, opened the hatch, and crawled onto the roof.

The sun beat down on him and heat came up from the tar, making the sweats worse. Jacob, groaning, climbed to his feet and looked around.

"Smith," Potestas shouted from below. "I ain't some hunting dog. I grow weary of this pursuit."

Coughing, Jacob ran across the tar-covered roof to the alleyward side. He stood on the ledge and looked down. Christopher and Charlotte stood down in the alley, looking back at the wooden slide Jacob had made. He saw only delegates with them.

"Why ain't you left yet?" Jacob asked quietly. "Damn people."

"Jacob Smith," Potestas roared from behind. Actual force came with the shout, like a cold wind on a January night, pushing roughly into Jacob's back. He reached down to the ledge and steadied himself.

Below him, down in the alley, his friends' heads snapped up. Charlotte waved at him, her arm raised over her head. Jacob waved a small wave back.

"Turn and fight me, Templar."

Jacob sighed. He turned and drew his sword. Potestas stood alone at the other end of the rooftop, his coat flapping in the breeze. Behind him, the haze of smoke drifted over the city. Turned out, the ladder had been Jacob's saving grace. Afflicted, apparently, had to take the stairs.

The teeth hung from Potestas's neck. They glint wetly in the sunlight, like the slather covered fangs of some ravenous beast. Jacob's eyes were drawn to the bloody smudge of warpaint streaked on Potestas's forehead. It seemed to throb with unearthly power. What was it? Where had it come from? And why was a Kukluxer even wearing warpaint?

The gunfire had slowed from its rapid tempo and almost completely quieted. No matter who had won the battle, the battle had ended. Well, it had for everyone else.

"Alright, Potestas," Jacob said, walking over to the thin blonde man. He stopped ten feet away. "Let's tussle." He tried to puff his chest out, but it didn't work too well. He just ended up coughing. Truth be told, he'd exhausted himself. The last three days, with only bits of chow here and there and hardly any sleep, was taking its toll.

The fever didn't help things much, neither.

"You look," said Potestas, advancing slowly on Jacob, "like something I once stepped in in a pasture, Smith."

"Do I now?" Jacob asked. "Well, looks can deceive, can't they?" He coughed again, spitting to the side. "Oh God, I do feel ragged," he said, a weak smile on his face.

"I can just kill you now," Potestas said, "and take the pain away."

"Nah," Jacob said, beckoning the Kukluxer with a wave of his sword's tip. "Let's have at it now. Put some heart into it this time."

Potestas made a slapping gesture with his hand, slapping downward to the roof. A wave of force, cold as the grave, slammed into Jacob's head and shoulders with the strength of an artillery round, flattening him to his chest.

Jacob grunted and called out in pain from the roof. He rolled over on his side, coughing.

"That weren't fair, you sumbitch," he yelled. "You wanna kill me? Fine. But, leave off them tricks of yours if you want it to be a real duel." He coughed again. "Jesus," he yelled, rolling over onto his chest and pushing himself up.

"Fine," Potestas said. "Fine, fine, fine. We'll do this your mortal way. No powers."

"Your word?"

"My word of honor."

"Let's go then."

Potestas roared and charged. Powers or no, he was still in as good a shape as Jacob. On top of that, a cursed fever hadn't attacked his body. Potestas drew closer. Jacob stood his ground. Potestas raised his sword when he was five feet away. He struck out with his cavalry saber, aiming for Jacob's head.

Jacob ducked the swing easily and sidestepped. He kicked out with his left leg, hitting Potestas in the side of the knee. Potestas lost his footing and went sprawling. He sprang to his feet in a flash, though, before Jacob could take advantage of his prone state.

Jacob advanced on him, striking mid-chest with his sword. Potestas parried and delivered a right cross to Jacob's face, knocking the Templar back a few steps.

Potestas's punch made a nag's kick seem weak. Jacob shook it off and recovered his stance. Jacob kept the blade of his sword up in the same defensive posture Henry Bennett had taught him when he'd first become a Templar.

Potestas went on the offensive, but Jacob blocked all his swings and stabs. Jacob countered every strike the other man made. More importantly, though, he studied Potestas.

Potestas didn't have a strong fighting form. He depended on his supernatural strength and endurance. Jacob had to admit that, under normal circumstances, that tact worked just fine for Potestas. That man could probably fight all day long and cleave through most crowds like they were lard. But he lacked finesse.

Jacob deflected a strike and spun around his opponent. He smacked Potestas in the back of his head with his chainmailed forearm, sending him to his knees. Jacob was too close for any forceful strike, though.

Instead of backing away for a better swing, he kicked Potestas in the back and knocked him flat. Jacob struck at him with an overhead, two-handed blow, but Potestas rolled out of the way and leapt back to his feet.

Jacob moved back from Potestas. The fever had reached his legs now. They were slowing.

Potestas charged him again. Jacob backpedaled. Time seemed to slow as Jacob stared at the red smudge on Potestas's forhead. The ritual they'd performed on Father Jacques? Maybe it was something similar?

Jacob's heels hit the edge of the roof. He brought his broadsword up and moved forward to meet Potestas.

Their swords clashed. Goddamn the man had some strength. Jacob grit his teeth, fighting against the Kukluxer bearing down on him. Their eyes locked.

"I see that bloody smudge," Jacob said, struggling to stay upright. "What ya got inside you?"

"Never you mind, race-traitor," Potestas said, shoving him back with the strength of ten men. Jacob's heels slid back on the tarring. He put the last of his strength, coiled it up from his feet and into his legs, into one final go.

He drove Potestas back a few steps and knocked him off-balance. Potestas stumbled backwards. Jacob dropped his guard and made a lunging grab for Mackandal's teeth. Potestas bent backwards out of reach, laughing out loud as Jacob's fingers barely brushed the artifact.

"Not close enough, Templar. This little game, I think, is finished."

He brushed his hand to the side. That same force from nowhere struck Jacob's sword, knocking it aside and almost from his grasp. Jacob tried to raise it as Potestas advanced.

Potestas's hand shot out and gripped him by the throat. Jacob struggled to strike with his sword, but he couldn't fight the unearthly energy. He groped with his free hand, first trying to uncoil Potestas's hand from his throat, then reaching for the other man's face and trying to dig a finger into his left eye.

Potestas extended his arm, holding Jacob farther away. Potestas drove him back against the ledge, knocking him onto his back, and pushing him out and over the institute's yard below.

"I'd almost say it's funny," Potestas said as Jacob struggled to breathe, "that you died this way. But there's not really any humor or irony in it. You're just going to die, Jacob Smith. Then I'm going to find that nigger of yours and kill him slowly. Make him suffer. We'll keep little Miss Gibson around for a while, though. She's right pretty. The boys'll enjoy her." Potestas gave Jacob a good shake, clamping down harder on his throat. "Finally, I'm going to take these teeth to every city in the north, then to Europe, and to the world."

Jacob, his vision fading, looked to the side. Charlotte and Christopher stood in the alleyway still. They'd waited for him. Now they'd get to watch him die. At least he wouldn't die alone. That would be worth noting in the annals.

Potestas shoved him backwards, coming closer, pushing down on Jacob as he held him out over the ledge. "You, Templar, will be just the first of many deaths."

A shot rang out. Potestas lurched backwards, his grip slackening. The bullet had struck him in the forehead, rubbing off some of the blood-red smudge, but not breaking the skin in the process.

Magic. It was strange.

Jacob took the opportunity. He lunged forward with his free hand and wiped a thumb across the smudge, smearing the

Kukluxer's forehead clean. A sharp shock of power shot up his arm, numbing his hand and forearm.

Potestas's eyes, now a plain mud-brown, went wide.

Jacob dropped his broadsword and kicked up his boot into Potestas's groin. Jacob grabbed hold of Potestas's left shoulder with one hand and the teeth with the other. He kicked him in the crotch again, pulling backwards and flipping him over the ledge.

Jacob didn't watch Potestas fall, though he dearly wanted to. He only heard him land. That was satisfaction enough, though.

The Cyclops landed on the fence separating the alley and the institute's grounds. It sounded like a tree trunk snapping in a hard wind. Jacob rolled over and looked down on the corpse. The fall into the fence had bent Potestas backwards. Blood already pooled below the body.

Jacob pushed back from the ledge and stood. He looked down at the artifact in his hand. He could feel the knowledge of all the afflicted in New Orleans. He could go down into them if he wanted, walk in their shambling footsteps. He knew this somehow.

That knowledge intoxicated. It was like a moldy black spot of power had grown on Jacob's soul. He heard whispers somewhere in the back of his brain, whispers of power. He ignored the coaxing from the artifact.

Sighing, he went and picked up his broadsword. He hefted its weight in his hand, and walked back over to the edge of the building.

He set down the teeth on the ledge. He struck down at the relic with a two-handed grip on his sword, swinging the blade's edge into the center tooth. Sparks flew. Jacob's strike had barely scratched the teeth.

Jacob raised his sword and, gathering up his strength, swung again. A thunderous crack of sheer power echoed over New Orleans as the teeth broke into a thousand shards. A staggering wave of energy slammed into him. Windows all over the city block shattered in a rain of glass.

The feverish heat began to leave his body.

Shaken, Jacob sheathed his sword and looked down at his hands. A sickly, amber-colored film seeped out from his skin. He watched as it evaporated into a fine mist and drifted into the air.

He walked back over to the ledge, stumbling over his own feet. He recovered and leaned out over the edge, looking down.

Christopher and Charlotte were examining Potestas's body. A half-dozen soldiers stood around it, rifles at the ready. They weren't taking any chances. Good.

Jacob stuck two fingers in his mouth and whistled weakly.

Charlotte looked up and waved over her head at him. Christopher glanced up, gave a cursory nod, and went back to watching the corpse like it was a snake he'd just found under a rock. Jacob waved back to Charlotte. He couldn't help but smile.

Jacob watched as Christopher stood and drew his sword. He motioned Charlotte back, then, bringing the sword back over his head, decapitated the corpse in a single stroke.

A piercing, keening wail rose up from the body. The horrible noise echoed all over the city, off the buildings, down the alleyways in between them, and through the streets. Jacob covered his ears, watching as Christopher, Charlotte, and the soldiers did the same.

A great, shadowy beast began escaping out from Potestas's stump of a neck. It didn't come as a mist, or as smoke. Instead, the demon-thing clawed its way out from within the corpse.

Black talons shredded the neck, tearing the orifice open and rending the skin and muscle beneath. Jacob's fellows downstairs stumbled back from the creature as it clawed free. It reached a hand as big across as a serving platter out into the institute's grassy turf and began to pull itself out into the New Orleans air, shedding the body like it was just a used up cocoon husk.

The keening wail continued, increasing in pitch. Jacob fell to his knees, his vision darkening. It was like nothing he'd ever experienced.

Jacob struggled against the fade and rose to his feet, legs trembling. He leaned out over the ledge, right hand over his ear and left on the pommel of his sword. The thing drew itself up to its full height.

The amorphous shadow towered over Jacob's fallen companions and the ruined corpse below. The creature must have been two-stories tall. It seemed to look up at Jacob.

A chill ran through Jacob all of a sudden. The chill made him desperate and full of rage. The thing stared long and hard at him, the keening wail rising as it did so.

Whatever it was took flight with a mighty vertical leap, rushing up past, and through, Jacob's head before he could step back.

Visions of a small frontier town flooded his mind. A wide thoroughfare lined on both sides by wooden buildings. A drugist on the left, two general stores, a livery at the end. He'd been there before, Jacob knew. He recognized the general store. That was where his pa had bought seed every season before the war. He'd buy penny candy for Jacob and his brothers when they went with him.

It was Lawrence, Kansas.

Jacob saw the town on fire. He heard people screaming. He saw men in mismatched, irregular clothing riding through town, setting the buildings afire and shooting down the inhabitants. It was a massacre.

It was the Lawrence Massacre, to be exact.

Next he saw a vision of a cold land of grey, blasted rock. Smoke and ash filled the skies. Armies of creatures marched and processed across the space, their numbers so great that to enumerate them would be like counting snowflakes falling in a blizzard. Impenetrable cold bore through him, numbing him down to his bone. This was a level of Hell.

The Ninth, to be exact.

The visions faded and so did the wail. Jacob shook his head and searched the skies, looking for the grave-cold shade on the New Orleans skyline. Nothing. His left ear felt warm. He reached up and felt something wet. He looked down at his hand.

Blood.

That wasn't good.

He shook his head again and looked down at the grounds between the back alley and the institute. The others all stood and hollered at each other. The soldiers looked to be in a tizzy. Jacob turned around and left the ledge.

He walked back to the hatch that led to the institute's third floor. He eased himself down the ladder, grunting with the effort. Corpses of the irrevocably afflicted packed the little closet. When the curse left them, they had just died. Jacob crawled over the fleshy pile in a daze. He heard sobbing coming from the hallway.

He crawled over the pile of bodies and climbed down to the floor. He poked his head out the door and looked left. A young, white lady, naked to the waist, sat on the floor with her back against the wall and her legs tucked beneath her. She wept into her gore-covered hands. Her greasy, blonde hair hung down around her head in an untamed mess. Jacob walked over and squatted down next to her.

"You alright, ma'am?" he asked softly. He considered putting a hand on her shoulder, but thought better of it. She was half-naked, after all. Wouldn't be seemly.

She uncovered her face and looked at Jacob with puffy, red eyes.

"I killed all them people," she said, tears streaming down her face and a trail of snot dangling from her nose.

"No, ma'am," Jacob said, sighing. "No, you didn't. That wasn't you. I was in the war. I killed people. You didn't. This ain't on your shoulders. A man was controlling you. He did those things, not you. It's on him."

She kept crying. Jacob sighed, turning his head away.

She reached out and wrapped her arms around Jacob's neck before he could pull back. She hugged herself to him.

"Hey," Jacob said, struggling at first, "what are you . . . ?" But he just stopped trying when she wouldn't let go. What was he going to do? Shoot her? Beat her? She'd been through plenty already. He tried a different tack. "Alright, ma'am, we're gonna get you some help now. Can you walk?"

"I think so."

"That's good. I don't reckon I can if we gotta go too far," Jacob said. "Gotta let go if I'm gonna stand, though."

"Okay," she said, letting go of him. Her tears began tapering off, too. That was good. "Oh, Lordy," she said, looking down at herself with wide eyes. "I'm naked."

Jacob stood first and helped her up. He took off his great coat and draped it around her, saying, "Now you ain't. Your virtue's intact, ma'am."

"You a soldier, mister?" she asked.

"Nah," he said.

"What are you, then?"

"Reckon I'm a knight."

"Shouldn't you'd be a bit shinier, then?"

213

"Ain't how it works, ma'am."

They helped each other walk down the long hallway to the stairs. Along the way they found more of those who had been cured of the curse. Most were corpses now, but they encountered a handful of survivors.

They roused most, but a few didn't respond. Instead, the survivors just stared off into nowhere with wide, indifferent eyes. Jacob had seen it on the battlefield. They wouldn't be coming back for a while, he reckoned.

"Leave them, ma'am," he said. "We'll send help up when we get outside." In the end, there was a trail of seven men and women, a mix of both white and colored, following behind Jacob and the young woman when they reached the stairs. Their little, ragged procession stumbled down to the second floor.

They met Charlotte at the foot of the stairs. A small detachment of soldiers escorted her and Dr. Beckett. Charlotte's eyes went wide at the sight of the young woman leaning against Jacob.

"Ain't what you think," Jacob said to Charlotte. She shot him a look. Jacob sighed. "Found her in the hallway."

"Oh, honey," Charlotte said, going to the young woman, "we gotta get you and these folks some help." She wrapped an arm around the blonde's shoulders, looking suspiciously at Jacob's jacket. "They're setting up an aid station downstairs. We should get you folks there. Corporal, you and your men take these folks down. They're fine, as I'm sure Dr. Beckett will confirm."

The soldiers and Dr. Beckett took over taking care of the folks, checking them over and leading them downstairs. Jacob sat down on the stairs as the soldiers led away the recently cured. He sighed.

Charlotte sat down next to him.

"He's dead," Charlotte said.

"I saw."

"Then you also saw the shadow?"

"I did. Flew right through me."

"Through you?"

"Yup."

"What was it?"

"Dunno. Certain it's some sort of devil, though. A powerful one."

"Yes," Charlotte said, her voice distant, "it was powerful." She turned and looked at him. "Your ear, it's bleeding."

"I know. It was. It's stopped, I think."

They sat silent for a minute or two. No more gunshots filled the air, just the sound of soldiers bustling in the meeting chamber. The cleanup effort had begun.

"What about Father Rousseau?" Jacob asked.

"Jacques? I don't know. I don't think he knows, either."

"We should get Christopher and go see him."

Charlotte sighed. She was as tired as Jacob, he realized. It had been a long week. They picked themselves up and walked down the hallway, Jacob leaning on Charlotte for support.

"Do you think," Charlotte began as they turned the corner to the stairs, "that the curse left everyone?"

"Yup. Those that weren't used up probably made it, just like the woman from upstairs."

They walked out onto the landing and looked down at the clean-up effort. Soldiers pulled the corpses of the afflicted from the stairs and dragged them out into the street. Christopher and the surviving delegates had started identifying and claiming their compatriots' bodies. Jacob and Charlotte walked down the stairs together.

They walked over to Christopher together. "Glad you made it," Christopher said to Jacob. "Was worried."

"I was too. Reckon I should thank you for that last shot on Potestas. Likely saved my life."

"Welcome, but it wasn't me," Christopher replied. He pointed at Charlotte. "You should thank this little sharpshooter right here."

Jacob looked down at her, smiling wanly.

"Told you I was from Texas," she said, looking up at him.

Damn, she was beautiful in more ways than one.

"Well," Jacob said, "I appreciate it. Thank you." He looked back to Christopher. "Any word on surviving Kukluxers?"

Christopher shook his head. "Most were killed or run-off. Baird's men won't let me near the ones that were captured."

"Think he'd let me?"

"Might," Christopher said, considering. "But it's doubtful. He's outside in the street."

"Reckon I should find out for sure. Charlotte, would you help me outside?"

They went out to the street, passing through the entryway. The corpses had been cleared already, but the walls and floor were dark with drying blood. Bullet holes pockmarked the stone. Boot prints crisscrossed the crimson floor. Outside, Jacob and Charlotte surveyed Common Street.

A circus of activity had overtaken the battlefield, and Maj. Gen. Baird served as the ringleader. Jacob watched him directing the disparate groups of soldiers on the hundred different tasks which needed doing. Jacob saw Maj. Overman talking to some of the surgeons. Charlotte and Jacob walked over to him.

"Maj. Overman," Jacob called, walking slowly to the throng of men. Maj. Overman turned and looked at Charlotte and Jacob. Jacob could see the strain on the major's face.

"Jacob?" Overman asked. "You still kicking?"

"A word, sir?"

Maj. Overman came over. He and Jacob shook hands.

"This is Miss Gibson," Jacob said. "Saved my life today."

"Helped save the city, too," Charlotte added.

"That too."

"Well, we're obliged for that. What can I do for you?"

"Wanna talk to them Kukluxers, Major," Jacob said.

"I'd love to," Maj. Overman replied, "but I can't."

"Why not?"

"They're already gone. Maj. Gen. Baird immediately shipped them off to Fort Jackson."

"Well, let me see them there, then."

"No," the major said, his voice flat.

"Joey," Jacob said, lowering his voice, "I thought we were friends. Old war buddies."

"We are," the major said. "And, I'm deeply sorry, but this came from the top."

"The top? Who?"

"I am not at liberty to say," Maj. Overman replied, shaking his head.

"But," Charlotte said, "what if we could get in for just a—"

"My final answer," the major interjected, "is no. I will not risk a court martial so you can see those men. I told you, my hands are tied and I have no recourse in this matter. Respect that I have ironclad orders, Miss Gibson, which specifically state no one is to speak to the prisoners."

"Not even you?" Jacob asked.

"Not even the major general. And, especially not you or Mr. Freeman, Jacob."

"What? By name?"

Maj. Overman paused a moment, looking around, before saying, "Those are my orders."

Jacob cursed. "Fine. Thanks for the aid today, anyway. Couldn't have fought all them off without you and your boys." Charlotte and Jacob shook hands with Maj. Overman again and walked back up the steps to the Mechanics Institute. Christopher waited for them at the front doors.

"Figure we need to see Father Jacques," Christopher said.

"Jacob and I," Charlotte replied as the two of them walked up, "were thinking the same thing."

"Then let's get," Christopher said, heading in the direction of Common Street. "It's a long walk back to Chartres, and the afternoon's almost over."

Jacob and Charlotte followed after him.

The three of them stood around Father Jacques's bed. The other priests had moved him into one of the small monk's cells in another building on the grounds. Father Pierre Cavey stood off to the side.

"How you feeling, Father?" Christopher asked.

"Could not be better," Father Jacques replied.

To say the priest didn't look good would have more than just missed the mark, it would've been like firing in the opposite direction. Black bruises circled his eyes, and his face was already thin. Containing the demons ate at his core. The room was warm, almost hot, but the priest lay beneath a pile of blankets and quilts, shivering as if it was on a mid-winter night.

"We wanted to let you know the fever's stopped," Christopher said. "The city's safe."

"Potestas?"

"Dead. Killed by Jacob."

Father Jacques nodded silently.

"Are they still . . . inside of you?" Jacob asked quietly.

"*Oui*," he said. A shadow shaped like a large slug passed under his skin, traveling from his jaw and down to his collar bone.

"They writhe, attempting to make their escape."

"We'll fix this," Jacob said. "Somehow, we'll fix it."

Father Jacques tried to shrug, but it required too much effort. He just sighed instead. The sigh turned into a cough.

"I believe," Cavey began, starting forward, "Father Jacques needs his rest now. You may speak to him later."

The Templars, Charlotte, and the priest stepped out into the hallway. Father Cavey shut the door gently behind them.

"I am sorry, gentlemen," Father Cavey said, turning to them, "but Father Jacques cannot stay here."

"What?" Christopher and Jacob asked in unison, their voices raised.

"Christopher," Charlotte snapped. "Jacob. I'm sure the father has a good reason."

"It's not my reason, Miss Gibson. It is Archbishop Odin's. I have no say in this matter."

"But why?" Christopher asked, hands spread. "That man saved all our lives."

"Helped save the city, too," Jacob said.

"He is a powder keg," Cavey replied. "Do you realize what would happen if those demons escaped? We couldn't protect this city."

The Templars, silent, looked at each other. Christopher crossed his arms and shook his head.

"So the Church wants us to take him?" Jacob asked.

"Yes. At least, at the monastery, he'll be safe. You would be capable of containing the demons should they escape."

"Fine," Christopher said, looking at Father Cavey. "It's not that I don't want to take Father Jacques. He's a good man, and I see no problem obliging him peace and protection. The Church not wanting to help him is what gets to me."

"As I said," Father Cavey replied, "it is not my decision to make."

"Fine," Jacob said. "You're clean on this one. We'll take him with us as soon as we leave."

"When will that be?" Father Cavey asked.

"As soon as we get passage on a steamer. A couple days at least. Army has the city locked down. Port's closed for a week while they guarantee the city's free of fever. No ships in or out."

"Until then, you should stay as our guests," Cavey said, walking past them and down the hallway. He stopped near the end of the hallway. "Please, enjoy the comfort of our hospitality."

"Sure you don't just want us around to kill demons if they pop out of the father?" Jacob asked.

Cavey didn't reply. He just turned and continued down the hallway, shaking his head.

"Was that necessary?" Charlotte hissed.

"Yup," Jacob said. "They abandoned Father Rousseau."

"It's the archbishop who made that decision, not Father Cavey."

Jacob just shrugged.

"Well," Christopher said, "we'd better get our gear from the hotel."

August 6th

The next week passed uneventfully. Charlotte received a telegram ordering her to the East Coast, near New York. The agency wired money to her with instructions to leave on the first steamer out of the city. The Templars booked passage on a riverboat heading north on the Mississippi. Their ship was due to leave before Charlotte's.

Charlotte walked the three men out to the dock. They came out on Levee Street. All those masts stretched out just like they had two weeks before, a forest just as thick as ever. Ships unloaded and loaded, carts trundled by. Barkers hawked their goods, and men dickered over prices. Life went on.

Christopher and Father Jacques walked out ahead of Charlotte and Jacob, the old priest's hand on Christopher's arm for support.. They'd wanted to get Jacques a carriage, but he wouldn't have it. He insisted on walking.

"I am not an invalid," he had said.

"Thank you, by the way," Jacob said to Charlotte.

"For what?"

"You saved my life twice this last week."

"Saved mine once," Charlotte replied, laughing. "Even if it did cause all this mess."

Jacob smiled and looked down at his feet as they walked. "So, they have you going to New York?"

"Washington first. They need the head of the OSW, I guess."

"Well," Jacob said, looking out over the ships, "you'll do fine, I reckon. You're a strong woman. Smart, too."

"Well, thank you, Mr. Smith. I greatly appreciate that from a church man."

Jacob laughed. "I ain't exactly a church man, you know."

"No? Guess I never did ask."

"Templars are separate. We ain't priests or nothing."

"Could've fooled me," said Charlotte. They walked quietly for a while. "Jacob, I have a question."

"What's that?"

"Will you write me? Letters, I mean?"

"I – I dunno. I ain't exactly a man for letter writing and such. I mean, I can write and all. Ma made us learn our letters and such, but I ain't the type to, you know . . ." Jacob stopped rambling and looked at Charlotte. She grinned from ear to ear.

"Just say yes."

"Yes?"

"Good."

They arrived at their riverboat's berth. Smoke bellowed from its boiler stacks. Charlotte quickly said her goodbyes to Christopher and Father Jacques. She shook Christopher's hand and hugged the priest tenderly. She and Jacob said their goodbyes.

Jacob didn't know what to do. He offered her a hand to shake. She laughed and took it. The three men gave over their tickets and Father Jacques began to lead the way up the riverboat's gangplank.

"Jacob?" Charlotte said from behind him.

He turned.

She kissed him. She had to stand on her tiptoes to do it, but she managed just fine. The kiss was a long, sweet one. Jacob couldn't remember the last one that had been so nice. There'd been a girl in Lawrence, back when he was a boy. Annie. But she'd been almost ten years ago.

He put an arm around Charlotte's waist and kissed her back. Feeling eyes on them, they broke the embrace.

"Write me," Charlotte said quiet enough for only Jacob to hear. A faint smile touched her lips.

"Yes, ma'am, Miss Gibson."

He joined the other two men on the boat. Charlotte stayed and watched the ship from the dock until it had pulled out into the river and joined the northbound traffic. Jacob stayed on the upper deck, watching her.

When he lost sight of her, he gave the same courtesy to New Orleans.

"You're in love," Christopher said from beside him. Jacob hadn't heard him come up.

"What?" Jacob asked.

"Seen that hangdog look before. Hell, see it every time in the mirror since I met my wife."

"I ain't in love."

Christopher laughed, clapping Jacob on the shoulder. "If you ain't, you should be. She's a good woman. Even I can see that."

Jacob grunted.

"Told you them pretty faces were trouble."

Jacob grunted again.

Their ship steamed north to Chicago.

CRAIG GABRYSCH

Lives and writes in Dallas, Texas, with his lovely fiancee and their ornery black cat. All three are very happy.

Visit him at www.CraigGabrysch.com

AVAILABLE NOW!

Available in both print and ebook format

Visit www.TwitPublishing.com for more details!

DIESELPUNK:
AN ANTHOLOGY

available now!

Available in both print and ebook format

Visit www.TwitPublishing.com for more details!

Twit Publishing

Dallas-based. Indie. Fiction. Awesome.

Want to find out more about Twit Publishing?

Then go to www.TwitPublishing.com

Read about the company, hear about upcoming releases, join our email list, and find links to our authors.

* * * * * * *

You can also find us at:

www.Facebook.com/TwitPublishing

www.TwitPublishing.WordPress.com

and

www.Twitter.com/TwitPublishing

www.ingramcontent.com/pod-product-compliance
Lightning Source LLC
Chambersburg PA
CBHW020325200626
46814CB00006BB/2416